GOODBYE RESERVATIONS

The Lost & Found Series
THE PREQUEL - PART I

JACQUELYN AYRES

ISBN: 978-0-9863069-3-8

Dedication

For my street team (The G-Team). I love you girls. I'm so blessed to have such loyal readers and, even more so, to be able to call them my friends. I hope I delivered another favorite for you!

Chapter One

1999

S tuck in bumper to bumper traffic, I glance over at my passenger seat. Against my own will, I feel my lips curving into a smile. *Pompous ass.* I grab the card off the Hydrangea arrangement and read it for the millionth time.

> Because it's not about the flowers.
>
> Under your spell,
>
> The Pompous Ass.

Add this to his amazing looks and sexy British accent and this would be romantic as hell; something to tell our grandkids one day. However, I feel pretty confident that I will never see him again. In hindsight, that's probably a good thing since he'd, most likely, give me good reason to choke him.

—Buck . . . buck . . . shake . . . stall—

"No!" I hit the steering wheel. My car stops spasming and passes out dramatically. "Goddamn it!" I yell—because clearly, that will fix the problem. It's okay; I'm only in the middle of Route 1 south, sitting in the fast lane like someone went ahead and pressed the pause button. "If you start for me, I promise to not call you a piece-of-useless-shit-on-wheels for *at least* a month," I beg as I whack the gear into park. Resting my head on the wheel—repetitively whispering, *"Please"* for dramatic effect—I turn the ignition off, say a final plea, and try to start her up again. She fights me, but I pump my foot on the gas and balance my comments from encouraging to threatening ones. *"You're a whore!"* I scream as she teases me with her attempt to catch. She doesn't though. I smack the wheel in frustration again. Grabbing the gallon of water off the passenger floor, I pop the hood of my shit-box-on-wheels and get out to see what I can do. I don't know why people, like me—who have no clue as to what they are looking for—bother to do this, but I can't seem to stop myself.

I stare—waiting for some kind of affirmation—or a genie (that's probably more realistic than the affirmation). Resolved to the fact that I don't know what the fuck I'm looking at, I unscrew the radiator cap. Leaning over, I start to pour water in.

"You might not want to do that, love. It doesn't look as if she's overheating," a man with a British accent says. I turn to find a giant, black man in my presence.

"Is there some sort of invasion going on that I didn't hear about?" I ask honestly.

"I'm sorry?" He gives me a look of confusion.

"Eh, never mind." I wave him off. "I don't know what else to do." I sigh in defeat and recap the water and radiator.

"First of all, you need to put your coat on; you're shivering."

I zip my hooded sweatshirt. "Done. Now what?"

"Do you not have something warmer?" he asks loudly as if I'm deaf.

"I'm fine. I see you have a cell phone." I shake my finger at it. "May I use it to call my friend?"

"How far away is your friend?"

"I don't know." I look around at all the traffic as if I expect Stacey to magically appear.

"Why don't you give her a go again? If it's your battery, I can give you a jump," he offers.

"See, I don't think it is because she died while running and when I tried to start her, she sounded like she wanted to catch." I shake my head and bite my lip, trying to figure out this mystery . . . well, other than my car being a piece of shit.

"Did you run out of petrol . . . I mean gas?" He follows me over to the driver's side.

Fuck.

I stare at him, unable to speak. Of course I ran out of gas. I wish I could help the tears that are building up but I can't. I work two jobs and yet, after paying all of my bills conservatively, I can barely keep enough gas in my car to get me through the week. That extra shift I did this week?—put me over the edge. *The irony.*

"Don't panic, love." He looks around. "There's a station right there. I will go and get you some gas; you just get back in your car and stay warm." He opens the door for me.

"No." I shake my head. "I have to call my friend. I left my wallet at home," I explain with a lie.

"I'm afraid you can't do that."

"Why?" I jerk my head back.

"It's cold out here. Obviously, there was an accident, stopping the traffic. You'll be waiting for hours. I'll take care of the gas."

"You don't know me, though." I back up a little. It's not that I feel nervous around him that's making my alarm finally go off, it's that I don't, and I think that scares me even more. I mean—who

3

does this?

"It's just gas, love."

"Well, you should excuse yourself; that's very rude." I laugh lightly.

He stares blankly at me for a moment, then throws his head back, laughing. "That was good!" he says.

"I'm Becca." I extend my hand.

"Derek—nice to meet you." He takes it.

"You, too."

"I know you now. Please get back in your car and wait while I run over to the station." He backs away from me and turns on his heel, heading across three lanes of traffic. Smart man, he left before I could argue—thank God. I watch as he gets further while talking on his phone. Ok, my lack of being creeped out by all of this is getting creepy.

Several minutes go by. Yes, I'm still standing outside. My passenger window won't roll all the way up so it'd be no different sitting in there. Besides, I'm impatient. I feel like if I stand out here, Derek will be back all the much quicker.

"You'll catch your bloody death out here!" a British voice booms behind me as a warm coat attacks my shoulders. I turn out of instinct; I already know who it is.

"What are you doing here?" I ask and, against my inner, stubborn chick, grasp his coat to wrap completely around me. *God—he smells incredible.*

"Same as you, playing in traffic." He grabs the lapels of his coat, closing it more and slightly pulling me toward him. "You're shivering," he says softly. "Come, sit in my car with me and warm up." The way he is staring at me is making me quickly come down with a case of butterflies in my belly.

"The guy who is helping me is British; do you know him?" I change the subject.

"He's British—of course I know him. I know everyone who lives in my country—on a first name basis, no less." He looks at me like I should've known that.

"Are you being sarcastic?"

"Yes, sweetheart." He cracks a slight smile.

"I told you earlier today, don't call me sweetheart." I look away from his gaze.

"I call every girl sweetheart—it's not a big deal—stop making it one." The back of his forefinger grazes my cheek lightly.

"Do you?" I turn back to him.

He opens his mouth but hesitates to say anything. "No," he finally spits out. "I don't call anyone that . . . anyone I don't know, I should say."

"You don't know me." I widen my eyes.

"I believe my soul must."

"You do realize how high you just jumped on the crazy meter with that statement, right?" I raise my eyebrow.

He laughs lightly despite himself, I think. "Yes, I believe I do."

"Does Derek work for you?"

"No. He's my friend."

"Why didn't you come out here to help me?"

"Because . . . if I had . . . I knew you wouldn't have accepted my help." He pulls me back, and my breath catches.

"I have a hard time accepting help from anybody," I offer honestly.

"Come—let us warm up in my car; it's just over there." He points.

"Ok."

"Yes?" He seems surprised.

"I'm freezing my ass off. If it were warm, I wouldn't go with you."

"I shall praise mother nature." He looks up at the sky.

"You do know how weird you are, right?"

"I am?"

"Yes."

"Let's go, sweetheart." He turns, placing his hand on my back and leads me toward his car. The driver gives me a curt nod as we pass him and get into the back seat. *Thank you God and baby Jesus;*

it's warm in here. "So, do you want to tell me why you're out in March with no bloody coat on? You trying to catch Pneumonia?" He seems cross. I shrug. He doesn't need to know my business. He exhales loudly and pulls out his wallet. Retrieving a few Benjamins, he holds them out to me. "Here—please—buy yourself a coat."

"I'm not a charity case, you asshole!" I whip his coat off and climb out the car.

"Becca!" he yells after me. "Becca, goddamn it—get back here!"

Honestly, I have never felt so insulted in my life. *Pompous ass.* I yank my door open, get in, and lock it. Checking my rearview mirror, I see that he was smart enough not to follow me.

I sit here for several minutes, trying to organize the many thoughts going through my head. First: I need to somehow get a cell phone. This fucking sucks! Even worse—what if I was in East Bumble Fuck when this happened? I'd be forced to walk to civilization and probably be that stupid female in horror movies who yells, *"Hello?"* when they hear a noise, then investigates it only to get slaughtered. I hate those dumb bitches. Second: Speaking of weak characters, why did he have to be stuck near me in this traffic? I think he's eating this shit up after I blasted him about his character, Jessica. Now here I am: damsel in distress.

A horn beeps behind me. I look up to see why. Seriously? The car in front of me has moved a few feet—that's all. Shaking my head, I throw my hazards on. Clearly, the guy behind me is experiencing road rage because he continues to honk at me.

Derek makes his way back to me, and I get out to open my gas tank. I flip the guy off and smirk. He looks at Derek and immediately looks away. "Not so brave now, are we?" I shout. Derek is jacked up—I don't care what color he is—this guy must've realized he'd have his ass handed to him.

"Why are you shouting at that bloke?"

"He's being an asshole, much like your friend, Grayson." I give him a double eyebrow raise.

"So, he came out of hiding?" He shakes his head then lets out a little chuckle. "Impulsive bastard," he adds as he begins pouring the gas into the tank.

"Derek, I'm going to need your address so I can mail you a check," I inform him.

"I told you not to worry about it."

"I don't take handouts. I especially won't take any from him." I cross my arms.

"I paid for the petrol. I don't care to be paid back." He taps the can to get the last of it before switching to the other.

"I care."

"Pay it forward." He smiles. *Christ—I can't even pay it backwards.* Clearly, I'm not going to win here, so I nod instead. "You know, Becca, he's not such a bad guy..." he trails off then glances my way.

"I'm sure he's not, he's just real shitty at putting his best foot forward." I kick lightly at my tire and bite at my bottom lip. Okay, my nerves are finally kicking in.

"He'll be worth the chance if you'll give him one." He pulls the empty can out and closes the tank.

"Look, I'm not in the market for any type of relationship right now. I have too much going on in my life." That should put an end to this. Suddenly, Derek laughs like he knows something I don't. Fuck if it isn't driving me crazy.

"I'm not going to ask why you're laughing." I walk past him and sit back in the driver's seat, leaving the door open. I pump the gas pedal then turn the key. I'd like to say she purrs to life but it sounds more like someone being strangled to death before the murderer lets go to allow air. "Yes!" I yell before getting out.

"I'll just place these in the back." He nods in that direction before opening the door.

"Thanks again." I let out a sigh.

"No trouble at all," he says as he closes the door.

"Well, you better get back to your car. The traffic's moving slightly and this guy back here may have a coronary if I don't move my car." I jerk my thumb towards the irate driver.

"It was very nice to meet you, Becca." He extends his hand.

"I'm a hugger, Derek—bring it in." I open my arms and wave him in. He doesn't hesitate. "You're a big damn teddy bear," I say as I'm swallowed up in his hug. He laughs and lets me go. "Bye." I smile.

"See you later." He waves. Huh? Nah—it's just a saying.

Climbing back in, I blast the heat then shift to head forward. I can't wait to get home.

GRAYSON

"Well, what did she say now?" I ask before he can even get fully into the car.

"Come off it, mate! We both know you listened to the entire conversation." He eyes me.

"I didn't catch the end. I was too bloody pissed off, watching you wrap your arms around her."

He laughs. "She asked for the hug. Maybe *I'm* her type." He waggles his brows at me.

"Oh please, for fuck's sake!" I roll my eyes and glance out the window, still able to get a glimpse of her car.

"What is it with her—I mean—she's pretty . . . and funny . . . but, I've never seen you act like this before." He smacks the side of my leg.

"I don't know, to be honest . . . just a feeling deep in the pit of my stomach."

I jump slightly at the sound of my mobile ringing. Expecting Derek's report, I pull it out of my pocket quickly. "Sorry, Jeffrey, I need to take this," I tell my editor. He nods, shuffling his fingers at me to go ahead. "Derek?!" I answer.

"Why do you answer like that?" He almost sounds irritated, and I half think he is, but he laughs through the question.

"Like what?" Honestly, I just want my update.

"Like you're ready for the world to end every time I call you with an update."

"You know why," I state tersely as I turn away from Jeffrey.

"If you're afraid she's going to start seeing somebody then do something about it . . . other than having me spy on her for you."

"Derek, please, we've been through all of this. Timing is of the essence." I run my hand through my hair before getting up, giving my editor a gesture that I'll only be another minute, and walking to the opposite side of his monstrosity of an office.

"You're being fucking creepy, mate, and I'm not sure how much longer I want to tag along for these charades."

"Ah, you have a nerve, don't you? After all I've done for you? I've never asked for help like this." I lower my voice more so. I glance back at Jeffrey, noting the suspicious look he has on his face. "I'll just take this in the hall," I say. He gives me a curt nod. "Derek," I start as I make my way out to the hall. "She's different. I need a way in. My usual stuff will not work on her and quite frankly, I'm glad it won't. Please, for the love of God, stop stringing me along and tell me what, if any, news you have," I beg. He lets out a big defeated-like sigh, and I know he will come through no matter how much he hates this.

"Everything's the same. She works a shitload of hours, mate; I don't know when she sleeps. Her car is way past being on its last leg."

"How do you know that?" I interrupt him.

"Because, she caught me following her at Barnes & Noble, read me the riot act, then yelled at me to jump her car since it wouldn't start up." He laughs.

"Why is that funny?!"

"Because, as she was telling me—and you, I might add—off, she headed to her car to take off, in what would've been a cool fashion, but it wouldn't start. She was *pissed!*" He chuckles.

"You didn't laugh at her, did you?" I close my eyes praying that he didn't.

"No, man—I wouldn't do that!"

"I know . . . I just had to ask."

"I'll tell you what I did do for you, though."

I lean up against the wall and rub my temple. "What's that?"

"I connected with her friend Stacey."

"What?! What did you say to her?" I'm half excited, half nervous.

"I told her who I was. Once I mentioned you, she went nuts— in a good way," he adds quickly.

"Well, how do you mean?" I straighten up and look at my watch.

"She wants to help you."

"What?—*why?!*" This has to be some kind of joke.

"She's never seen Becca get so bent out of shape over anyone before, especially a guy. She believes Becca is secretly interested in you," he finishes then pops—what sounds like—the tab of a can. My eardrum is filled with the sound of him gulping, obnoxiously, I might add. I pull the mobile away from my ear slightly, taking this time to let this information settle in my head. *Interested in me?* So . . . I do have a chance in hell. "You there?" he asks, bringing my attention back to the conversation at hand.

"Yes, sorry. How does she intend to help?" I ask and quickly glance at my watch again.

"Not sure," he says in a jumbled voice.

"Could you please stop eating while talking to me, you big donkey?!"

"I'm hungry," he states defensively.

"Look, I'm in a meeting with my editor. Is this all the info you have for me?" I try to take my tone down a notch. Here he is, helping me, and I'm doing nothing but getting short with him.

"I'll just text you her number. She's expecting a phone call from you."

"Really?"

"Yes. Try not to mess it up by being . . . you know . . . you!"

"Yes, I'll try my best." I laugh. "Thanks, Derek," I add.

"You owe me."

"Put it on my tab. Catch you later, mate." And with that, we hang up.

I take a deep, cleansing breath and head back into Jeffrey's office. "Sorry 'bout that."

"Everything all right?"

"Yes, I'm sorry; personal matter I had to attend to. So, you were saying?" I quickly change the subject as I reseat myself.

"I was saying that you have, yet another, solid piece of work here; minimal corrections." He smiles and hands me my script.

"No plot issues? No flaws in the character development? *Nothing?*" I can't help but question him like this.

"No, Grayson. Why all of the questions?" He jerks his head back.

"Just curious. A serious writer is always looking to perfect his craft."

"Well, I don't see how you could get it any more perfect than it is." He gives me a huge smile, and I have to say—for the first time—I notice how fake it is. *Well . . . shit.*

"Yes, right-o!" I pop out of my seat, script in hand. "Have a lovely day, Jeffrey, we'll talk soon." I put my hand out for a shake before leaving.

Three months ago, I wouldn't have had a second thought about this meeting, his sincerity, loyalty to me, or his lack of drive to aim for the best. I've become another script on his desk he needs to rush through to put a dent in the never-ending pile.

"Hey, Sam." I nod as he opens the door for me. I climb into the back of the car.

"What's the matter, sonny?" Sam asks as soon as he gets behind the wheel.

"Not a hundred percent sure yet, Sam. I'll let you know as soon as I figure it out." I keep my eyes on the manila envelope as I open it and pull my script out. I start slicing through the pages for notes—anything. All I manage to find are punctuation corrections, which are few and far between.

"Do you need anything?" Sam pipes up again.

"Yes—Becca Campbell," I answer. Sam lets out a small laugh. Yes, I have been driving he, Susanna, and Mum a little nuts about her. Seriously, though. If I were to put this script in her lap, I bet my eyes she'd rip it to shreds. I need that . . . that raw honesty. Yet, another reason I have to have Becca Campbell in my life. Christ, Derek's right; I sound creepy. In my defense, I have never been hung up about a woman like this before in my life. One meeting and just like that—karma! All the fecking crap I write about in my novels—poof—real life.

"We're home, sonny," Sam announces as he turns the car off.

"Oh . . . right!" I pull myself together, shaking all thoughts of that beautiful brunette. *Her green eyes. An arse that could make a grown man cry.*

"Grayson?" Sam interrupts my thoughts again.

"Yes, I'm coming now." I get out. I really need to get a grip on myself.

"Man up, Grayson!" I say under my breath and sit on my bed. I've been staring at Stacey's number for a half an hour now. "Feck it!" I hit the green call button.

"Well, if it isn't the infamous Grayson James," she answers after the third ring.

"How'd you know it was me?"

"I had your buddy program your number in my cell, so I wouldn't ignore your call. If I don't know who's calling—I don't answer," she explains. I'm just as put off by the ease in which she speaks to me as I'm glad for it. I feel my nerves settle down several notches. "So . . . what can I do for you, sir?"

"Well, Derek told me you were willing to help me with your lovely friend, Becca," I tread lightly, still unsure of her intentions.

"I am . . . as long as your intentions are sincere. In saying that,

I have a few questions for you before I agree to anything." She stops talking and replaces the sound of her voice with the tapping of something.

"Please—*what is* that noise?" I bite.

"Ooo . . . testy." She laughs. *Shit. Well, this is going wonderfully.*

"Sorry," I sigh.

"That's ok. So! Ready for question number one?" I can almost hear her smile. *Weird.*

"Yes, go on, please."

"What *are* your intentions—I mean—do you just want to fuck her?"

Good thing I wasn't drinking anything, I surely would've spat it out. "Well, let's not beat around the bush, aye?" I laugh nervously.

"Blunt is the only way to go, Grayson. I don't have the time nor the patience to dance around shit."

"I happen to agree with you, Miss . . . eh…" I trail off.

"Walsh; just call me Stace, though."

"Miss Walsh," I repeat with a nod (more for myself).

"Grayson?"

"Yes?"

"Answer my question, please."

"Oh, sorry," I say quickly. "I only have the best of intentions toward your friend, Stace. Also—I would love to shag the hell out of her. All in due time, love."

"Yep," is all she says.

"Eh . . . yep?"

"You're perfect for her," she informs me.

"I'm glad for your vote of confidence; however, I fear your friend lacks the same passion in your conviction." I guffaw.

"Don't laugh," she says, unable to hide the amusement in her voice. "I'm as serious as a heart attack; no one knows Becca better than I do. Besides, you've got a huge plus on your side already."

"What's that?" I'm half scared as to what will pop out of her mouth next.

"You're British. She has a thing for Brits. The accent does things to her that should be deemed unnatural."

"Well then, I shall be extra British around her!" This has to be one of the most amusing conversations I've ever had. I can see how she and Becca are best girlfriends.

"Yes—more British—less pompous."

I roar with laughter.

"Oh, gotta go—duty calls!"

"Wait—what?" What happened to the other questions she had for me?

"Hey, Becca!" she calls out.

"Oh . . . right, then. Well, please, call me when you can talk again," I plead.

"Will do. Thanks for your help, Brian; it's working now."

"Great . . . and . . . thanks, Stacey," I say quickly before she hangs up.

Am I really that much of a pompous arse?

Chapter Two

BECCA

"Jesus, Becca, you look like shit!" Stacey never holds back in the compliment department.

"Shut up," I grumble as I head to the fridge.

"You have to stop working all of these hours; you're going to kill yourself." She reaches past me for the yogurt.

"Ugh. God. I know." I close my eyes and allow more of my weight to be held by the fridge door. "I just need to suck it up for a while; I need a new fucking car," I remind her. "Fucking shit-box-whore..."

"Hey! Don't call me that anymore—I've changed my ways!"

I can't help but laugh a little. Stacey always knows how to pick me up.

"How is it that you only work one job, cry poor, *yet*, never run out of money? Your bills are always paid, and you go out *every* weekend!" *No, really, how in the fuck is this possible?*

"Cause I have myself a sugga-daddy, baby." She bats her eyes, sashays her silk robe, and winks at me as she turns on her heel and exits the room like she's mastered the art of channeling Blanche Devereaux.

Oh, she's *golden*, all right.

She's also full of shit. Max is a full-time student and broke as a joke. *Whatever…*

I head off to my room. I don't even have the energy for mindless TV tonight. Besides, I have to be up in six hours to do another double at the nursing home. Lately, I don't know why I even bother to come home; I should just sleep there.

It's ten o'clock and I've just finished the last of my rounds for the night when I find Jimmy Boland, one of my favorite residents here, sitting alone in the foyer near the nurses' station. He's snacking on a package of Lorna Doones and a small glass of milk. It's not often that he does this, but it generally means that something's bothering him. "Hey, Jim-Jim," I greet as I plop next to him, slap his knee, and steal a cookie. "What's up, buttercup?" I ask before I take a bite.

"I'm worried," he simply states, then proceeds to dunk a cookie into his milk.

"About?"

"You."

"Me?" I jerk my head back.

"Yes, you." He pops the whole thing into his mouth. I know it'll be a few before he elaborates—dentures.

Just then, Jeremy approaches me with the two big binders we record all of the residents' ADLs (activities of daily living) in. "Here you go, baby girl." He smiles as he places them in my lap.

"Thanks, Jer," I say as I pull out my pen. Most of the time, I try to avoid Jeremy's eyes. He's a good friend, as far as work buddies go. Problem is: he wants more. I don't. Put aside that I have no time for a boyfriend—whatsoever—I'm just not interested in him. He's not my type. I'm not exactly sure *what* my type is, but I know enough to say that he isn't it. I'll leave it at that.

"Numbnuts…" Jimmy trails off under his breath. I giggle. Jimmy is *not* a fan of Jeremy at all.

"Stop." I nudge him.

"Ehh! Why doesn't he pick up his damn pants? Nobody wants to see his ass or his shorts." His hands wave out in frustration.

"Okay, let's get back on topic, otherwise, we'll run out of Lorna Doones up here."

"You really want to hear it?" he asks, but it's more like a warning.

"Jimmy, are you *really* giving me a choice, buddy?" I eye him.

"No."

"Carry on, then." I flip open the first book and start recording what happened on my shift.

"This is the third week you've done doubles most days—even your days off. And when you haven't, I know it's because you're at the bookstore. It's too much, Becca! Why are you trying to kill yourself? You're young! You should be out making memories." He taps on the page I'm working on.

"Ah, Jim, I have to. My car's on its last leg. Pretty soon, I'll be starting nursing school. I won't be able to work like this. I need to get all of my ducks in a row." I give him the same speech I've given several of my residents over the past week. It's frustrating, yet, I love how they always think of me. I've become their family and they, mine.

"I'd argue with you about that, but I know it will fall on deaf ears, so…"

"So, what?" I ask, though, I'm not certain I should have.

"Tell me about the nice fellow who sends you flowers here every day."

"It's annoying," I offer.

"Yes, I see that it annoys you." He nods. "So much, that you can't hide the little smile that crosses your lips when you see a new bunch," he adds.

"I don't do that . . . smile," I say suspiciously as I slowly bring my gaze up to find his.

"Don't you?" His brows pop up.

"Do I?" I furrow mine.

"Every time." The creases in the corners of his eyes deepen in amusement.

We find ourselves engulfed in awkward silence. This would be because it's really my turn to speak and I have nothing to say. At least, nothing I'm willing to admit to.

"What's his name, sweetie?" Well, clearly Jimmy isn't going to let the silence fly.

"Grayson James," I answer dutifully like a good daughter. No, he's not my dad, but he's got that cap on real good, if you know what I mean. Truth be told—I love that about Jimmy. He reminds me so much of my own dad.

"Tell me about him."

"There's not much to tell," I say but decide to carry on, so this poor guy can finally go to bed. "I met him at the bookstore. At first, he was fine but then, we got into a heated debate." I stop right there, hoping that's enough.

"About?" he asks.

"Let's put it this way, this guy is used to people kissing his ass and telling him what he wants to hear. I didn't follow suit. Because of it, he almost caused me to get into trouble at work."

"What was the argument over?"

"His book. He's an author." I finally give in. "His character was weak. I told him so. We argued."

"And now, he sends you flowers every day? Sounds to me it's as if he values your honesty."

"He's bossy." Easier to say that then acknowledge that maybe Jimmy is right.

"Is he? Or, are you just stubborn?" He shakes a finger at me then taps my nose with it. Before I can even answer (not that I have one for him), the next shift starts slowly coming through the stairway door next to the nurse's station. "Eh . . . here comes the zombie apocalypse." Jimmy sighs and I laugh as he gets up. "Night, sweetheart." He kisses the top of my head. "Go home and get some rest."

"Yes, Dad," I tease.

"If only I were that lucky." He gives me a soft wink and a warm smile. Jimmy has three sons. He calls them his "vacaysh-sons" because they only manage to see him on their vacations; not a one lives out of state. It pisses me off.

Pulling myself together as he strolls back to his room, I head over to the station and pass the buck, so to speak. Honestly, I'm so tired, I don't know how the hell I'm going to make it home; I live thirty minutes away.

Just as I get outside, I see Jeremy leaning up against the driver's door of his car that he, strategically (I'm sure), parked next to mine.

Great.

Don't get me wrong; he's a nice guy. I'm just tired and done!

"Let's grab a drink, boo." He nods toward his car. Fuck—I hate when he calls me that.

"I'm exhausted, Jer . . . maybe another time?" I wince.

"A—ight!" He smiles as if he's trying to not be disappointed.

"Jer . . . can you just—talk normal around me?" Oh, I need to go home; I'm about to take everything out on him.

"Er . . . yeah." He shifts from foot to foot and turns his cap straight. It was shifted to the right. I have no idea if that means anything other than, "I'm a dumbass." Shit—Jimmy's rubbing off on me.

"I'll see you tomorrow," I say quickly, offer him a smile and climb into my "dead-car-driving." I turn the key. Fuck my life. I turn it again. "Please . . . please turn over or I'm gonna go all Karate Kid on your ass!" I plead; my weekly routine.

I turn the key.

She belches and dies.

I don't even have enough energy in me to cry. I get out.

"You need a ride, boo, eh—Becca?" Jeremy kicks his foot at my tire. Just as I'm about to say yes (God, help me), I notice Derek out of my peripheral vision, trying to be incognito.

"Actually, I'm good. My friend, Derek, is right over there. This is perfect. I forgot he was coming tonight." I offer a white lie before heading in Derek's direction. "See you later, Jeremy!" I wave and then jog over to my stalker in shining armor.

"Becca, please don't read me the riot act." Derek holds his hand up, begging me before I fully make it over.

"I need a ride," I say as I head over to the passenger seat, open the door, and plop in.

"Finally died?" He looks over at me.

"Yup."

"Okay, buckle up," he instructs. I pull my seatbelt across my chest and offer my car one more derogatory remark before Derek gets us out of the parking lot. "Are you off tomorrow?"

"No. But, I don't have to be in until three—thank God."

"What are you going to do?" He looks over at me before turning right.

"Try to get a rental, I guess." I shrug. We both sit in silence for a few minutes. "Please don't tell him," I finally say. He looks over at me with a raised brow, and I know there was no point in me asking.

"Are you hungry?" he asks after a beat.

"Yes, but I'm too tired," I say around a yawn.

"You really need to take better care of yourself, love."

"Thank you, Derek, that's the fifth time I've gotten that memo in the past twenty-four hours." To say I'm getting a little irritated with everyone mentioning this would be an understatement. He shrugs. Smart man. I stare out of the passenger window, watching row after row of different strip malls go by. Signs are lit, but stores are all closed, with the exception of a sporadic Walgreens. I feel myself giving in when my eyelids get heavy.

"Becca . . . Becca," I hear my name and feel someone slightly nudge me.

"Hmm?" I open my eyes.

"You're home, love, time to go in." Derek gives me a sympathetic smile.

I give him a nod and just as I'm about to get out of his car, I turn to him instead, "No, seriously—why are you doing this? Why do you follow me around like you're my own personal Secret Service agent?" I ask calmly. I've asked him this once before— well, screamed it at him, really. I started noticing him parked in the Barnes & Noble parking lot when I was working. One day, I suddenly lost my shit and went off on him. I never did get my answer. And even though I screamed my head off, he was still kind enough to jump my car after and not laugh at my circumstance. Derek's a good guy, the type that emanates that right away.

"He doesn't *force* me. I do this because he's my friend; I owe him." He turns the car off like he knows our conversation is going to take longer than he should let his car idle.

"You can't owe him that much that you stalk the girls he likes for him." I jerk my head back.

"First, you are the only girl he's ever asked me to do anything like this for. Second, thanks for making me feel like some sort of creepy psycho." He laughs lightly.

"Well . . . you know—if the shoe fits…" I trail off, teasing him again.

"I have to say, this shoe would be a lot more uncomfortable if you weren't the person you are," he says with a relieved tone.

"That sounds as if it is, indeed, a compliment. If that's the case, I'm so happy to make your stalking experience a pleasant one." I break off into a laugh. "Christ, I can't imagine anyone else in the world having this exact conversation," I add.

"Nope—no way!" he agrees.

We settle into the amusement of it all for a moment. I then slap his arm, "So, tell me; why do you owe him? For what?"

"He saved my life. It's that simple." Gone is the hyena chuckle.

"How?" My voice cracks. I wasn't expecting that answer.

"Grayson and I went to Uni together," he starts.

"As in brow?" I ask straight-faced.

"Yes. Wait—what?!" He catches what I actually said.

I laugh. "Go on. Sorry. What's Uni?"

"University," he clarifies.

"Ah . . . ok." I nod.

"My parents..." he trails off, takes in a deep breath and puffs it out harshly, like he's trying to fight something off. I wait, understanding the need to articulate, in your head, what you want to come out of your mouth. I can't say that I'm always successful—but, I understand. "They did a lot of missionary work over the years. The last trip they made was to Sudan. Several weeks into their mission, I received word that they were taken by rebels—"

"—Oh no!" I gasp.

"I was more or less told not to expect to ever see them again," he continues.

"Derek—no! I can't imagine what you must've been going through at that moment." I lay my hand on his shoulder. I know they are in the middle of their Second Civil War there. It's been going on since the mid-eighties and from what I have seen or heard reported; it's bad with no end in sight. The casualty count, whether killed, lost, or forced into slavery, is gut-wrenching.

"Oh my God, I was destroyed, Becca. It wasn't just my parents; they also had my baby brother, Jasper."

I cover my mouth, trying to conceal another gasp. "Well . . . ?"

"Well, time went by with no word. No optimism to pass along to me, either, I might add. I felt helpless. Someone out there destroyed my family, and there was nothing I could do about it. Well, except, . . . destroy myself." He grabs his coffee and takes a swig.

"What did you do, Derek?" I ask apprehensively.

"Let my grades go, started hanging out with the wrong people, and then proceeded to miss lectures, deadlines, and defy any rule I could. I was almost kicked out. Grayson swooped in and saved the day," he states, a smile pushes through.

"How so?"

"He and I were best friends already—but—with me going

through this, I tossed our friendship to the side."

"That makes sense," I say quickly between his thoughts.

He jerks his head back, "It does?"

"Sure. If he was already your best friend, then he was really more like a brother to you. Pushing him away was your way of protecting yourself from another loss, especially, one out of your control. That's what it all came down to, right? Your behavior was all about what you *could* control," I explain.

"Grayson's right."

"Huh?"

"You are brilliant." He smiles thoughtfully.

"He said that about me?"

"All the time."

"He . . ." I shake my head, so full of confusion, it might explode. "He doesn't even really know me."

"That will change. He's a persistent fucker."

Yeah, no shit!

"Well, let's get back to you. What happened?" I try to get us back on track.

"Oh, so he talked to the Dean and got me a reprieve on the condition that I'd be under his care. He verbally beat the fuck out of me." He starts laughing.

"What?"

"He's just funny. However, he was the first person to actually give me hope. He said to me, 'Derek, you fucking wanker, get your head on straight, man! Your family is out there! You need to find them! And, what a piece of shit you will prove to be when they come back only to find you've shamed their fecking name by being an arsehole. Pull your shit together and let's find them!'" He stops, trying to collect himself. I can see the formed tears that he's now pushing away.

"Did you?" I inquire.

"Did I what?"

"Find them?"

"Yes—with Grayson's help, in a year's time, we found them—

alive."

I let a sob of happiness escape as I reach to pull him into my embrace. "I would've never found them if it weren't for him giving me a swift kick up the arse. I thought they were dead. Christ—that's what I was led to believe. I wanted to die with them. I was ending up there—in my own way. He saved my life. He saved the lives of my family. I will *forever* be indebted to him," he carries on; all the while, I continue to hold him in my embrace, crying tears of joy.

Suddenly, Derek's door jerks open. "What's this, now?!" Grayson barks. Yes, I know it's Grayson. No, I haven't bothered to look for confirmation.

Derek jumps, but I hold him tighter. "Eh, uh, Gray . . . this isn't what it looks like, mate," he stumbles through. I laugh and finally release him.

"The *bloody hell* it isn't!" Grayson's rage only heightens.

"Thanks for the ride home and for sharing that with me, Derek." I kiss his cheek, completely ignoring Grayson. I grab my bag and get out of the car. Grayson stays where he is—seething. Once again, he's acting like a complete ass. I want to walk away, just walk inside and let him fester. *But*—all I can think about is what Derek just told me and my talk with Jimmy. I pull my bottom lip in, letting my teeth hold it in place as I think about the next, *very crazy*, move I want to make.

Fuck it.

I saunter over to him. Poor guy; his face is going through phases of his predicament. Jealousy—with no actual right—equals jaw twitching. Then, his face softens as I walk up to him, but he still seems on guard someway.

Completely in his space now, "Grayson," I say formally.

"Becca." He stares into my eyes. I toe up and softly kiss his lips once. Just as I pull back, he quickly grasps my lips with his again.

"Goodnight," I say as I pull away.

"What . . . what was that for?" He seems unsure.

"Goodnight," I reiterate and back up out of his embrace.

"Night, sweetheart. I'll see you tomorrow." His hand slides down my arm till it reaches mine. I'm not going to lie; I'm having all kinds of crazy feels, fluttering from my belly to my heart.

"Why?" I stop.

"I have an idea I wanted to run by you." He squeezes my hand, and I feel myself being tugged ever so slightly toward him. "But, I understand you've been working a lot of hours." His left hand grasps my right hip gently, closing in on our personal space again, "I'd rather you get some rest tonight. What I want to talk to you about can wait." He leans down. And, just as his lips almost reach mine, I turn my head.

"Goodnight, Grayson," I say quickly and gasp in air as he squeezes my hips and lays his forehead to my temple. "Please, I need to go in," I add.

"And I need to taste your lips again," his words above a whisper. Inside, butterflies swarm in such a frenzy flight, my whole body shivers. Before I can think of a reply, his hands grasp my face and shift it up to him. His mouth attacks mine. I *may have* just let my lips part for his tongue. I *may have* just whimpered, feeling that very tongue caress mine. And, my hands *may have* just slid up his chest, around his neck. I feel my fingers thread through his hair and pull him closer to me. It's like I'm in the middle of an out of body experience. There are a million alarms going off in my head—*HE WILL CRUSH YOU!* Fuck if I listen to the warning. Just as I'm about to turn the volume of the alarms completely off, he pulls away abruptly. We both stand here, gasping for air like we've run a marathon.

"Get some rest, darling." He finally steadies his breath.

Yeah—right.

"I'll be around late morn, so stay put." He chucks my chin.

Stay put?

"I have things I need to do tomorrow," I snap lightly, my head finally clearing up.

"Trust me. Just stay here and wait for me . . . please?" He cups my face.

I jerk back. "Goodnight," I say again for the five millionth time. But instead of lingering, I turn and quickly take off, pulling my keys out to open my apartment door. I don't even look back. Safely inside, I lean up against it.

"Jesus! Where've you been?" Stacey turns quickly from the fridge, grabbing her chest.

"The fucking shitbox finally croaked!" I roll my eyes.

"How'd you get home?"

"Derek," I say as if that should've been obvious. She knows he's around, lately, more often than not.

"Now what?" she asks.

"I have no idea. I need to see if I can get a rental for tomorrow." I saunter toward my room, omitting all other information.

"Hold it!" She comes around the breakfast bar that separates the kitchen from the dining/living room.

"What, Stace, I'm tired?" I complain.

"Why is your mouth red?" she asks, looking at me suspiciously. "You know your boyfriend, Grayson, wouldn't like it if you were kissing someone." She smirks. "Wait! Were you kissing Derek?" She grabs my arm, a look of panic on her face.

"First of all—he's *not* my boyfriend! Second of all, no, I wasn't kissing Derek. Thirdly, I'm pretty sure Grayson would be happy about the state of my lips since he's the one who made them like this." I pull my arm away.

"What?!" she shrieks excitedly.

Oh. Fuck.

"Stace, I'm exhausted. I don't want to have a pow-wow about this right now. I don't even know what happened. All I know is that it shouldn't have, and I'm going to bed." Before she can say another word on it, I go into my room, close the door, and lock it.

"Alright, but I'm gonna grill your ass tomorrow!" she yells through my door.

"Whatever," I mumble and head off to my shower.

Plopping onto my bed, I pull the covers up, ready to fall fast asleep. I don't think that thought is unrealistic; I've had four hours of sleep a night this week if I was lucky. Yet, here I am, letting my fingers graze over my lips again. His kiss was so rough and so gentle at the same time. I'd be lying if I said I've had better in the kissing department. Ugh . . . God, but why did I let that happen? Why did I initiate the possibility of it getting that far? I need to do something to fix this. I'm not really sure what "*this*" is exactly—only an idea of what I think he wants. If that is the case, I need to make him realize that I'm not the girl for him. No way can I get emotionally invested in someone. I just . . . I don't have it in me. I've hurt too much this past year to invite someone in whom *I know* will end up hurting me. Nope—I'm going to nip this in the bud!

I close my eyes, finally feeling ready to accept sleep, but instead, I'm haunted; my parents' faces flashing like a slideshow. I hate when this happens. I hate not having control over my grief. I just want to turn my brain off and go to sleep. My brain and my heart have other ideas though and instead, I cry myself to sleep once again.

Chapter Three

GRAYSON

"How do you think she'll handle all of this?" I ask Derek as we head up to Becca and Stacey's door. This is my first official visit to Becca's apartment, and I have to say, I'm a bit nervous. Last night proved to be a huge leap of progress that I, quite frankly, wasn't expecting. I'm not sure how "cool" I should play it or if I should just let myself pounce. Christ, I just want to pounce; claim her as mine once and for all. I've also just realized that I've gone completely mad.

"I'm not sure exactly," he replies, snapping me out of my thoughts.

Becca lives in a quaint building with four apartments (two on each side). The doors are at an angle, facing the parking lot, yet greeting their neighbor's door. The whole development is like this. I follow my friend's lead as he heads to the bottom floor apartment on the left and knocks. After a few minutes, we're greeted by a guy with blond hair and a nice physique. The only reason I notice that is because he's answered the door in only his PJ bottoms.

"Can I help you?"

"Who are you?" I ask quickly, as I feel the green monster stirring inside of me, wanting to get out.

"Dude, you knocked on my door." He jerks his head back.

"You live here?" I point to the location as if any of us were unsure.

"My girlfriend does, what's it to you?" He crosses his arms and takes a wider stance.

"You're not Becca's boyfriend, are you?" I try to keep my voice unaffected, although, I've probably blown my "cool" cover when I nearly jumped down his throat a moment ago.

"Stacey's; Becca doesn't have a boyfriend, just a crazy stalker," he says, and we all just stand here, staring at each other.

"Derek," I turn to him, "You really mustn't do that anymore; it's getting creepy now."

"Right—I'll try to control myself," he plays along.

Just then, the door swings open all the way. "You gonna stand out there, hoping someone notices how pretty you are or are ya gonna come in?" Stacey (I'm assuming) enquires.

"Several passersby have already commented, so I believe I've met the quota and can come in now. Please do grab me a glass of water. It's hard standing out here and being gorgeous at the same time." I wink.

"It must be. Entrée." She moves aside, allowing us in.

"Thank you." I nod as I head in.

"Hi, Stace." Derek, who's already met her, gives her a hug. I, of course, skipped that step, being too focused on scanning the home for a sight of Becca.

Completely. Fucking. Mad.

"Please tell me that she did not leave already," I almost groan. I wouldn't put it past her.

"Nope. I went in and turned off her alarm clock so she'd sleep in." She clicks her tongue and shoots me a wink. "You boys want anything: coffee . . . a spot of tea?" she does a terrible impression of an English accent.

"She's still asleep? It's eleven!" I ignore her offer.

"Yeah, which just goes to show how exhausted she is." She frowns and shakes her head.

"Speaking of . . . and since she's . . . *sleeping*," I whisper the last word (not really sure why). "Do you have that stack ready for me?" I waggle my brows.

"What's wrong with your brows, man?" Max shoots me a strange look.

"Shh, Max!" Stacey swats his arm. She gives her attention back to me. "Yes, I have it over here." She heads to a desk in the living room, opens a drawer, moves folders out, and retrieves a manila envelope. "Here, they're all in here." She hands them to me.

"You're sure she won't notice?" I hesitate.

"Nope. She's got like five of each. If she gets to any of them, it's one and only once a month." She gives it the final push into my hands. I give it to Derek as he sets and opens my briefcase on the table. He places it in the top file, away from the other stuff I will be sharing with her today. "This better not come back to me; she'll kick my ass." She wags her finger at us.

"I won't say a word. Now, can I go see about waking her up?"

"Oh, I wouldn't miss you doing that for the world." She laughs.

"Are you trying to frighten me?"

"No, no—that laugh is for Becca."

"I've come to realize, in a short time I've known you, that you're a very good friend . . . in an evil, twisted sort of way."

"Yes . . . yes, I am." She grins. "Her door is on the left, through there." She points to the hallway through the threshold in front of me. "Good luck," I hear her say as I head to Becca's room.

At her door, I take a deep breath then open it slowly. I step inside. Immediately following the entrance to the room is a tall chest on the right. Keeping at the same pace, I move in further and more of her bed is revealed. As soon as I get a full view of her, I bring my fist up to my mouth and bite.

There she lies; her left leg out and straddling around her comforter. She's hugging her pillow in the same fashion. Of course, this brings on the fantasy of me taking the place of her bedding. But the actual fist-biting is due to the fact that she has gone commando under her jammies. I know this for certain because her left arse cheek is poking out of her fecking shorts! I have been mesmerized by her arse since the day I met her. *This* is sending me to a place I'm not sure I can control. I feel myself cave in to my desire as I make my way over to her and—suddenly—find myself nibbling on said cheek.

"*What the?!*" Becca jumps and quickly turns to face me—her eyes wide.

"Jesus! I'm sorry, Becca." I'm completely flustered. "You have to understand, I came in to wake you. I love your bum, and there it was! And it called to me. It said, '*Graaaaysonnnnn, please nibble on me.*' It was like some sort of mind control because before I knew it, I was tasting and biting that fantastic arse of yours for twenty glorious seconds of my life," I blather on. I have no idea if any of that made any sense. "I'm terribly sorry . . . that was very rude of me." *Oh, fuck it to hell with my Goddamn eyes blinking away as if they're seizing!*

Becca sits up, staring at me and the oddest thing happens; a smile bursts through the pissed off look she had a minute ago and a giggle is released (also, with a good amount of lip biting that is driving me completely mad). "Wow, that is one magical ass I have," she says through her giggles.

"Ugh . . . you have *no* idea!" I plop onto her bed, dramatically. "Good morning, sweetheart." I smile over at her.

"Morning." She offers a shy one back.

"All right then, time to get up." I smack the mattress and get back up onto my feet. I turn and balance on my fists as I lean in for a proper morning kiss. A confused look crosses Becca's face, and she moves her head back away from me. "Your sense of direction is terrible, darling. This way," I coach her, crooking my finger.

"This needs to stop." She's so quiet, I can barely hear her.

"We've barely begun." I sit back down, in front of her this time, and grab her hand.

"Grayson," she starts. "I'm going to be very honest with you." Her eyes meet mine and hold their attention.

"Go on, then." The suspense is killing me.

"This year has been very difficult for me. I've lost two of the most important people in my life: my parents." Her eyes fill up.

I reach to palm her cheek. "Oh, sweetheart, I'm so sorry. What happened?"

"Car accident; nobody knows exactly what happened that caused it." Her chin quivers and she pulls her hand away to wipe her tears.

"It's an awful pain, isn't it?" I stare off in the direction of her bathroom, thinking of my own father.

"Did you lose your parents too?" She sounds almost surprised.

"My dad—lung cancer—five years ago. Although, I did get the chance to say goodbye. However, watching him suffer for so damn long," I take in a deep breath, "I honestly don't know what's worse or what's easier; watching someone you love suffer or have them go quickly but never having that closure."

"How's your mom?" she asks, her hand finding a home on my shoulder.

"It's tough on her. He was the love of her life. Through it all, she's remained her cheerful self." I turn back to her. "You'd love her—everybody does."

"I'm sure."

"So . . . do you want to finish your earlier thought or explanation as to why you're pulling away from me?" I pat the hand she has on my shoulder.

"Right!" She pulls it away. "Sorry, I get easily distracted." She reaches over to her nightstand and grabs a tie for her hair.

"Leave it down, Becca; it's so beautiful." I reach to touch her dark, wavy hair. She leans away.

"So, as I was saying," she wraps it up, "It's been a very difficult year for me; I've had to handle all of this on my own. I had to take a leave of absence to sort their estate out. It took a lot longer than I had planned, which has now given me a lot to clean up in my personal life. I *need* to do this before I start nursing school in the fall. So what I'm trying to get at is that I have no time for whatever it is that you would like *this* to be. I need to focus on my life right now and getting to where I need to be." She stops. My God, I'm not sure if she even took a single breath during her whole speech. "Do you understand where I'm coming from?" She grabs both of my hands and squeezes them.

I yank her forward and swiftly kiss her lips, "I'll meet you in the living room. That is, unless, of course, you need help getting undressed." I smirk.

"Grayson?!" She sounds exacerbated.

"Five minutes—tops!" Another kiss and I'm up and heading for the door.

Heading back out to the living room, I find Stacey, Max, and Derek at the breakfast bar, eating. "Hey." I tap on Stacey's shoulder. "Why didn't you tell me about her parents?" I almost whisper.

"Uh . . . that would be because she doesn't require any help in using her crutches," she states then pops the rest of her sausage link into her mouth.

"What?"

"She uses that excuse for everything. Don't get me wrong— most of it's legit, but the rest is bullshit." She waves her hand.

"You're so poetic, baby." Max smiles and rubs her back.

"I feel awful about her parents, though, and I can understand the grief."

"So, you're gonna back off then?" She raises a brow at me.

"Certainly not!" I scoff. "And if she thinks that, well, I'll be correcting that assumption straight away."

Just then, I turn my neck at the sound of a door clicking open. Soon enough, Becca pads her way into the living room. "There she is." I smile at her. "Have a seat, I'll fetch you some coffee." I place my hand on her back and gently guide her to the last barstool. I head around the bar into the kitchen and proceed to hit every cupboard before finding the correct ones. I shan't mention how convenient it would have been, had someone gave me some sort of direction. I go about making her coffee: two and a half spoons of sugar and extra half-and-half. Placing it in front of her, I wait for the taste of approval. In slow motion (so it seems), she brings the mug up to her perfect lips, her eyes bore into mine. I don't even think she realizes how seductive she can be; it's effortless.

Taking a sip, she gets a confused look upon her face and sets the mug back down. "How did you do that?" she asks.

"Do what, love?"

"Make my coffee perfect without asking me how I like it."

"Easy," I begin. "I made it how I see you: sweet and—"

"If you say creamy, I'm gonna barf my breakfast all over you!" Stacey cuts me off.

"And full bodied," I say through my chuckle.

"Well, what do you mean by 'full bodied'?" Becca gets defensive.

I come back around the bar, stand next to, and lean down. "It means, I fecking love your body, Becca," I say in a stern, yet, full of desire, tone. I'll have none of that insecurity she had brewing a moment ago. She responds only with erratic breathing. She picks her mug up for another sip. Looks like I successfully squashed that. Now, if only I could stop the tightening of my trousers, I'd be sorted. "Now, there is some food left that Stacey cooked. Shall I fix you a plate?" I push some of her hair behind her ear. She moves her head slightly away.

"I don't eat right away," she states. And with that, she gets off the stool, cup in hand. "Excuse me." She looks up at me. I take a step back so she can head over to the living room. She sits on the sofa, curling her legs underneath her. "So, what did you want to discuss?" she asks after making herself comfortable.

"Right!" I run my hand through my hair and head over to her, grabbing my briefcase on the way.

"Oh, Stace, will you be able to get me to work today? I thought I set my alarm to get up in time to get a rental but apparently I didn't." Becca leans her neck forward to look past me.

"Uh..." Stacey starts.

"I've got your ride all taken care of," I inform her.

"I bet he does!" Stacey pipes in, her statement covered in naughty thoughts.

"Max, shove something in her mouth, will you?" Becca complains.

"No problem—I wouldn't mind a twofer!"

"Ugh . . . eww—shut up!" Becca cringes then laughs. I prop my head on my fist and just watch her, intoxicated by her laugh. Noticing my intrigue, she abruptly stops. "Sorry."

"I love the sound of your laughter; no need to apologize."

"What do you want to talk to me about?" She takes another sip of her coffee.

"Yes!" I slap my knee before retrieving my manuscript out of the briefcase.

"What's that?"

"A copy of my next book. Let me explain." I put my hand up. She nods, and I continue. "I really appreciated how honest you were with me when we first met. Did I whole heartedly agree with you? No—not at first. *But* then I re-read "Timeless" and found myself seeing it through your eyes. I was shocked. You were the only one to point out *anything* that may be looked upon negatively. I have to say—it hacked me off. At this point, the publishers already had this script," I pick it up, "in their hands. So, I anxiously awaited the edits to see if it was just a fluke. Here," I hand it to her, "nothing. Well, with the exception of a few grammatical and spelling errors." I watch as she flips through.

"Grayson," she looks up, "I'm not really understanding the point of you coming to me about this. Isn't this something you should talk to your team about?"

"Well, that's just it!" I raise my voice. "I've come to realize that they are not really *my* team. I'm just another author to them. One that earns them a lot of money to boot! They've become lazy when it comes to making sure I am putting my best out there. I need your help." I get to my point.

"How am I supposed to help you?" she pleads, seemingly confused.

"I need you to do what you do best—criticize me." I didn't mean to say it *exactly* like that, but it is rather to the point if I do say so myself. Becca's shoulders begin to shake as she seemingly tries to contain her laughter. Her eyes are full of mirth, and I feel my chest tighten, watching her. This is the first time I'm getting a glimpse of this side of Becca—I love it. I want to see more of it. I want to be the cause of it.

"Well, when would you need it back by? I might not be able to get it done in time with all the hours I work." She cringes.

"One month long enough?"

"Yes, I think so."

"Then I have five more for you to review after."

"What?"

"This is a job, not just a favor. I am paying you to proofread. As a matter of fact, I have a sign-up bonus for you." I smile.

"I don't know what to say…" she trails off.

"There's nothing more for you to say—you've already agreed. Want to know what your bonus is?" I bite my smile back.

"What?" She seems unsure.

"I've bought you a brand new car, sweetheart."

"Wha . . . why would you do that?" She pushes herself back further on the couch but gets no further as she is at the end already. It's almost as if she's trying to get away from me, like I'm going to harm her or something.

"I've told you why, that and I'd feel much better knowing you were driving a safe vehicle. Becca, why are you responding this way?" I shuffle my finger at her.

"I'm not going to sleep with you," she says in a low, accusatory tone. I have *never*, in my life, felt my blood come to a raging boil as it does so at this very moment.

"Let us get something straight, *darling*. I have *never* bought, nor needed to buy, a woman expensive gifts to have at her. Contrary to your belief, my charm affords me all the comfort I could want and then some. There is never a shortage, and there are plenty of flavors to choose from. Do I make myself clear?" I seethe.

"Very," she agrees with a smirk almost like she's claimed my king. All of the sudden, I realize what I've just done. I have loaded her weapon with the ammo for her to keep me away—emotionally. Brilliant! *Just fucking brilliant, Gray!* "So what kind of car is it, boss?" Her stolid expression makes me slump; square one.

"Honda Accord; I wanted you safe, and it's one of the safest cars on the market." I'm flat; excitement is all gone.

"Well, that definitely cost more than what you'd pay me to proof six scripts. Can we set up a payment plan?"

"It's a bonus!" I snap.

"Ok," she sighs.

"Here." I toss her a cell.

"What's this?"

"It looks to me like it's a mobile phone, Becca!" Clearly, I have no ability to hide my anger.

"I know what it is! Why are you tossing it on my lap?" she bites back.

"It's yours—don't be so daft!" I get up. "You are to answer all calls and texts from me!" I bark. "I need to take a walk," I say before she can bother with a reply. "Derek, show her the new car, please?" I ask then head right out the door. *Bloody fucking hell—* she drives me mad!

I take to the sidewalk, heading off as if I have a clue or a plan as to where I will end up. I don't care if I get lost. Honestly, it'd be a whole hell of a lot better than sitting back there, being torn to shreds every chance she gets. Does she think I behave like this for sport? Does she find me to be the desperate sort? Christ, I'm fecking rhyming now. *Shut it, Gray!*

I know she is feeling the same pull I feel, her behavior and the way she kisses me tells me that much. I need a different approach. But what? I'm afraid to admit it, but I believe I've become a bit spoiled; always having my way. It's been a long time since I've had to *work* towards a goal, to actually achieve it. Maybe—just may-be—I'm working too hard! That's it! She's got used to me panting over her. It's time I mix things up a bit. Yes—that's it—that's just what I'll do.

I return to her apartment, surprisingly without incident. Bec-ca and Derek are walking back to the door as well. My guess is, they've just finished going over her car.

"It smells like a new car!" she screeches at me and does a little happy dance. The excitement on her face is at full capacity. I can't help but smile. I can't help but forget why I was so mad at her a moment ago. *Stick to your guns, Grayson!*

"Glad you like it." I cut my smile short and give Derek my attention. "Ready to go, mate?"

"Uh…" he trails off unsure like. I get it; we aren't booked to leave till tomorrow. She doesn't need to know that, and there's no point to hanging around here.

"I've got lots of work I need to finish up before our flight," I inform him quickly as I head through her front door and grab my briefcase. "Nice meeting you Stacey and Max!" I shout, assuming they are in her bedroom.

"Bye!" they both yell back.

I turn only to bump right into Becca. "Oh, I'm sorry."

"No, that was my fault—sorry."

"Okay, well . . . I'll see you in about a month, then." I clear my throat.

"Okay." She stares up at me.

Don't kiss her. Don't you dare kiss those fecking gorgeous lips of hers!

"Excuse me." I gesture with my briefcase that I need to get through.

"Oh, right—sorry . . . again." She shakes her head and moves to her left.

"Good day."

"That's it?" she asks just as I make it to the door.

"What's it?" I turn.

"This is how you're leaving?"

"This is how one usually does." I look at her as if she has five heads. "Would you prefer I climb out the window instead?"

"Don't be a smartass." She crosses her arms. "You're not gonna…" she adds almost hesitantly.

"What? Kiss you goodbye?"

"Yeah." I can hear the vulnerability in her tone.

"No. Because I should've never kissed you 'hello'." And with that, I turn and walk out the door.

"You want to explain to me what's going on with you?" Derek asks as soon as I make it over to him.

"Trying something different." I walk past and get into the passenger side of the car. He follows my lead and gets into the driver's seat.

"So?" He looks over.

"So?"

"What's the new plan—the something different?"

"No clue, but I'm cutting back on my attention." I shrug. "We'll see what happens from there."

"Does this mean I get to go on holiday?"

"Oh please! Where've I been holding you back from? I'm surprised I haven't had a call from them, thanking me."

"Haha . . . jerk!" He throws a side punch to my arm, and I laugh.

"To answer your question—yes, you're a free man."

"How do you feel about that?" he asks as we head out of the complex.

"Not sure. Guess I'll find out soon enough."

Chapter Four

BECCA

"Off to work?" Stacey asks as I enter the living room.

"Nope . . . these are my 'hot date' scrubs." I grab my purse and shuffle through it for the keys to my new car. I can't believe it—*I have a new car.*

"How do you like it?"

"What?" I pull them out.

"Your new vibrator—*the car*, asshole!" She throws her pen at me.

"Are you paying bills again?" I look at her funny.

"No. I'm writing my sponsor child a letter." She holds her hand out for her pen.

"Your what?" I widen my eyes in shock as I hand her pen back.

"Yes . . . I sponsor a child. Kenede; she's from Zimbabwe." She looks back to her letter.

"Uh…" I trail off.

"What?!" She turns back. "It was late, I couldn't sleep, and those bastards with the infomercials! My heart broke. For less than a cup of coffee a day—"

"—Stop!" I cut her off. "Do not recite their commercial to me." I laugh.

"It's marketing genius! The guilt hooked me right in." She shakes her head.

"I don't feel guilty. Probably because I can't afford to buy a coffee every day."

"Oh, shut up now. Tell me about the car!" She smacks my arm.

"It's silver, four-door with all the bells and whistles."

"I'm just going to put this out there—you were such a bitch to him." She grabs an apple out of the fruit bowl and chomps into it.

"Look, I was just stating a fact. I'm not doing this with him. I don't want this—not right now—not with him." I cross my arms and lean against the bar.

"I'm gonna call bullshit on that. But, either way, I don't think he's going to let you get away with that behavior."

"Well, it seems to have worked. He didn't even attempt to kiss me goodbye. So, put that in your hat!" I say matter of factly.

"Yeah . . . good luck with that." She humors me.

"Whatever; I have to go. I'll catch ya later." I pull my purse strap up and over my shoulder.

"Have fun," she says as she gets back to her "child."

"Yeah, right."

I rub the towel through my hair again in an obnoxious manner. I'm about eight paychecks overdue for a haircut, and I get paid biweekly. To say I'm itching to cut it would be an understatement; it's not just long, it's thick and wavy. *Eh . . . soon, Bec.*

I forego brushing my teeth and head out to my room and the nice glass of merlot waiting for me. I can actually relax tonight after a long shift at work. I'm working at Barnes & Noble tomorrow, but I don't have to be in until two. So, I'm going to stay up real late tonight to guarantee I enjoy the benefits of sleeping in tomorrow.

Besides, I've been itching to start Grayson's book all day. I won't tell him that, though. Not that he'll be asking me—at least not tonight. He hasn't called me once since giving me the phone this morning. No flowers today, either. Suddenly, Barbara and Neil are blasting the chorus to "You Don't Bring Me Flowers" in my head. "Ugh . . . so dramatic, Becca." I shake my head and climb on top of my covers, setting my pillows up to sit against them. Getting myself situated, I grab my wine and take a long swig. "Ok," I sigh. "What do you have for me, Mr. James?" I put the glass down and pick up the script.

He writes very well. I mean, I knew he did, I just thought a lot of it was polished off by his editor. He's right; there aren't too many corrections as far as I can see, and I'm already thirty pages in. I wonder if I should text him to give an update. No. *Just keep reading!*

After another ten pages, my hand finally grasps a pen to make its first marks. Nothing major, just the character stood up when he never actually sat during this scene in the first place. Suddenly, I jump from the not-so-subtle way Stacey bangs on my door before opening it.

"Whatcha doin'?" She saunters over and plops belly down on my bed.

"Going over his script," I reply without looking up.

"Ooh . . . is it good? What's it about?" She smacks my leg.

"Ow—stop!" I rub it. "So far, it's good."

"What's it about?" she asks again.

"Um . . . it takes place during World War I in England. The hero is a barrister—"

"—He works at Starbucks?" She gives me a quizzical look.

"You better change companies for your hair dye; the bleach is getting into your brain. A *bar-rist-er!*" I worry about her sometimes. I really do. "He's a lawyer in England in the higher courts. Believe it or not, our world existed once without the likes of Starbucks or Dunkin' Donuts."

"Our poor fore fathers." She chuckles.

"*Anyway*—Rupert also operates in higher society, getting his jewels shined by whomever he chooses." I waggle my brows.

"Go on." She flutters her fingers, encouraging me.

"But, he's bored! He's tired of these high-class whores, basically."

"Basically?"

"Well, he doesn't come right out and say it—not yet. But, you can sense his boredom in his tone and behavior. Grayson does a really good job pulling the reader in to gain that kind of perspective. Anyway…" I shake my head and hands to get myself back on track. "I've just come to the part where he's met this lovely girl, Lydia. She's the niece of his maid, whom he's rather close to. Lydia is getting ready to go on trial for supposedly killing her attacker. But, she has no money for a proper attorney or as they call it: a solicitor. So, fearing for her niece's life, the maid begs Rupert to step in." I stop to drink some wine. "From the moment their eyes lock, he's a goner. And when she speaks to him so eloquently; an educated woman—it floors him. That was the least he was expecting."

"He thought she would be uneducated because her aunt is a maid?" Stacey asks defensively.

"Yes. But, it's the right thinking for that time. Usually families all worked at the same station level."

"So glad to be here in the nineties!"

"Yeah…"

"Well?"

"Well, what?"

"What happens?!" She slaps the mattress.

"I don't know. It's just now stepping into his growing attraction for her; what he's going through," I explain.

"What he's going through?"

"Yes. This is unchartered water for him. He's never had an instant connection to a woman before. It's hard for him to handle these feelings all the while, trying to fight them off, thinking it's lust."

"But it's not."

"Nope."

"Hmm," she hums.

"Hmm? What's that about?"

"Just reminds me of someone." She passes it off.

"Who? I know all the 'someones' in your life." I remind her.

"Someone you're overlooking." She winks. I stare. "Grayson!" She smacks my leg again.

"Huh?"

"When did he write this?"

"I don't know." I shrug. "Why does it remind you of him?"

"He's crazy about you!"

"He doesn't know me."

"Rupert didn't know Lydia." She points out.

"I haven't finished the book; they may not end up together."

"I bet they do." She sits up. "Grayson will see to it," she adds.

"Whatever. Look, I need to go to bed; I'm tired."

"You're just dodging an uncomfortable bullet." She stands up, giving me room to stretch out.

"Um . . . I'm guessing that all bullets are uncomfortable," I suggest as I close his script up and put it on my nightstand.

"Knock it off; you know what I mean."

"Look, I'm not going to deny that I'm attracted to him. My problem is: I'll fall and have my heart shattered. After losing my parents this year, I don't think my heart could take anymore."

"I love you, Becca, and I loved your parents too, but I'm not gonna let you pull this cop-out bullshit with me." She gives me "The Look" complimented with her hands on her hips.

"What cop-out?" I snap. I'm seriously not in the mood.

"You're using their death as an excuse to avoid everything that has to do with living; anything enjoyable, at least." She points out.

"I don't know what the hell you are talking about! Am I working a shit ton of hours? Yes. I have no choice—you know that! So no—I'm not living my life to the fullest right now, but I don't see what any of what I'm going through has to do with Grayson except for the fact that I don't need him to be another item on my already overflowing plate!" I actually feel as if my head is about to explode.

"News flash, Bec—bills will always be there, lurking. Your twenties won't be. I highly doubt your parents would want you to run yourself into the ground like you have been. I'm also pretty damn sure that they wouldn't want you to push away your chance at love."

"Love?!" I practically shout.

"Yes! Love! In *any* capacity! Don't get all 'happily ever after' on my ass! I'm just talking about allowing yourself to experience the possibility." She throws her hands out.

"This is all well and good, Stace, but true to form, you are over exaggerating the situation." I roll my eyes. If over exaggerating was a sport, Stacey would be the world champ—hands down.

"I'm not over exaggerating! I am trying to open your eyes!" She gives a last ditch effort. However, her delivery has lost its thunder. "Look," she starts up again. "I know you are going to end up doing what you want to do, I'm just asking for you to try to open up your mind a little. And, for God's sake, be a little kinder to Grayson. I don't agree with this wall you have up, but I understand it. However, you need to stop and think of the words you use when conveying a message to him. He's really into you, and he's trying to do everything he can to show you. I kinda feel like he's your knight in shining armor."

"Uh…" That's all I've got. I'm so beyond confused right now. Stacey's not usually so pro "be nice to the stalker guy." I'm beginning to think I'm in a really bad episode of *The Twilight Zone*. "Stace, can we go over a few facts here?" I wait for a response. She's silent, so that's like anybody else screaming into a megaphone. "Okay, first: I've only known him for a little over a month. Actually—correction—I met him a little over a month ago. I've known Derek since then. Secondly: I've seen him a total of four times since I've met him. Doncha think his behavior is a little . . . I don't know—overbearing?! I mean, who acts like this?" Just as I finish my sentence, the "Bat Phone" sounds off. We both stare at it then look at each other. An unexplainable giggle erupts from both of us.

"That's fucking weird!" she finally says.

"Right?!" I grab it; my eyes open wide at her.

"It's also kinda hot," she adds.

"Shut up!" I wave her off before I answer. "Hello?"

"Oh good, you're still up!" he states with some relief in his voice.

"Yeah, barely; I was just getting ready to go to bed," I let on. Stacey shoots a glare at me.

"Oh . . . uh . . . er . . . well, I'll let you go then," he stammers.

I don't know if it's the guilt coming on from my conversation with Stace or the fact that Tevin Campbell (no relation, of course . . . that I'm aware of anyway) is blaring "Can We Talk" in my head, but I blurt, "I started your book tonight."

"Really?" He perks up. "Okay . . . let me have it."

Jesus, the way he just said that . . . I'm crossing my legs. I swallow hard and glance back at Stacey, who has a devilish grin on her face. I flash my sight word at her. She kisses one off to me, in return, before waving and heading out of my room. "I'm only about fifty pages in, I think. So far; so good. There're a few corrections I made note of," I offer.

"Fifty pages?" He sounds surprised.

"Yeah."

"That's a lot. Are you . . . are you sure you took enough time to catch things?" I can tell he's trying to tread lightly.

"Yes, I promise. I'm a fast reader, but you're also a wonderful writer. You're very smooth, your flow is great; it makes me all that much faster," I say softly.

Grayson chuckles lightly.

"What?"

"If you weren't being such a pain in the arse about having a relationship with me, I would so feed off that statement you just made," he states in such a regretful tone, as if he wishes he could just say *fuck it!* and let, whatever it is he wants to say, out.

"Pain in the ass?"

"Yes. You're a pain in the arse. Fear not, darling, I am up for the challenge."

"Thanks, Shakespeare." I throw my sarcasm his way.

"Hmm . . . all right, enough of that. You need to get some rest, gorgeous."

"I'm gonna let you slide on that comment for two reasons. One: I'm feeling generous. And two: I honestly don't think you can help what comes out of your mouth."

"I have to get off the phone with you now; I find your telephone voice to be rather annoying," he says nonchalantly as if he weren't hitting me with an insult.

"What?!" I snap.

"Yes, love, it's incredibly sexy. So much so, it's annoying the fuck out of me that I was too stubborn to kiss you before I left."

"I wouldn't have kissed you back," I scoff.

"Yes . . . you would have." He's so cavalier, so confident . . . so sexy. *Shut up, Becca!*

I clear my throat. "Grayson, I am your employee now, you can't behave like this—it's inappropriate." I try to steer the conversation.

"Too right, Miss Campbell," his voice laced with mirth.

"Okay, well . . . goodnight," I say with some hesitation.

"Before you go; how was your first day with your new car?"

"Filled with awkward silence." I laugh.

"Why's that?"

"I didn't scream one profanity."

"That's good." He laughs. "And, I trust you were warm?"

"Yes," I say quietly.

"I worried about you . . . um . . . being warm." I can hardly believe how vulnerable he sounds. I notice my breathing trying to keep up with the butterflies in my belly. "You were so cold that day, I had to fight off the urge to pull you into my arms to warm you," he adds.

"I have to go, Grayson," I say quickly. I simply *cannot* stay on the phone with him.

"Of course you do," he's short. "Goodnight, Becca."

"Night…" I trail off and hang up.

"Becca, dear, can you come in here and fix this damn TV again?" Jimmy pulls me out of my thoughts.

"Sure. The movie over?" I ask as I get back from lunch physically. Mentally—I've already clocked out for the day. I am beyond grateful that I only have to work until three today.

"You okay, honey?" He pats my shoulder as I switch the TV back to cable. "You've been very off lately."

"Oh, I'm okay, Jimmy. I've had a lot on my mind." Of course, I fail to mention that it's been Grayson on my mind. I haven't talked or texted him in three weeks. I don't know Grayson well at all, but I think I know him *well enough* to guess that he isn't very happy about this.

I am really enjoying his book. Although, I do agree that he needs a new team; a lot of discrepancies were missed. My problem is: the characters have taken on the form of Grayson and me. I'm having a difficult time separating my feelings . . . my attachments from the story to real life. Lydia is *so* much like me, it's creepy. I know he had written this before we met, which creeps me out even more. My avoidance of him really comes down to me needing time to process everything correctly. I don't want to make an ass out of myself. I need to keep this professional.

"Well, as much as I love seeing you all of the time, I'm glad you're not working as many hours." He smiles warmly.

"Me too. It has been nice to catch up on sleep." I grab the remote. "Ok, court shows?" I ask.

"You know it." He winks.

"All right, try to stay out of trouble." I eye him as I place the remote down.

"I won't make any promises I can't keep." He holds his hands up. I laugh lightly before heading out of the main living room to start my afternoon rounds.

Chapter Five

GRAYSON

"She is not going to be happy with you," Derek warns me for the umpteenth time.

"I don't bloody fucking care!" I bark back at him. "I'm not happy with her!" I add. "I'm here; I'll ring you later."

"Good luck, mate," he says, sounding apprehensive.

"Right-O!" I hang up and head into the nursing home she works at. I inform the receptionist, in the little room, on the left, that I'm here to meet with the administrator for my tour of the facility. I can't believe the levels I've had to sink to, to get this woman's (this woman being Becca Campbell) attention. I sit in a huff.

"Bad day, son?" The older gentleman, a few seats down, peers over his paper at me.

"I'm sure it's going to be," I grumble.

"Things could be worse." He shrugs.

"How so?"

He gets up and shuffles his way towards me, taking the seat

next to mine. "You could be that putz," he says secretively and shuffles his paper out in the direction of an orderly who, for some reason, seems to be losing his pants. I bite back a need to laugh. "I can't say he's worth the weight of that gold chain he's got wrapped around his neck," he adds. I observe this fellow he's pointing out again and do indeed notice a very thick chain. "Just wait until you hear him talk . . . it's magical." He whacks my leg. I go to say something, but he shushes me. I turn my attention to the "putz", waiting in anticipation.

"Yo, yo! Here comes Scooter G, out prowling for da ladies!" The putz announces as a resident comes down the hall in his electric wheelchair.

"Shut up, moron!" Scooter G says in a disgruntled tone and offers Putz a middle finger.

"You gots spunk, son . . . dat's what da ladies like. Go get yours, Scooter G!" Putz carries on as if this is a friendly exchange. I believe it is on his part, actually.

"They say English is required to work here, but I have no idea as to what that was."

"How does he keep his job here, talking like that?" I ask him in disbelief.

"I'll tell you how," he starts, "because my Becca girl, over there, saves his ass constantly."

I jerk my head quickly at the mention of her name to search for her. There she is. *God, she's lovely.* I watch as she walks hand-in-hand with a very slow walking female resident.

"Beautiful, isn't she?" the fellow asks lovingly.

"Well, she's a bit old for me, mate, but that one walking with her knows how to stop my heart in an instant," I joke.

"Ha ha ha!" He laughs so loud, I'm afraid it will grab Becca's attention. "I like you! What's your name, son?"

"It's Grayson." I smile at him. Funny old fellow, you can't help but like him.

"Becca's Grayson?" He jerks his head back.

The air gets knocked out of my lungs. "Wha . . . what?" Surely

I misheard him.

"Becca's Grayson . . . the one who sends her flowers every day, putting a smile on her face. Well, at least, he used to." He pauses. "Why don't you send her flowers anymore?" he asks.

"They make her smile?" I ignore all questions.

"Oh boy, do they! She doesn't even notice it, but I keep a close eye on her. I see how they make her feel."

"That's a bit creepy, eh…" I trail off for a name.

"Jimmy. And no, it's not creepy!" He smacks my leg again. "Becca lost her parents this past year; I keep an extra eye out for her. Her dad asked me to, last year, when her parents were up visiting. Now, we're her only family. That's just how she makes us feel, too." He starts to get teary-eyed. "You've got a great girl on your hands; don't mess it up. And don't you hurt her!" He pokes me. "She's all some of us have."

"I'll resume the flowers immediately and I'll muster up more patience with her. You know, Jimmy, she hasn't made courting her very easy at all. I've been getting quite discouraged of late." I pour my heart out.

"She'll be worth the wait, son. Just give her time. She's stubborn to the core, but that's part of who she is and you have to love every part of her, not just the appealing parts," he advises. I can't help but let my mind wander to Becca's *very* appealing parts.

"Damn, Boo, you are beautiful!" I hear the putz exclaim.

"And, for the love of God, keep this moron away from her!" Jimmy begs.

"Did he just call her 'Boo'?" I ask without masking any of my annoyance.

"Yeah. I keep asking him if he's a ghost." He shakes his head. A burst of laughter escapes from me before I can contain it, bringing Becca's attention to me. A look of disbelief crosses her face. Someday, I hope excitement is the only thing that crosses her face when she sees me out of the blue. The fact that she didn't this time saddens me—disappoints me—I don't know which. All I know is that it's powerful enough to make me look away from her, uncomfortably, I may add.

"Grayson, what are you doing here?" she asks under her breath when she and the lady approach me. I don't have to look up to know she's also said it through her teeth.

"Mr. James," an enthusiastic female voice greets me. I look up, acknowledging the very-put-together woman. "I'm so sorry to have kept you waiting." She holds out her hand. "I'm Joanne Kerns, the assistant administrator here. I'll be happy to take you on your tour now." She extends her hand out, after the greeting, to lead the way. Becca, with her front row presence to our exchange, gives me a confused look. "Did you need something, Becca?" Joanne asks her quickly.

"Um . . . no. I was just coming over to check on Jimmy," she flusters, then moves to the side more. "C'mon, Lillian, let's grab you a seat next to Jimmy." Her attention now focused on the little lady with a jewel-beaded hairnet.

I follow Joanne's lead, though my head is cranked to the left to watch Becca. As if she can sense my stare, her eyes find mine. I pucker up and send a small air kiss her way. She rolls her eyes angrily, I believe, and refuses me anymore of her attention. I turn mine back to Joanne, who has chatted me up without missing a beat.

Bloody fucking hell! I was beginning to think that this tour was never going to end! Joanne talks your ear off as if it were a sport and she wants to maintain her MVP status. Christ—I've been here an hour and a half now!

"So, Mr. James, do you think this would be a great fit for your grandmother?"

"I think it would be." *If she were alive...* "You've definitely made it to the top of my list. Why even just observing that lovely nurse you have, Becca?" I ask.

"Yes, Becca! She's one of our best nurse's aides here. All of the residents adore her." She beams.

"You can tell the feeling is mutual; that's what grabbed my attention!" *Sure it was, Gray!* It definitely wasn't all of her "appealing parts."

"Oh, it is! She's a gem, that girl."

"Yes, well, I'd like to thank you very much, Joanne, for taking the time out of your busy schedule to accommodate such a last minute tour for me." I extend my hand out for a farewell shake. "I'll be sure to let you know my decision. I'll show myself out."

"It was my pleasure, Mr. James." After a quick shake, she heads off to her office, saying hello to some of the residents on the way.

Quickly, I begin turning on my heel in search of Becca. "She went downstairs for a smoke," Jimmy alerts me.

"A smoke?!"

"Yeah, she only does it when she's stressed. I get after her for it, though." He eyes me over his glasses as he rumbles his paper to fold it.

"This way?" I point to the door right near the nurses station.

"Yep." He gets up and walks over to me. "Let her know I went in for my nap, will ya?" He pats my back.

"Sure thing." I nod then head out the door and down two flights to the door leading outside. "Put it out right now!" I command as she's about to go in for a drag. She stops. I walk up to her. "Put it out!" I reiterate. "You think I want to kiss an ashtray?" I bite. Becca slowly brings the fag up to her lips, takes a good long drag, and inhales. Cool as a cucumber, she proceeds to blow it into my face. "Very cute." I lean down near her ear. "If we didn't have an audience right now, I would have a seat at this picnic table here, throw you over my lap and spank the feisty out of you."

"Don't you threaten me!" She pushes at my chest with her free hand.

"Ha! Not a threat, doll, more like a promise." I stare her down. "Put it out!" I say through my teeth.

"Yo, dawg, don't be talking to my boo like that!" The putz finally formulates a sentence, or, at least, something that resembles one.

I turn to him. "My name is Grayson—not dawg." I try to sound like him. "And she's not yours, she's *mine!*" I poke my chest.

"What's he talkin' 'bout, Becca? You with him?" He seems a bit hurt. "I thought we was workin' toward somethin'." He adjusts his cap.

"I think you should *work* your way towards an English class." Whack.

"It needed to be said," I defend myself as I rub my stomach where she just whacked me.

"Jeremy, I…" Becca begins but trails off.

"Are you?" he presses.

I watch as her eyes go back and forth between us. Finally, looking at him, she nods slightly—avoiding me. Fuck if my heart cares; it's leaping in my chest. I grab her free hand, squeeze it, and then trace the top of it with my thumb in slow circles.

"Later!" Jeremy (the putz has a name!) stops as he walks by us and whips the door open.

Becca fidgets as if she wants to stop him but decides not to. Instead, she looks up at me. I give a pointed look at the smoking fag still in her hand, hoping I don't have to repeat myself again. She rolls her eyes and puts it out. "You almost done for the day?" I push some fly-aways behind her ear with my free hand.

"Yeah, in a half an hour."

"Ok then, I'll head out. But…" I bring my hand across her jawline. "I'll be over later to start on the book. We'll order in." I chuck her chin. She stares into my eyes, nibbling on that delicious lip of hers. "I'm extremely tempted to kiss a dirty ashtray." I let my head lean down towards her. Her eyelids start to close as if the closer I get, the more they are weighed down. Just as I'm about to reach her lips I change course and plant a kiss on her cheek before I bring my lips to her ear. "The only time I will appreciate your dirty mouth is when I'm between your legs, soliciting the filth from it." I nip at her lobe, enjoying the tempo change in her breathing. Straightening up, I see an expression I was *not* expecting. Her nostrils are flaring.

And as I come to the conclusion that the change in her tempo was not due to desire, she shoves me.

"I'm only going to say this once to you, so listen closely." She gets back in my face. "I am not one of the whores, you have lined up, waiting with baited breath for the next moronic thing you say! You better keep your goddamn manners in check when it comes to me." She shoves my left shoulder. "Do I make myself clear?" she adds. Dear God, all I can think about is how gorgeous she is when she's angry, and how I bet she's bloody fucking brilliant in the sack when she is too. "Answer me!"

"I apologize. It won't happen again . . . or, at least, not until you're used to the moronic things that come out of my mouth. They'll roll off your back much easier then." I give her a half smile, hoping I've lightened up her mood a little.

"Grayson, you're overbearing. You've got to take it down a notch. I'm a very independent woman; your take-charge attitude only pushes me away. It makes me uncomfortable." Her veracity hits me like a ton of bricks.

"My intention has never been to make you feel uncomfortable." Reaching for her hands, I lace my fingers with hers.

"I don't want this." She raises our hands a bit. "Yet, you keep pushing it on me." Her voice is almost pleading.

"You say this, yet, you just told that idiot that you're mine." I release her hands. "Constant mixed signals with you! You're confusing the hell out of me!" I snip. "You know what? You don't want this—fine—I'll stop. I'll keep this completely professional." I wave my hands out like an umpire calling a play safe. That's the point really, aye—she's "safe" from me trying at her anymore.

"I don't buy it!" she scoffs.

"No, I'm serious, Becca." I tap the picnic table. "You want to talk about uncomfortable? I've been completely out of my box since I've met you! You think I always behave this way? I can tell you right now the answer is a big, fat *no*! I hate this! I hate the way I think about you all of the time! I hate most of the things I've been doing just to get close to you! For Christ's sake, my grandmother has been dead for five years! And here I am, taking a bloody tour for a woman who couldn't care less what they serve for lunch because *she can't fecking eat it!*" I yell, reaching the pinnacle of my crazy. Becca clamps her teeth down on her entire bottom lip in an effort to not laugh. "It's not funny!" I stomp my foot. *No, really . . . I can't even believe I just did that!*

The laughter hits her eyes without any sound from her mouth. She then winces and raises her eyebrows at the same time. "It's a little funny." She raises her hand, her thumb and forefinger giving measurement.

"It's not." I steady my voice.

"It is."

We stare at each other for a long moment of maybe five seconds before we both begin to laugh.

I just made her laugh.

This makes me happy and yet, I feel sadness creeping in. "Why did you tell him you were mine?" I ask, my laughter gone.

"Because I definitely don't want to be his. He's a very good hearted person, but he's not my type. I've run out of ways to explain that to him." She shields her eyes from the sun that has just peeked out from behind the clouds.

"So . . . I'm the lesser of two evils?" My heart sinks once again. *God, I'm such a bloody fucking idiot.* She confirms my inner thoughts with her silence. I take in a deep, cleansing breath and blow it out forcefully. "Ok then, you need to finish your shift. Jimmy asked me to let you know that he was taking his nap. I'm going to head off. I'll see you later, so we can get to work. Drive safe," I ramble on before turning for the door and briskly leaving the scene, not giving her a chance at a word, if she decided to even have one.

Damn it! Every time I tell myself I'm going to back off, I get near her and all plans shoot out the window. I *have* to pull back; it's simply not working this way.

BECCA

My car gets me home on autopilot. It's kind of scary when that happens; you arrive home with no memory of the ride. I know what has me so distracted today, though.

If I'm going to be honest with myself, I really don't know what the hell I'm doing. I hate it. I hate that I'm sending him mixed signals. I wish he had shown up at a different point in my life. Stacey says I'm using my parents as a crutch, and I can totally see where she's coming from. However, I *am the one* who suffered a great loss. I need to work through it the best way I can. Having another person in my life, soliciting deep feelings from me, is not what I need right now. I can't even begin to explain the anxiety I have over losing anyone else close to me. Why throw someone else into the mix? But still, at the end of the day, I look and feel like a bitch when it comes to him. I don't mean it; I just don't know what to do about it.

Suddenly, there's a rapping on my driver's side window, causing me to jump and yelp. "Solving the crisis in the middle east?" Stacey has her tone dialed up to loud and obnoxious. At least she didn't say anything about sex. "Or are you solving the crisis in the middle of your thighs?" *Spoke way too soon!*

"Shh!" I open the door and step my foot out.

"Oh, nobody's listening to us." She waves me off.

"That's what you think." I raise a brow.

"So, what's the scoop; what's going on with you?" We begin to walk toward our front door.

"Grayson made an appearance at my work today." I snort. "Boy, he sure knows how to make awkward moments happen at the drop of a dime."

"What do you mean?" She sticks the key in, turning the lock.

"He just . . . I don't know how to explain it other than to say that he suffers from foot-to-mouth syndrome terribly."

"So when do you think you'll see him again?"

"Tonight—soon, I think. I need to jump in the shower." I plop my purse down and head to my room without ending the conversation properly.

Glancing at my alarm clock, I rush through my lotion regimen. It's a little after five in the evening. Dinner time for my family was always at five, so that's what I'm going by since he never gave me an exact time. I slip my black, lace panties on and reach for the matching bra.

"Christ!" I hear Grayson say under his breath as I'm about to hook it.

After my initial jump at the sound of his voice, I take a deep breath and let it out slowly, hooking the last hook. There are two ways I can handle this situation. One: completely flip out. Or two: make him squirm. I decide to go with option two, calling upon my inner sexy bitch. Besides, it's not like I'm naked, more like I'm wearing a bikini. I wish I were standing in front of my dresser with the mirror instead of my nightstand; I'd love to see his face right now. Reaching up to my hair, I undo the clip, allowing my long locks to fall as I turn. "I was thinking about cutting my hair, Gray, what do you think?" I ask as if this was a normal situation for us.

"It all depends, sweetheart." He takes slow, confident strides toward me, like a predator.

My adrenaline finally kicks in. "Depends on what?" I look up into his chocolate-brown eyes as he approaches me.

"On how my opinion will actually affect your decision." His hand sweeps over my shoulders to scoop my hair up. "If I were to say to you, 'Darling, I love your hair; like you—it's gorgeous.' Does that mean tomorrow I'd have Joan of Arc greeting me? If that's the case," he lets it fall again, "I have to say it's hideous, that I can't stand long hair on a woman." He cups my face.

"You prefer it on a man, then?" I raise an eyebrow.

"You cheeky thing, you." He leans down and rubs his nose against mine so lovingly it knocks a few bricks down from my wall.

"I don't know what that means but it sounds like a compliment."

"Hmm . . . could be," he says with a smile in his voice. There may be one across his lips but with him so close, my eyes are shut in anticipation. My inner sexy bitch is wobbling on her legs apparently made of *Jell-O*. "God, Becca, why can't you just let us be? Doesn't this feel so right . . . so perfect?" He sounds as if he's trying to muster up enough strength to not kiss me. I feel his pain; I'm fighting the same battle. It *does* feel right. And because of that, I fear it's all wrong.

"Oh, Grayson . . . please," I beg. It's more of a plea really. My defenses are so weak. Grayson has the type of presence where he could be completely all over you without laying a finger on you. Before I know it, my lips are consumed by his. Parting them to protest only gives him the full access he is looking for. His tongue glides over mine with expertise. I may have slightly moaned into his mouth. My fingers thread into his hair. His hands travel down to my waist and around my back. "Gah!" I gasp, breaking away from the kiss as I get a double slap to my ass and then a squeeze before he lifts me up. My legs wrap around him, pulling him closer as he attacks my lips again. With one swift turn, my back meets the mattress, and my body is crushed by his weight in the most delicious way.

"Let us be," he encourages in an almost whisper when he pulls back from our kiss. I close my eyes again, not saying a word either way. I'm too focused on not knowing what to do, that and the slight shakiness I'm feeling from adrenaline overload. His mouth moves down my jawline, my neck . . . clavicle, painting my skin with savoring kisses. I suck in a deep breath as he rolls his hips, pushing his excitement into me. The slight shakiness turns into a shiver that I can't seem to keep at bay. He pulls my right bra strap down, gliding his mouth over the top of my breast. My hand finds its way back into his hair to both encourage and stop him; I don't know. My teeth start to chatter lightly. I can't control it. My nerves are going crazy.

Still not aware of my shakiness, Grayson uncovers my breast, the warmth of his tongue sending another shiver down my spine. Pulling my nipple into his mouth, I yelp when he grinds it between his teeth. "Too rough, darling?" He looks up at me. "Becca?" He jerks his head up. "Becca, why are you shivering like this?" he asks in a panic, flying off of me. He re-covers my breast and quickly pulls my blankets around me, wrapping me in a cocoon. My teeth are full on chattering. I couldn't get a word out if I wanted to. Grayson pulls me into his arms, comforter and all, and rubs me down, trying to warm me more.

After about ten minutes or so, I'm finally back to normal—*whatever that is.*

"Did you eat today?"

"Yes."

"Are you diabetic?"

"No."

"Are you not feeling well?" He places his palm on my forehead.

"I feel fine . . . I mean . . . I don't feel as if I'm catching something." I look up at him.

"Has this ever happened to you before?"

"No . . . well, yes."

"Which is it, sweetheart?" He seems annoyed. I did just give him blue balls, so I think I can understand his frustration.

"Yes, but never that bad."

"Do you know why it happened before?" He pushes a loose strand of hair behind my ear.

"Nerves . . . anxiety." I look down, feeling embarrassed.

"Right!" he says abruptly, then climbs off of the bed. "Look, Becca, if you didn't want me to touch you, the simple use of the word 'stop' would've sufficed. I don't want you to think you should let me have at you because of my recent generosity. It just makes me feel more foolish than I have already been feeling." He's not even looking at me. "Just . . . get yourself together and meet me in the living room. I have dinner for us, and we should get to work. What I just did," he finally looks at me, "I can assure you, it won't happen again. I may not have wanted to hear your words, but your negative response to my touch spoke volumes more. Consider yourself understood." And with that, he's out the door. Except, he doesn't understand. My nervous behavior was not because of him, per say, but because of my inexperience and, most likely, my inability to make a decision as to what I want. I didn't want him to stop, yet, I felt I should tell him to. Then, there's the whole embarrassing part. I mean, who the hell is still a virgin at almost twenty-three?

After a few deep breaths, I dress myself and head out to the living room, grabbing his ms on the way. Grayson is sitting on the couch with his knees supporting his elbows. His head is down and his hands are buried into his hair. I pad quietly over to him and sit. His head jerks out of the position it was in, and he looks at me like a deer in headlights. I'm pretty sure it's surprise from not hearing me.

"Grayson." My hand slides up his bicep. Grayson definitely works out; he's defined and strong but not bulky. *He's perfect.* "My reaction had everything and nothing at all to do with you," I say softly, raising my eyes up to his.

"What does that even mean, sweetheart?" His right hand reaches up and palms my cheek. I close my eyes and lean into his touch naturally.

"I don't want this. I can't. And you…" I stop, trying to gather what it is that I'm trying to say.

"I make you second guess yourself?" he searches.

"Yes . . . something like that."

"Good." He moves his hand. "Let's get to work now—chop, chop!" he says assertively. I sit here—dumbfounded. "Let's go, Becca, I haven't all night and I'm waging war with a deadline." He grabs the ms out of my hand, sits back, and takes it out of its envelope. "Notes in the margins?" he asks as he begins flipping pages.

"Uh . . . yes." I shake my head, trying to climb out of my stupor.

"Hmm…" he trails off when he sees my first note.

"What?" I try to look but have trouble, so I readjust myself onto my knees, trying to peer over his shoulder. "How tall are you anyway?" I ask; he's like a mountain. *I want to climb that mountain.* Shut up, Becca!

"Six-four," he states simply then points to my note. "This was a good catch; drives me bloody mad when I see that in a book."

I look. "Oh yeah, I actually came across that several times; characters sitting down when they were already seated. At one point, Lydia is outside, picking a flower as she continues to talk."

"What's wrong with that?" He turns his neck, giving me a strange look.

"She never stepped outside. She was talking to Vanessa and pointing out the window, showing her that the peonies bloomed. A few sentences later, she was suddenly picking one. There was point A and C with no B," I explain. I have to say, it's a little difficult, with the way he's looking at me. I can feel the heat rise to my cheeks. "Grayson . . . please stop looking at me like that." I look down.

"Hungry?"

"Um . . . yeah."

"I brought you Chinese."

"Thank you." Realizing that I'm still leaning against him, I fall back a bit. He places the ms on his other side. He grabs the brown bag off the coffee table and starts pulling out containers. "I'll get forks," I offer.

"You will not!" he scoffs, then hands me a set of chopsticks.

"I don't know how to use these."

"Well, tonight, you will learn so that you can eat Chinese food properly." He grabs the pair back from me, rips the package open, and separates the sticks before giving them back and doing the same with his. "Now, watch how I hold mine," he instructs. I humor. Seemingly happy with my hold on them, he grabs the first container and turns to face me. With his leg bent and resting on the couch between us, he holds the container of rice and chopsticks up, ready to instruct. I giggle lightly at his serious behavior. A slow smile creeps across his lips, and I don't actually believe this but a hint of shyness (?) flashes across his face. "Now," he clears his throat, "pay attention, sweetheart."

"Yes, sir." I mimic his seriousness. His eyes smile at me. *I love it when that happens.* Shut up, shut up, Becca! Fuck if I'm not losing this battle. No willpower.

He dips his chopsticks in and grabs himself a decent amount. That looked easy enough. "Open," he commands, holding the bite in front of my lips. I open my mouth and let him guide the food in. I chew, which takes forever because I'm under his gaze. I can feel my cheeks firing up again. I go to take my turn. He lowers the container and leans forward, his lips barely touching mine. "A kiss for good luck," he quickly says before pressing his lips to mine, my lower one getting sucked in slightly between his. The butterflies in my belly do their best to escape their cage.

"I'm eating with chopsticks for the first time, not going for gold at the Olympics," I joke—a nervous tendency of mine when I'm overwhelmed.

"The smallest achievements are the stepping stones to the greatest accomplishments." His seriousness is killing me.

"Is that what you did before you became an author?" I bite back my smile.

"What's that?"

"Write for the fortune cookie companies?" I laugh.

He shakes his head at me. "Come on and feed me, woman, I'm hungry!" He slaps my lap.

"Ok, ok." I stifle my laughter and try to concentrate on the task at hand. Thinking I've achieved absolute success, I bring my chopsticks up. We both stare at them for a moment. "Well . . . I hope you're *really* hungry," I finally say as straight-faced as I can.

"Honestly, I'm overwhelmed at the moment, sweetheart." He shoots me a look of nervousness. "I mean, that is one *ginormous* piece of rice."

"Shall we cut it in half?"

"No, darling, you need to watch your figure." He guides my hand up to bring the lonely speck of rice to his mouth. I'm fighting the internal battle of "was he saying that in jest?"—I hate being a girl sometimes; we're so quick to lose our confidence over our appearance. "Incidentally, I've been watching your figure since we've met." He dives his chopsticks back in.

"You have?" my voice quiet.

"Oh yes, of course! I have a deep appreciation for fine art." He offers me his successful attempt.

Man, he's smooth…

I can be smooth.

I gently grab his wrist to hold it steady as I slowly lean in with an open mouth. I close my lips around them and take my time pulling back all the while, eyeing him suggestively (well, I think it is.).

Grayson returns the stare as he feeds himself, then me again. This ritual carries on for the next ten minutes in silence. Well, all except for the slight sound of more bricks falling off my wall.

When not another bite of food can be eaten by either of us, we package up the leftovers, and I grab them to put in the fridge. "I bought wine. Let us have a glass," he calls over.

"Where is it?" I look around.

"Bag on the counter." With his back against the arm and his legs stretched out, he throws his glasses on and carries on with the script.

I retrieve two wine glasses from the cabinet, open the wine, and pour us each a glass. "Here you go, Clark." I hand him one when I get over to him.

"Don't be so formal; call me Superman." He takes the glass from me with a wink.

"I think I'd need to see evidence of that identity." I sit between his legs after he puts his right foot to the floor and pats where I should park it.

He pulls me back up against him. His mouth, hot at my ear. "I tried to show you that very evidence bout thirty minutes ago with no success. Shall we revisit for the possibility of a different outcome?" His hand slides up to my breast. His mouth, making a hot trail down my neck.

"Please . . . please stop," I pant. His hand slides back down, and he plants one last, big kiss on my neck. He brings the ms up for us to both go through. And just like that, we're all business, though, a more relaxed version.

Chapter Six

GRAYSON

"Gracie? Gracie? Oh, there you are!" My mum says as she pokes her head into my study. It's actually my make-shift office right now. My real office is upstairs, loaded with boxes. I haven't a clue as to how I want to set it up and haven't spared the time to hire someone to do any designs for me.

"Hello, Mum," I greet her.

"I wasn't sure if I'd actually find you here, you've been jetting off to Boston so much lately without any notice," she says this with a little laugh but I know she's actually put out about it (says a little birdie named Susanna).

"Yes, Mum, I know. Come have a seat, let us have a chat." I try to distract her.

She wastes no time taking me up on my offer, finding her favorite chair. "Now, son, let's start off with her name." She eyes me.

"What makes you think there's a woman involved?" I play.

"I know my son. Now spit it out; I haven't all day, you know?"

She pours herself a cup of tea from the pot which Suzie brought in 'bout half an hour ago. She brings it up and stirs the spoon around slowly, waiting.

I let out a big sigh, get up, and head to sit across from her, joining her for a cuppa. "Becca Campbell," I finally give her the info she's so desperately waiting for.

"And?" She stares over her cup.

"And . . . I'm arse over tits," I admit.

"I know that, you wally. Tell me about her."

"Well, she's absolutely amazing and frustrating all at once," I vent. She remains quiet, so I continue, telling her about the last few months: Our work arrangement, her denial of her feelings even though she lets her guard down, contradicting herself. How I have to set up dates with her through her best friend.

"Go on, now! Why can't she sort them out with you?" Mum scoffs.

"Because they're bloody surprises!" I growl. "She won't actually commit to a date, so I have to show up at the cinema or wherever and sort of take charge."

"Gracie, I don't understand why you're wasting your time with someone like this. You deserve better—you're a great catch!"

"Yes . . . we both know *exactly* the type of woman that tries to 'catch me'." I give her the air quotes. "Becca's not like that. She doesn't care about all of this." I wave around. "She works too hard, Mum." I let my voice falter. I hate it. I've paid off all of her bills (unbeknownst to her), except for college because it's the only thing she keeps on top of, so she'd know. I've given her a brand new car. *Yet*, she continues these crazy hours. I don't really understand it.

"What's her deal then?"

"She's scared, simple as that. She lost her parents tragically a year ago, and the trauma is causing her to push away anyone new that she may end up caring deeply about. She doesn't want to suffer a loss like that again," I relay Becca's usual spiel. The same one I'm very tired of listening to, though, I understand it. "I am slowly breaking through her wall, I think."

"What makes you say that?" She places her tea back on the table.

"Tonight's date night and I'm not showing up." I bite back my smile.

"You sure she'll be expecting you?"

"Oh yes, I haven't missed one yet. That ought to piss her off."

"Why do you want to piss her off?" She shoots me a quizzical look.

"It's all a part of me helping her to realize that she already has feelings for me. My hope is that she will be disappointed, and *that* will piss her off."

"Grayson, this all sounds like too much work, love." She shakes her head in disapproval.

"If you met her, Mum, you'd know she's worth it. I know she'll be different once I get her over this idea that she has."

"She can't control life. She can only live it to the fullest." Mum sighs. "I'm very sorry for her loss and I hope you are right about her, Gracie. I'd love to meet her—I'm intrigued. Now, what's the plan for the gala?" She pours more tea.

"Ugh . . . bloody hell. I wish I didn't have to go," I groan.

"You need a date." She raises a brow.

"Yes. Charity has agreed. I'll be picking her up at eight p.m."

"Does she know that you are involved elsewhere?"

"I've only mentioned Becca to her a million times, but you know Charity..." I trail off. Why I ever chose to have a sexual relationship with her is beyond my understanding. I mean, she's a beautiful woman and a great shag, but she's had us married off, in her mind, since the first time for fuck's sake! Can't even get rid of her because she's Mum's best friend's daughter. Yet, she's reliable for last minute date needs . . . or shags. In the past, that is. I haven't looked at another woman, let alone touch one since I've met Becca. To say the man downstairs is unhappy about this would be an understatement.

"Well, I'll have a word with Trudy."

"Thanks, Mum." I stand up, then lean down and kiss the top

of her head. "Speaking of, let me go get ready for that delightful torture."

"Invite Becca out here for a work weekend," she suggests quickly.

"Ooh . . . the old *weekend away for work with the handsy boss*—I like it, Mum! I shall work on that straight away!" I laugh when she smacks my hip. I leave her to her tea and head off to get ready. But first, I text Becca a quick message. It's something I've been doing every day the past month or so. Just a simple something to tell her what I love about her, on her, or just that I'm thinking about her.

> **Me:** Sometimes, when you fall asleep, while we're working, I stare at you in awe of God's skill to create something—someone so beautiful, it makes my heart leap all over my chest every time I look at you.

Within moments, my phone pings.

> **Becca:** Thanks, Shakespeare.

> **Me:** Knock, knock.

> **Becca:** I'm not playing.

> **Me:** Knock, knock.

> **Becca:** Ugh . . . who's there?

I plop onto my bed and enjoy my favorite sport—pissing her off.

> **Becca:** Who's there?!!

> **Becca:** Grayson?!

> **Becca:** Asshole!

> **Me:** Go to your door.

I wait several minutes.

> **Becca:** There's nobody there.

Me: I didn't think so.

Becca: Why did you make me go to the door?!

Me: You wanted to know who was there.

Becca: You are so weird! Leave me alone, I have things to do.

Me: You listened! Who's the weird one? What things do you have to do?

Becca: *blows raspberries* I have a date to get ready for.

Me: Is it with that good looking bloke you've been seeing for a few months now?

Becca: No clue as to whom you are talking about. I'm going out with Kris tonight. I'll talk to you later.

Me: Your girlfriend from work, right?

Don't fall for this, Grayson, don't fall for it!

Becca: Kris, the pharmaceutical rep. He's been asking me for a while.

Me: Have fun!

Nope—not falling for it. Sure my hands are balled up in fists; I have to do something to prevent myself from calling her and ripping her a new arse.

"Charity, please—stop making a scene! Have some self-respect!" I snap as I push her off of me once again.

"Come on, Gracie, let me make it all better," she coos, sliding her hand back up my leg.

I have never slapped a woman in my life (well, outside of the bedroom and definitely not across the face), but Charity is surely pushing me to the edge. I can't believe she behaved so pathetically back there. If I told her once, I've told her a hundred times—I'm off the market! She doesn't want to "get it" but tonight was the worst yet. She took full advantage of the media coverage. At the most opportune time, she shoved her tongue down my throat for a photo op. I froze in utter shock, the sounds of flashes from cameras snapping me back.

"You are off your bloody trolley!" I push her again. "Sam." I turn my attention to him. "Pull over and let me out. Take Miss Newman home, and then come back for me." Just as I finish my sentence, he pulls over in front of a small coffee shop.

"Gracie, you can't be serious," she pleads.

"Don't *you* call me that! Go home, Charity, and get yourself together!" I assert as I get out and slam the door in her face.

At a fast, determined pace, I head into the shop, find myself a table and sit down. The waitress comes over, and I order a coffee regular before pulling out my mobile. It was vibrating quite a bit earlier. *Ah . . . several texts from Stacey and one from Becca.* I'm not ready to look at Becca's; I'm sure I'll hear her screaming at me.

> **Stacey:** Annnnnnd she's looking around for you nonchalantly.

Well, that just brightened my day.

> **Stacey:** She just asked me if I knew where you were. I told her that I let you know that we were going to the movies but haven't heard from you.

Wow . . . she asked.

> **Stacey:** Ok . . . I think she's getting pissed now.

Well done, Grayson, well done!

> **Stacey:** She's barely paid attention to the movie—keeps looking for you.

And that's where her texts end. I feel bad now, although, Becca needed to learn a lesson. I tap on hers next.

> **Becca:** Are you ok?

I'm an arsehole...

> **Me:** Yes. I'm sorry I missed our non-date. I had to stay back here for a charity function. It was terribly boring and a bit nightmarish. I wish I had been with you instead. I rather enjoy you pretending you have no interest in me being there. ☺

I put my phone down and sip my coffee. It's only going on nine, and I'm dead tired. My eyes glance back down at the sound of a ping.

> **Becca:** Ok. Goodnight.

Really? That's it?!

> **Me:** Please don't be mad at me, sweetheart.

I wait about ten minutes. Nothing. I ring her. Nothing.

> **Me:** The way you giggle when I pepper your neck, under your ear, with kisses—I love that sound.

Just then, Sam rings in, letting me know he'll be here in a few.

BECCA

I plop belly down onto my bed. Okay—he wins. As if my reaction to him not being here tonight wasn't enough, he sealed the deal with that last text. He's a persistent fucker; I'll give him that. Drop dead gorgeous—I'll just put that out there since I'm being all honest with myself. British—no need to explain what that does to my panties! *Panties!* That's it! He was getting back at me tonight for the last time. He didn't have a function. I bet he stayed back just to watch me get aggravated! This should really piss me off . . . I should be fuming, except I deserve it.

Honestly, I can't believe he still talks to me after what I did a few weeks ago. I can feel the ache grow between my legs just thinking about it...

"Grayson," I panted.

"Shh, darling... Let me make you feel good," he barely whispered. I was asleep. The sensation of his fingers gliding up and down my center, ever so slowly, is what woke me up. "Do you feel how wet you are for me?" he asked as his finger took a shallow plunge into my opening, retrieving evidence and sliding it up to my clit. Slow, agonizing *circles around my clit took place. I felt my hips buck up to his touch—traitors. "Mmm . . . feel good, sweetheart?" he hummed into my ear.*

"Gray . . . I . . . oh God . . . no . . . you . . . um."

"Becca, besides tasting you, I will not go any further. I won't take you until you are ready to fully commit to me. Do you understand?"

It was just . . . his fingers . . . oh God—so slow and methodical. I wanted him to hurry up and not rush all at the same time.

"Answer me!" he commanded and smacked me in my sensory overload department. The little tightness that was building up exploded and I writhed against his hand. I may have yelled out gibberish—it's all an orgasmic blur to me now. *His mouth assaulted mine, his tongue lapping against mine, comforting me as I rocked against his hand.* I have never let anyone touch me like this before. I didn't even *let him.* But, he went ahead of his own accord to touch me there, like it was his to do so. Truth be told, it felt that way too. *Just as my body slowed down, my breath regulating itself, he began again; slow, caressing fingers up my center. It didn't take long to climb again, not between his fingers doing naughty things to me and his teeth grinding my, then exposed, nipple.*

I came so hard and fast. "Oh God, baby . . . oh God!" I whimpered, holding onto him.

That was when I really knew I was in trouble, with my heart that is. He heard me. I called him "baby." I don't call anyone that. We had just recently discussed this topic over breakfast a few weeks prior. It was all of us: Stacey, Max, Derek, Grayson, and I. Derek was sweet on the waitress; he called her "baby." I cringed.

"What was that look for? Gray asked after wiping his mouth.

"The word 'baby' is sacred to her. She hates when people use it so casually," Stacey offered before I could say anything. She's always thought I was silly about this. To a point; I guess she's right. But, it's just how I feel.

"Why's that, sweetheart?" Grayson seemed intrigued. So, I sat back and explained my feelings on the subject. "So, you've never called anyone that? Not a boyfriend?" He poured me more coffee and fixed it the way I like it—without asking. I always say this, but it's true—it's the little shit!

"No. I've never had deep enough feelings for someone to call them that." He actually seemed relieved when I told him that. I wasn't sure why—I'm still not.

"She's saving 'baby' for marriage." Stacey laughed.

"Shut up!" I threw a creamer at her which spurted onto her chin.

"Well, that's the second time that happened to you today, Stace," Max teased and wiped her chin.

"Eww! You're fucking gross, Max!" I cringed then laughed with everyone else, including Stacey, who did manage to get a good elbow into his ribs.

When my body finally stilled, my breathing trying to mimic, Grayson rested his forehead to mine, his hand still caressing my nether region. "Do you have . . . any idea . . . how you've just . . . made my heart leap . . . out of my chest?" He was panting. I was wondering how I was going to backtrack. Instead, I focused on my breathing. "I want to hear you call me that again. I need to," he said against my lips before pulling on them gently with his own. I closed my eyes and continued to concentrate on my breathing as he began the slow descent down my body. My legs voluntarily opened for him, exposing myself fully. The vulnerability, alone, had me so hot, I could feel myself start to drip with anticipation. No nerves whatsoever. He could've taken me. I had no thought or concern about trying to stop him. Maybe it was because he already said he wouldn't that I was so relaxed; I'm not sure.

His tongue replaced his hand, and I was done for. So was he. "Bloody hell, you taste fantastic," he groaned as he ripped his mouth from me. He sat back on his knees and grabbed the waistband of my pajama shorts, finally freeing me of them as he whipped them off.

Note to self: Unless you want him to have easy access like this, you should probably wear underwear with your PJ shorts.

He pushed the sheet and comforter off the bed as if they would get in his way as well. It was kind of comical, but I didn't have time to laugh. His arms scooped under my bum, reaching his hands around to my front, his fingers opened me, and he buried his face. This position held my hips still but the rest of me was flailing. I mean . . . he didn't even come up for air. He feasted on me like a starved man. I about ripped my hair out, begging him (not sure for what but I won't be questioning the heroines when they say this in the many books I've read; I sooo get it now!) and using my sacred word despite myself. He ripped three orgasms through me this way. When he was done, he climbed back up my body. He took my hand and placed it over his heart. "Do you feel that?" he asked. It was pounding.

"Yes."

"It only beats for you." And with that, he gave me a chaste kiss on the lips. "I'll be right back, darling." He cleared his throat, "Need to go take care of something," he added.

I wanted to offer, but I was nervous that I would be crossing my own line (as opposed to him always crossing it) and . . . I've never done anything like that. I thought I'd probably be terrible at it.

At twenty-three, it's more embarrassing than it is impressive. I mean, I have no plans of becoming a nun. Besides, that "Come to Jesus" moment, I'd assume, is much different than the one Grayson had given me. Pretty sure I'd like his version better.

Grayson climbed in next to me when he had finished in the bathroom. He pulled me to him, and I settled into the spoon position, his arms around me. I haven't said it once, but I do rather like the way we happen to fall asleep together while working. It's gotten to be so that we just get ready for bed and hop in with the laptop and notes. Way past the part of pretending we'll separate.

Except that morning, he woke up to an empty bed. I was nowhere to be found. I didn't answer his calls or his texts. I simply stayed away. Why? Because I'm an asshole. That, and I really needed time to think about everything. Things had gone too far, and my fear of falling for him was coming to fruition.

That's when the daily texts began, telling me something he loved about me. *Nail in the coffin.* Pretty sure he knows it too! I'm also pretty sure him not coming tonight was to cement that nail—make me truly see my feelings. Thing is, I already succumbed to them and tonight was the night I was going to let him know; the chase is over.

I've never been one to flip-flop like this, and if I could've stepped out of my body and slapped some sense into me, I would have. Forget everyone else—I was driving myself crazy! But, I'm done. And now . . . I have to wait. *Damn it.*

> **Me:** I love the way your eyes blink rapidly when you're nervous.

Take that, Grayson!

Chapter Seven

A week has gone by. A week filled with texts and voicemails that would make anyone cynical about love want to vomit. I don't care—it's been amazing to let all of my previous hang-ups go. I've even scheduled myself to have a week off. I never ask for one, so they didn't give me a hard time at all. Grayson's bought me a plane ticket to come out by him, and I can hardly wait. Not just to see him, but I've never been to California!

"Becca, honey, I'm ready for my shave," Jimmy calls out to me, pulling me from my thoughts.

"Oh . . . sorry, Jimmy." I shake my head, trying to snap out of it.

"That's okay. It's nice to see you smiling so much." He holds out his arm for me. I take it; such a gentleman.

"Happiness really is all they have it cracked up to be." I squeeze his arm to me.

"You should tell the putz over there." He nods toward Jeremy. "Is it strange that I miss the old moron? He's not himself at all anymore," he adds.

He's right. Jeremy hasn't been himself since the showdown with Grayson. However, since I caved with Gray a week ago, and the happiness in my decision pouring out in everything I do, Jeremy's gotten even worse. He barely says hi to me. When I need help with a resident, he helps but then he's out of there. It used to be that we would help each other with our assignments, especially on the nights where one of us would get behind. No more, though. Yesterday, he spoke to me the most he had in weeks. One simple sentence: "He's not what you think." That was it—no other explanation—nothing.

"You getting excited for your trip?"

"I am!" I burst. At this, Jeremy snaps his head up.

"I wrote that list down of the places Grayson should take you. My wife and I spent a lot of time, over the years, out there, with her being from California."

"You can't go out there!" Jeremy pleads. I'm taken aback.

"It's just for a week. I'm not moving or anything," I offer, thinking this is what's upset him.

"He's *not* who he says he is," he reiterates his comment from yesterday.

"Jer—"

"—Google him!" he cuts me off. And with that, he heads down the hall in a huff.

"What the…?" I trail off.

"He's losing it." Jimmy slaps at the nonsense in the air.

"I think you're right. Okay, let's get that handsome face all shiny and new." I take him into his room, distracting us both from what just unfolded.

I pace. I chew on my thumbnail. I stare at our computer, sitting in our living room. I walk away. *This is absurd!* I walk back to it. I pace, chewing on my nail. *Oh, for the love of God, Becca, stop being such a wimp!* I sit and turn it on. The familiar dialing sound of AOL chimes up (because we're too cheap—read: broke, to get broadband). Well, this shit's gonna take forever, might as well go to my regular mailbox. What the fuck is *Google* anyway? Everyone is talking about it.

I run out to the mailbox and retrieve the mail. Aww . . . Grayson sent me a letter! I love letters! I stop and have a moment of silence for all those cynical people out there, so they can purge. Closing the door behind me, I plop all of the other mail down on the half hutch we have and rip open his letter.

> Dearest Sweetheart,
> I'm counting the days until you are in my arms again. I can't wait to touch your skin, smell your hair, and feel the warmth of you in my embrace.
>   You are more than I have ever dreamed of (you royal pain in the arse, you!).
>
> I'm so smitten.
>   So very done for.
>   You were worth the wait.
>
>   All my love,
>   Grayson

He is so getting laid! Whoa! Where the fuck did that come from?!

"You've got mail!" the robotic AOL man says.

Right.

I head over to the computer and take a seat, still on cloud nine from his letter. I find the Google website and put in Grayson's name. All of this wonderful information pops up: his books, the movies based on his books, where he lives, that he's about to become a father, his charities—wait! What?! I scroll back, trying to ignore the ball of vomit sitting in my throat, like a man standing on a ledge ready to jump. I click on the link.

"Charity Newman, Grayson James's on again off again girl-friend, has confirmed that she is pregnant with the bestselling author's baby. The news was released immediately after a recent charity event, where the couple did not hold back on the PDA."

I scroll down to the pictures of them all dressed up—kissing—last Saturday! I shut down the computer the irresponsible way and run to the bathroom. The sound of my sobs changes to sounds of heaving. How could he do this to me? Why? Why did he make me fall for him just to turn around and do this to me?

I wish I never looked. Ignorance is bliss, right? Oh God . . . it hurts. My heart hurts. I'm such a stupid fool. I knew falling for him would be a big mistake. Unable to control my sobs, I make my way over to my bed, climb up, and curl into a ball. I give in to my tears until I'm so wiped out, everything fades.

"Hey, Becca." Stacey shakes me. I turn and look at her, though I can't see anything since my room is pitch-black. "You okay? You're never in bed this early."

I shake my head, feeling a bit disoriented. "No . . . I'm not feeling good." It's not a lie.

"Well, here. Grayson's worried about you; your phone sounds as if it will destruct." She hands it to me. I scoff.

"Thanks," I say, then curl back up. When she leaves, I dare to look at his messages.

4pm Gray: How was your day?

5pm Gray: Are you doing a double today?

5:30pm Gray: At Barnes & Noble?

6pm Gray: Sweetheart, where are you?

9pm Gray: Why are you sleeping? Are you poorly?

Me: I'll send your script to you tomorrow as well as a check to go toward payment for the car (I've been saving to pay you). I will then send you a check each month until it's paid off. Take me off your phone plan. Don't call me anymore. It's over.

I hit send, and the dam to my tears breaks again. Within a few minutes, my phone pings again.

Gray: Very funny. Can you talk? I need to go over a scene with you. Missed you today!

I turn the phone off. Another few minutes go by, and the house phone rings. I glance over at the caller ID . . . of course—relentless bastard.

"Bec! What the fuck is going on?!" Stacey, who normally loves to be in the middle of my shit, hammers through my door, making me jump. I turn on my lamp so that she can actually see my face. "Whoa . . . what the hell happened?" she asks me. "What *the fuck* did you do, Grayson?" she yells into the phone. "Well, by the looks of your girlfriend here, you've done something!"

"Stacey," I pull her attention away from whatever he's saying. "Please tell him that I wish him and his girlfriend, Charity, all the happiness in the world with their new baby. Then, please hang up and never take another call from him," I say as calmly as I can.

"You *motha fucka!*" Stacey yells into the phone—less calm. *Hello, London—I'd like you to meet Boston.* Stacey reams into him as she heads out my door. Within a minute, she's back. "Bec . . . I'm so sorry. I had *no* idea." She sits on my bed and pulls me in for a hug.

"Well, if something's too good to be true…" I trail off with a shrug, trying to hold back from crying again.

Epic fail.

GRAYSON

"Gray?" Derek pulls me out of my trance.

"Wha . . . were you already almost here?" I ask bewildered.

"You called me fifteen minutes ago." He looks at me curiously as he walks in and takes a seat by me. I didn't realize that much time had gone by.

"I've lost her. I've lost Becca," I choke on my words.

"Wait—what do you mean? Was there an accident?"

"Oh, the irony of that question," I say angrily through my teeth. "No. I didn't lose her in that respect. I've lost her in every other way."

"What happened?" He furrows his brows.

"I'll tell you what happened! Charity fucking Newman and her false allegations!" I get up and swipe everything off of my desk angrily. "Fucking lying *whore!*" I scream. I take a moment, running my hands through my hair, trying to calm down. I rub my face then throw them out in a plea. "I was going to tell her, you know I was. But, I was waiting for the air to be cleared. Somehow, someway, Becca found out." I sit back down. "She didn't even give me a chance to explain," my voice cracks. "I don't know what to do, Derek. I can't lose her. I love her…"

Derek sits there, fisted hand leaning against his mouth. It's what he does when he's coming up with a game plan. "This is what we'll do." And now he shakes a finger at the sky. "You handle everything the way you have been, to clear the air here and get the truth out. I will handle the rest. Book me a flight to Boston; I'm not using my miles." He tries to lighten the situation, but I'm too far gone.

"I couldn't ask for a better brother." I slap his shoulder.

"Everything is going to be okay," he encourages.

"God, I hope so." I retrieve my laptop from the floor, praying it still works.

"Grayson, you have to eat something." Susanna slaps the table.

"I just can't." I push the plate away.

"Just give her time, she'll come around." She sits across from me.

"It's been a week. She won't listen to anyone, not even Stacey. She's still crucifying me for something I didn't do and have been cleared on. I'm devastated," I'm barely audible. "And, damn it—I'm mad!"

"She just needs to be confronted by you in person. Once you get out there, you'll set it right." She pats my hand.

"I hope so. I need to go get ready to leave."

"Piece of toast—please!" She hands it to me.

"Alright!" I give in, grabbing it from her. I take a hearty bite before heading off to my room.

Within the next hour, Sam is driving Derek and me to the airport. My plan is to stick with what works. Stacey and Max are dragging Becca out dancing tonight. Becca loves to dance, so it doesn't take much to twist her arm. I'm going to show up as her date . . . as usual. If she wants to go head to head with me, I'll welcome it. I need for her to know the truth.

Club Axis is pretty packed tonight. I'm grateful that Stacey informed Derek that they would be upstairs. As we work our way up there, I notice that it's a lot less crowded up here. Suddenly, Max jumps in front of me. "Let's get out of here!" he yells.

"What? No! I want to see Becca!" I yell back.

"This isn't the place for this!" he yells back. The music is so loud; it's all we can do to hear each other.

"He's right! Let's go!" Derek, after he had faced the room we were about to walk in, turns and yells quickly. I don't know Max too well, but I know my friend—something is *not* right. I push them to move out of my way and head into the room. I don't have to scan the room long before I see what they were trying to have me avoid. There she is—the woman of my dreams—in the middle of the dance floor, grinding her body into the putz, no less. What's worse is watching his hands run all over her. All I see is red. I go to move forward, to rip his bloody arms from their sockets, but I can't move. Derek and Max have a firm grip on me. As if she can sense me, Becca looks in my direction. I stare at her angrily; I feel as if I'm about to explode. Instead, the wind gets knocked out of my lungs as I watch her cover his mouth with hers. I can't believe my eyes. I'm completely fucking paralyzed right now. Becca pulls back from the kiss and looks at me again with a smug look on her face, but it suddenly drops. My guess is that the heartbreak I'm feeling right now is all over my face. She just deliberately hurt me. She's no better than all of those girls who come after me for my money; she doesn't really care about *me* either. I'm utterly shattered.

"Let's go!" I yell to Derek, and they allow me to turn and leave.

BECCA

I pay no attention to Jeremy's mouth, working at my neck. Although, it's kind of hard to when I feel all kinds of slobber there. All I can really think about is the crushed look I just saw on Grayson's face. Instantly, my heart broke all over, this time for him. I glance around the room once Grayson is gone from view and lock eyes with Stace. If I were a dart board, she'd totally get a bullseye with the daggers she just shot at me. *Wait—whose side is she on anyway?!*

I nudge Jeremy off and make a beeline for her, pushing up my imaginary sleeves. She grabs a hold of my arm and drags me to the bathroom. "What is your problem?" I yell once we're in there.

"You, you dumbass!" she gives it back. "You haven't wanted to listen to me all week, but you're gonna listen now! He *did not* cheat on you! He *did not* get that chick pregnant! *You* are a *fucking* asshole!" she yells each word as a verbal poke.

She's right; I haven't listened to anyone—I wouldn't. I'd like to defend myself, give her reasons why I don't believe what she just told me, but I can't. I do believe her. I don't know if it's because she's my best friend—she'd never hurt me—or because of the way Grayson reacted. It's probably both. I *am* a *fucking* asshole! What's even worse: I just used Jeremy. Now I have *two* bombs to defuse. *Fuck!*

"I have to get out of here!" I panic. "I have to find him."

"I'm pretty sure he'll find you when he cools off." She unzips her small clutch purse aggressively and turns to look in the mirror.

"Can you tell Jeremy that I got sick and went home?" I plead.

"And ewww . . . why in the fuck did you let him get up on you like that? Then, you kissed him!" She curls her lip up in disgust.

"I know. I need to go home and shower," I state, completely not impressed with myself.

"Go!" she commands.

"Okay, I am! Thanks, Stace!"

"You owe me!" She pushes her eyeliner back into the tightly packed purse.

"I'll make dinner every night this week."

"You always make dinner!" she guffaws.

"I guess we're already even then." I give her a wink and head out before she can say another word.

All I have to say is—*Thank God* I brought my own car! Parking can be a bitch, but I knew I didn't want Jeremy to pick me up because then he'd want to bring me home, and then I would've had another battle on my hands, getting him to leave. Now I just have to battle traffic in downtown Boston . . . on a Saturday night. Ugh!

The whole way home to Winthrop, I sing one line over and over again—*a three-hour tour.* Since there's no skipper, captain, movie star, etcetera involved in my scenario, the rest of the lyrics to *Gilligan's Island* are irrelevant. I should be thinking about other things, focusing on what needs to be done. Instead . . . I'm wondering why the fuck it was Gilligan's island? He wasn't the only one to land there. I'm sure there was an episode explaining this, but I don't remember. Furthermore, who the hell names their kid Gilligan in good conscious? It's like they looked at their baby, deemed him awkward looking, possibly the kid to be bullied on and they thought better than wasting the "good" name on him. Why did the rich people have luggage with them on a three-hour tour? It's a conspiracy. And why didn't anybody ask these questions (or the million others) in the 60s, when the show was a hot commodity? That's a little scary.

Not as scary as pulling into a spot at my complex without remembering much of the drive. At least I got here safely. I turn the car off and grab my purse before getting out. I rush to my apartment, keys in hand. "No nightcap, then?" Grayson barks behind me, causing me to jump. *Shit.* Without answering, I continue to unlock the door. I walk in and hold it open for him, unable to look him in the eyes. He grabs it, slamming it shut after himself. "I want you to get in the shower to wash his bloody stench off of you right now, Becca!" he orders me in an extra British tone. "I command you!" *Don't laugh at that statement, Becca, don't laugh.*

I look up at him. God, he's so angry; I've never seen him like this. "Yes, Grayson," I say softly and watch his hard gaze lighten up. His right hand reaches up as if he's about to palm my cheek, but he stops, grits his teeth, and fists his hand as he takes a step back to let me through. "I'll only be a few moments." I keep my same tone and place my hand over his heart. It's pounding. "Please don't leave, Grayson. I really want to talk this out with you," I beg with my eyes more than my words.

"Go." He jerks his head toward the hall, his voice barely audible. I nod and head off.

I scrub myself clean in record time. I may have scrubbed a little too hard. I may look like Meryl Streep in *Silkwood* after the decontamination scene. I apply the lotion that he bought me after he noticed me appreciate it in the store. I've been realizing, lately, that he always does stuff like this. He's not elaborate about it either, usually leaving stuff like this for me to find after he's gone. My stomach turns. Why didn't I just listen this week when everybody (and their mother) was trying to tell me about Grayson? I think . . . well, I was hurt. And—Goddamn it—I had the right to be upset! He should have told me from the get-go! Well, then, I'm going to hear him out but I will *not* let him bulldoze me. With a new purpose in my step, I yank my bathroom door open. I gasp slightly at the sight before me. Grayson is sitting on the edge of my bed, facing me. His legs are crossed at his ankles casually. I feel the heat rise to my cheeks as his eyes drink the sight of me only wrapped in a towel. I look away, noticing his six manuscripts we've been working on, piled up next to him.

"What's this? What are you doing?" I walk up to him, pointing to them.

"I want the car keys," he simply states.

"Wh . . . why?" I stammer.

"We're through. Car keys, please." He stands up, towering over me.

"No." I stare up into his eyes.

"No?" His brows furrow angrily.

Shaking my head slightly, I take his hands in mine. "We need to talk."

"Now you want to talk?! Don't you think that would have been a wiser decision a week ago?!" he growls and jerks his hands away.

"Yes. Just like it would've been a wiser decision to tell me what happened—when it happened!" I give it back to him.

"I wanted it all resolved before I told you! It's not like you were completely committed to me! You've got some bullocks to your logic, sweetheart!"

"But that was the night I did. I texted you back about your blinking. That was my flag," my voice cracks, and I feel my eyes sting with threatening tears.

"Your flag?!"

"Yes!" I cry. "You can't deny that I was different after that. I let you buy me a plane ticket to come out by you."

"You let me?!"

"Yes! Damn it, Grayson, stop answering me with a question!"

"You allowed that bloody fucking idiot to touch what is *mine!*" he roars, his face so red, like it's on fire. "You looked straight into my eyes, all smug, and let him taste your mouth!"

"I'm sorry . . . I . . . I was devastated . . . you have no idea how much I was hurting. I felt like a fool. I wanted to hurt you back . . . make you feel some of what I was going through," I plead.

"Some?! Hurt me back?! I can't fecking believe you!" He pushes me slightly out of the way and begins to pace my room, pulling at his hair. I wait patiently, watching him and trying to collect myself. "*All. You. Have. Done,* since I've met you, is hurt *me!*" He points an accusing finger at me.

"I have not!"

"Oh yes you have, Becca! Comments you've made, the constant back and forth with your feelings!"

"What comments?"

"Oh—we'll go with my favorite one about me not getting laid just because I was giving you a car and a job!"

"Well, I just had to put that out there," I defend myself.

"Yes, yes you've done a grand job, putting out there that you are a *complete* bitch! Well done!"

That moment, a few minutes ago, when I was trying to pull myself together, is completely lost on me now. My heart hasn't ached like this since my parents. It's a different ache because he's standing right in front of me, but it still hurts at this level of losing someone you love. *Oh God . . . I love him.*

"You're right, Grayson. You deserve better than me. Let me get dressed and I'll clean out the car," I offer softly, not sure of my own voice. I turn to my dresser to grab sweats to throw on.

I feel his hands slide onto my hips. "I don't deserve better than you. I deserve for you to give me a better version of yourself." He kisses the top of my head. I lean back against him, relishing in his touch. "We both just need to cool down. I know I need some time. I'll leave the scripts and the car—for now. Do not let me hear even a whisper of you being with someone else." He squeezes my hips.

I turn quickly and throw my arms around his neck for a hug. "Not even a whisper, baby." I use my sacred word. "I promise, you're the only one in my heart . . . on my mind." I reach up on my toes and plant a few gentle kisses on his neck. I can feel the tension in his body. Not sure whether to feel happy or sad about that. Happy that he seems to be fighting the need to touch me. Sad that he isn't giving in. Attempting to help him with that, I bring my face back to look up into his eyes. They're hooded and almost black compared to the usual dark chocolate color. I focus on his lips and nearly groan when he licks them slowly. I reach up further. *I need to kiss him.*

"No." He turns his head. "I have no desire for you to share Jeremy's germs with me."

"I brushed my teeth until my gums bled, Grayson. I scrubbed my skin sore." I am now going to chalk this up as one of my most embarrassing moments.

"I don't care. That's all I see when I look at you at the moment." Just as he says that, my towel loses its ability to stay tied together and it falls to the ground. *Jesus—seriously?!*

"Well, I'm sure if you look again, you'll see a lot more now." I giggle at my predicament. He bites back his smile but loses his battle as his body shakes with mirth. We both give in, laughing as if we hadn't argued at all—as if we weren't on shaky ground.

"I will be checking out your bum, even though I'll be pretending not to. It can't be helped; I fancy it so.

"I fancy having your hands there." I lose the humor.

"Christ!" he hisses. Before I know it, I find myself gasping from a delicious sting on my left bum cheek. "Did you fancy that?" he asks, his voice smooth and sexy, his hands cupping my bottom in a gentle, yet possessive manner.

"Yes." I breathe rapidly, matching the beating of my heart.

"I'm going to leave now before I end up throwing you on your bed and taking you." He closes his eyes and seems to be trying to talk himself down.

"I wouldn't oppose."

"Sex will not solve our problems, Becca." He looks me in the eyes.

"It'll solve that itch we both need scratched." I smile wryly at him. *Um . . . knock, knock, Becca! Do we need to put a little Madonna on to remind you of your prior sexual experience? Or give you a short list (only kind available)?* Who are you and shut up?!

"Goodnight, love." His lips apply pressure to my forehead, but I'm focusing more on the aggressive way his hands are caressing my ass. "God, I love this arse of yours," he groans.

"I love you..." Who said that? Who *the fuck* just said that?! Because this moment hasn't been awkward enough?! I hate you! *You're welcome.* Before I can answer (as crazy people tend to do), Grayson slams his mouth against mine. Not only do I welcome it, I open for him to deepen the kiss, threading my fingers into his hair, pulling him closer. I whimper into his mouth after my ass gets a double slap and squeeze. But, he's not picking me up like the last time.

He growls and rips away from me. "No! We can't! I can't." He paces then stops and looks at me. "You're bloody fucking gorgeous. You have *no* idea how badly I want to taste you right now, sink deep inside of you." He shakes his head. "I have to go. We'll talk soon." Before I can utter a word or breath, he's out the door. I grab my robe, throw it on, and go to stop him, but he's already left. I open the front door and step outside. I hear a car door slam, an engine start, lights flash on, and he backs out to leave, taking my heart with him.

Chapter Eight

GRAYSON

"Have you cancelled Becca's plane ticket yet?" Derek asks before he brings his beer up for a sip.

I've been waiting for him to ask me again. Since we came home, two weeks ago, I've barely discussed her with anyone. This is the only matter he's brought up—several times. He's not really smooth about it, either. I'm pretty sure he has something up his sleeve. It's why I won't cancel her tickets. I miss her . . . terribly.

I've been the most stubborn I have ever been in my life. She messages me every day like I did with her, telling me things she likes about me. Comments about my books, as well. I haven't responded to any of it. No. I've needed this time to really think about everything and to see if I could truly function again without her in my life. So far, I've failed at an embarrassing rate. I can't even brush my teeth without her popping into my head. With her being completely naked, the last time I saw her, I've recently spent a lot of time with the bloke below, reminiscing the teenage years, if you will. How I ever had the strength to walk away from that vision, I'll never know.

"Well?" he pries.

"Same answer as last time, mate." I grab the remote and turn up the game. Manchester United is up against Real Madrid. It's an important game, mostly because it will distract Derek. Me? I'm distracted, all right—thanks to him. It's something that replays the most to me. It's more like a constant echo of her saying it. I still *can't* believe she said *I love you.* She almost seemed like she regretted it after, not so much that she didn't mean it but like she was afraid I'd freak out or something.

I love you...

It was such a beautiful sound, coming from her lips.

"Can I have your extra ticket for the premiere this weekend?" Derek interrupts my thoughts again.

"Sorry. I'm already using it."

"But . . . you were taking Becca." He turns his focus to me swiftly.

"Yes, I was. Now I am not."

"Are you taking your mum?"

"No."

"Susanna?"

"No."

"Who then?" he asks . . . a bit hostile.

"Why is it so important to you?"

"Why are you being so secretive about it?" He slams his bottle down on the coffee table.

"What are you on about?"

"There will be paparazzi, Gray! You get snapped with another woman, instead of Becca, I'm not helping you clean up the mess again!" I can't remember the last time I've seen Derek this angry.

"Well, Becca and I are through, so, there should be no issue." I point out.

"Right!" he snaps in a condescending tone, grabs his beer, and sits back to watch the game. I try to keep my smug smile at bay. He just confirmed what I thought all along—I will see Becca in two days. I can't wait!

BECCA

"Are you nervous?" Stacey asks as she sits next to my suitcase on the bed.

"Yeah, I am. What if this is a mistake?" I stop going over my list of things to pack and look at her.

"He wants to see you, otherwise, he would've cancelled these tickets," she delivers the same speech she's given me a million times this week. I blow out a big gust of air, trying to help my nerves. "So…"

Just by the way she trailed off; I know what she's asking. "If things get that far, then yes, I will be coming back here a woman." I puff out my chest.

"You're finally ready?!" she asks excitedly.

"Yeah . . . I have been. But then, all of this shit went down."

"Shit *definitely* went down." She widens her eyes. "So, have you seen him naked?"

"No . . . I mean half, obviously. How is it that he's seen me three times now?!" I huff as I throw on a pair of jeans.

"But have you felt it when he's grinding against you?"

"Yes! It feels like it's huge. He gets so hard, it feels like steel." *Man of steel!* Coincidence?—I think not! "So, if you hear a faint scream, that'll be me, yelling from California, while I'm getting some." I laugh.

"I'll keep an ear out so I can drink to you!" She joins in my laughter.

"Teasing aside, I don't know when or how to tell him." I throw the last item in and zip up.

"He knows," she says nonchalantly.

"Wait—what?!" I stop from pulling it off the bed.

"Max told him."

"How does Max know and when did he tell him?" I get excited. Not *that* kind of excited, more like an "I'm going to rip your fucking head off!" excited. Stacey and I have a history of arguing over this topic. I thought we'd finally come to an agreement on it. See, she had this terrible habit of always telling people I was a virgin. It would piss me off. She always said I was overreacting, that I should be proud, not embarrassed. The last time we argued over it, it seemed to have finally sunk in. I explained to her that she was, in fact, telling people how many partners I've had. *"But you haven't had any," she said.* I then reminded her that zero, last I checked, was still a number. It wasn't anyone's business how many people I slept with whether it was zero or a hundred. But, if she wanted to continue to inform people then I would let everyone know her number. She didn't think I knew them all. And then, the light switched on when I proceeded to give her every name (even a few she had forgotten about). Now I'm not saying my best friend is a whore; her number is pretty average for this day and age. But, that stigma is *still* there (no matter how much Madonna has tried to bury it) and women, in general, never brag because of it. Needless to say, she finally conceded. I haven't had this problem since.

"He figured it out; he's around you enough to know you're not waving your vagina in anyone's face." She throws her hands out.

"He had to have confirmed it with you before telling him." I'm *not* letting this go!

"Yes—but—I only confirmed because one: you are close to him and two: besides you, he's my best friend. It wasn't malicious or even cavalier."

"Whatever; tell me what Grayson said." I mean, what's the point in carrying on about it?

"I guess he cursed under his breath, a little freaked out." She shrugs.

"Did he actually say he was freaked out? And when did Max talk to him?" It's official—I'm mortified! I would've never thought Grayson would freak out. Maybe that's why he refuses to talk to me or Derek about me.

"Max talks to him every day. They've become close friends over the past few months. There's actually something to be said about that; we all know how Max is with 'new' people." She does the air quotations. Knowing Stace, "every day" is probably an exaggeration. But still, the idea that he's talking to Max and probably going through him to "check on me", makes me feel a million times better. That, though, will totally piss Derek off, I know that for sure! "As far as saying he was freaked out, no. Max just said he sounded that way."

"Okay." I pull the suitcase down.

"Hey," She grabs my arm. "Everything will work out," she encourages.

"I hope so."

"It will. Now, I have to go and call Guinness." She gets up.

"The beer company?" I shoot her a confused look.

"No, the world record company. I have to tell them to take your name out of the running for the oldest virgin in the world. No need to be on snatch watch anymore." Stacey's delivery would leave the mass millions to believe her serious. But, I know better and grab my pillow to whack her with it.

Walking to the baggage claim at LAX, my eyes are peeled. There's a huge part of me that is hoping he is here to surprise me. My eyes light up just the same to see Derek waiting for me. Sign in hand reads: P.I.A. JERSEY GIRL. I flip him off and enjoy the sound of his deep laughter. I kinda love this guy (in a best friend or brother sort of way). As soon as Grayson and I get ourselves squared away, I'm gonna work on finding Derek a nice girl. He's a great catch!

When I reach him, he pulls me in a big bear hug, lifting me off the ground and swinging me around till I can't control my laughter. "Put me down, you big, vicious teddy bear!"

Two weeks ago, this guy was practically spitting nails at me with his words. He's never displayed his angry side before. I gave it back, though. It took a few days, but we let it go and started mapping out this plan. That, alone, tells me he believes I'm the one for Grayson, otherwise, after the anger he displayed with me, I wouldn't be here. Grayson is his brother through and through. And I know from having Stacey in my life, that a brother or sister by choice can be ten times more symbolic than the one you're born with. "I'm just glad you're here!" He gives me another squeeze before putting me down. The belt starts moving for the luggage.

"Ooh . . . that's mine!" I point it out.

Derek heads toward it and looks at me over his shoulder. "Is this your bag, baby?" He imitates Austin Powers (more with the facial expression since he's already got the "Brit" thing down pat).

"Why, yes it is, love!" I give him my best impersonation of an English accent. He cringes, then laughs at me as he grabs my bag.

"I'm banning you from ever watching *Mary Poppins* again," he states, walking up to me.

"Not good?"

"Dreadful."

"I'll work on it."

"Please don't."

"Jerk!" I elbow him, laughing as we head out of the building. Within fifteen minutes, Derek has us pulling out of the airport and heading to his house.

"So, you haven't talked about it in a while; how're things going with your security company?" I've been meaning to ask him this for some time. Derek, being a whizz at computers (he's an engineer) and a weekend warrior for the British Army a few years back, has been working hard on setting up his own security company.

"Eh . . . there were a few hiccups but things are moving along smoothly now, and I'm in the process of hiring and soliciting for work. Grayson, of course, is my top client." He puts his sunglasses on as he cruises down the road.

"Oh, so you'll be handling all stalker needs, as well as protection?"

"Shut it!" he says, then laughs.

"Well, just make sure you always have a job for me in case I fall in love with this place." I gaze out the window and begin forming my first impression of California.

"Ha—like Grayson would ever let you work!" he scoffs.

I shift my body toward him. "You talk as if it's a done deal. How can you be so confident?"

"I know my friend, Becca. When he looks at you, he sees forever. In all the years I've known him, I've never been able to say that about another girlfriend of his."

I straighten back, deciding on silence instead of a response. It's not long before we pull up to Derek's house. "Derek, who in the fuck lives here with you?!" I stare at the monstrosity before me.

"Staff..." he trails off.

"Are you compensating for a small penis, Derek? You can tell me; we're friends." My tone is so serious, I'm proud of myself.

"Oh, shut up—can't stand you!" He laughs.

"Yes, you have me staying with you for the week," I remind him.

"Ha—get that out of your head! He won't let you stay here—trust me," he says before he gets out of the car. I follow suit. He grabs my luggage and leads the way inside. "Here's your room until he demands for you to be at his house." He shows me into the first floor guestroom.

"Did you just move in?" I ask him this because his house has barely any décor and everything is white.

"I've been here for two years, why?"

"Are you friggin' kidding me?"

"No, why?"

"It looks like a damn hospital in here!" I wave my hands around.

"It may need a woman's touch," he concedes.

"I don't think it's concerned with gender as long as someone is touching it!" I say exacerbated.

"Alright, alright." He holds his hands up in defeat.

"Let me help while I'm here; I have an eye for decorating." I raise my hands up and clasp his.

"Deal."

"Yay!" I cheer and dance around a little.

"What am I gonna do with you?"

"You're gonna love me and hug me and call me George!" I say excitedly.

"In the great words of *Charlie Brown*—good grief!" he boasts.

"Stop!" I swat him. "Is there a bathroom in here? I need to run the shower to steam my dress for the premiere. I'm so nervous; I hope no one asks me who the dress is by." I am *really* worried about this. I tried going to all of the consignment shops I could find. But, no one had any designer dresses . . . at least any I could afford. I had to settle for a pretty evening gown from Macy's.

"Becca . . . I wasn't able to get his other ticket for the premiere." Derek is looking everywhere but at me.

"Why?" I feel my heart dropping.

"He's using it."

"His mom?" I ask, hopeful.

"No."

"Who?" I sit on the bed and feel the rise in my anxiety. *Oh . . . what am I doing here?*

"I don't know. But listen, you are still to get dressed. The after party is at his house, and you will be going to that." He grabs my suitcase and puts in on the bed.

"No."

"Yes! I promise; you won't regret it," he assures me before heading into, what I see now is, the bathroom and turns the shower on. "Let's get that dress out." He claps his hands together as he walks back in. I unzip my suitcase and hand it to him. "The hairdresser will be here at five pm. Do you want to take a nap?"

"Yeah." I offer a meek smile. I don't really need a nap, just alone time to analyze all of this.

"Alright then, love, you get some rest. I'll wake you at four." He stands before me, his fists sitting on his hips, his legs spread apart. I start laughing. "What?"

"You're standing there like a Goddamn superhero—Daredevil Derek!" I add quickly.

"Why do I get the feeling that I will now be inundated with all sorts of Daredevil paraphernalia?" He looks up at the ceiling, sighing in defeat.

"Because you know me so well," I quip. "Now, leave me be! I need to get plenty of rest before I'm completely humiliated tonight." I get up and shoo him toward the door.

"I won't leave your side, Becca." He turns to me before finally leaving.

"I know. Thank you. I'll see you in a few hours." I give him a quick hug and let him leave.

"I'm gonna throw up," I say for the fifth time as we pull up to Grayson's home. It's rather large as well. However, unlike Derek's contemporary home, this one is a Mediterranean ranch.

"Everything will be fine," he repeats.

"Why is there no one here?" I look around.

"We're here first to make sure the security is all set." He pulls into the massive garage.

"Right; that makes sense." I unbuckle when he turns the engine off. I try to calm my nerves but it's pretty hard when you know that you're probably not expected or worse . . . wanted.

"Let's go." Derek opens my door for me. I didn't even realize he got out of the car.

"Well, here goes nothing," I breathe, take his hand, and climb out. He leads me to the door I'm sure leads inside the house. The moment we walk in, I hear a ton of commotion coming from another room.

"Uh oh, Susanna doesn't sound happy," Derek states as if I already know her well. He leads me toward the yelling and slamming of stuff. "Susanna, what's the matter?" Derek rushes into the kitchen ahead of me.

"What's the matter?! The caterers *your* friend hired apparently booked us on the wrong date! I didn't think anything of it since Grayson said he had handled it, but when they still didn't show up an hour ago, I called. They have no one they can send, and it's too late to get anyone else! I have to come up with several ideas for hor d'oeuvres for well over a hundred people that will be here within the next two hours!" If it weren't for her beautiful olive complexion, I'm sure she'd be beet red. Thankfully, her shoulder-length, salt and pepper hair is pulled back into a low ponytail, otherwise, I think she'd be pulling it out.

"Susie, honey, please sit down for a moment; you're turning the color of an eggplant." The gentleman (I'm guessing her husband) with the kind face, dark hair, and same olive skin tries to coax her to a seat.

"Sam, how can I sit when I have so much to do?" I can tell she's on the verge of tears the way her voice is shaking. I glance around the kitchen (trying to avoid my need to mentally remodel it), noticing a shitload of grocery bags on the counters and floor. I head over and start peeking inside of them. There's every kind of *Pillsbury* dough in a can you can find. Chicken, graham crackers, cream cheese, hot sauce, blue cheese; the list could go on forever. I start pulling out the bags of potatoes and setting them in one area.

I look over my shoulder at them, "Take a seat, Susanna, I'm going to separate everything. Then, we'll figure out what we can make that will be quick, easy, and fantastic," I offer her a smile. She gives me a quizzical look. Derek leans into her ear and her eyes widen, a slightly surprised smile crosses her face before she slowly takes a seat. I turn back to the task at hand. In between sorting, I turn the oven on and raid the fridge as ideas pop into my head, seeing if the final ingredients I need are there. Several ideas seem like they are gonna pan out—woo hoo! Finding big pots, I start filling them up with water for the chicken to boil as well as pasta.

"Ok, what's the plan? I'm calm now." Susanna walks over to me.

"Did you have any ideas?" I ask not wanting to push any of her thoughts to the side.

"Too frazzled; I couldn't come up with anything solid. Just sent Sam to the store with a crazy list; I was hoping I could figure it out when I was looking at it all." She looks around. "Nope—I've completely crashed."

"No worries; I have several ideas and because of your brilliant list, they will all work out. Right now, we have to prep the hell out of this shit. Can you start to clean the mushrooms and pull the stems?"

"I'm on it." She winks and starts grabbing the containers. I throw the chicken in and start on the potatoes.

Over the next hour, Susanna and I find a nice groove that I believe would make others think we've been working together for years. We even put Derek and Sam to work. All the initial prep has been done and we're onto putting the hor d'oeuvres together for the final phase of cooking. Now, it's just a matter of watching and waiting—for the food and the guests.

"I'm heading out, honey." Sam sneaks up behind Susanna and kisses her cheek. I've known them a whole hour and a half and I'm already full of admiration for both of them. You can see how much they are still in love. *My heart just sighed.*

"Where's he going?" I ask as I scoop mac and cheese into the mini muffin pans.

"To pick up Grayson and Hazel."

"Hazel went to the premiere with him?" I ask trying to hide my hopefulness. Hazel is Grayson's mom.

"Yes. Didn't you know that?" She stops mixing the cream cheese mixture.

"No. I was supposed to be his date tonight," I answer truthfully.

"I know that. Did he know you were coming? I am certain he would've taken you, had he known." She places her hand on my forearm.

"He never cancelled my tickets, so I'm not sure. Playing things by ear here." I shrug lightly. While I've enjoyed getting to know Susanna, I do feel a little uncomfortable discussing this. I can't help but wonder what she thinks of me now. I do feel quite pathetic, come to think of it.

"It's good you came; he's missed you." She smiles warmly.

"He has?"

"Oh yes! He won't admit it, though. But, he always leaves the evidence out."

"Huh?" I ask, confused as hell.

She laughs. "He has a framed picture of you two. I've caught him holding it several times these past couple of weeks, lost in his thoughts." This warrants a massive amount of silence from me. Why didn't he respond—just once? Why, if he was just as miserable, did he embrace this misery? Was he teaching me a lesson? Was he trying to get over me? Did he leave those tickets viable, hoping I would come here? Were these two weeks just a "cool off" period for him? I have so many questions.

"Oh Susanna, I can't believe this has happened!" A woman's voice travels to us from the entrance to the kitchen, behind us. I quickly look at the clock, noticing twenty minutes, of me being lost in my sea of questions, have gone by. We both turn toward the woman heading in. "What can I do?" she asks. She has the most gorgeous, pure-white hair I've ever seen. Her powder-blue eyes compliment her well-styled hair and pale skin.

"We actually have it under control, Hazel." Susanna hugs her. "The Lord sent us an angel." She holds her hand out for me to grab when she pulls away from Hazel. I smile timidly, while taking her hand.

"Oh good! I'm so glad your boss was able to send you our way." Hazel beams, clasps her hands and looks up towards the big guy in the sky.

"She's not from the caterers." Susanna bites back her smile.

"No?" She looks between us.

"No," Susanna says. I look down and play with my fingers nervously. "I guess I'll make the introductions since it seems your son is avoiding my wrath," she starts. "This beautiful, young lady is Grayson's Becca."

I look up quickly with how she said that. *Grayson's Becca . . .*

"So . . ." Hazel leads in. I bring my attention to her. She studies me for a moment. "You came? Even though he's been avoiding you?" she asks.

"Yes, ma'am." I nod.

"I assume you are dressed for the premiere—the same one he asked you to but, in fact, did not take you to," she continues. I'm not sure what she's getting at, but I'm feeling that foolish feeling coming over me again.

"I am."

"All dressed up for a ball the prince promised, yet pulled out from underneath you…"

Can someone please point me toward the nearest rock?

"Still, you swooped into save the day when he needed help, without batting an eye?"

"Hazel, you have no idea how she saved the day. She just jumped right in," Susanna champions me. I stay silent.

"Well, this can only mean one thing." She lets out a sigh. "Gracie was right about you and I was wrong. I *hate* when he's right. I'll never live this down."

"I see where Grayson gets his riddle talk from." I giggle, still slightly confused.

"Sorry." She laughs. "He told me that you were different and that I would love you the moment I met you." She beams.

"Oh."

"It's so nice to finally meet you, Becca." She pulls me in for a hug. Funny, hugging her doesn't feel awkward at all.

"Susanna!" Grayson booms, causing Hazel and me to jump. "I'm so sorry, love. I thought everything was squared away." He walks up to and kisses her cheek.

"Thank God Becca was here, I would've been lost without her." She reaches for me again. She's such an affectionate person.

"Yes." He stares at me. "I'm very familiar with that feeling."

Sade comes strolling into my head . . . "No need to ask . . . he's a smooth operator . . ."

"Hi," I manage.

"You're looking fancy tonight; going somewhere?" he asks.

"Grayson!" Susanna and Hazel gasp in unison.

"Why, this old thing?" I look down. "Just my usual Saturday night rags . . . minus the tiara, of course."

"Is it off for appraisal?"

"Oh no . . . I realized I may be working in the kitchen this evening, so I left it off knowing my hand would be too tired to do the Queen's wave all night. I see you've got your Clark Kents on." I step out of Hazel's space and work my way closer to him.

"Well, yes—I had to. At least, I thought I did. But alas, no buttons from my shirt have been sacrificed; my real identity—safe for another day."

"I'm sure we can come up with a just cause to sacrifice them," I suggest, inching closer to him.

His hands palm my face. "Now *that* would be super," he states before softly collecting my lips in a simple "my mother is standing right next to us" manner. He rests his forehead against mine. "You look abso-fucking-lutely gorgeous," he breathes.

"You clean up pretty good yourself." Just then, the oven dings, pulling us out of our moment. I turn to find our audience, Susanna and Hazel, staring at us as if they are watching a movie. "Excuse me, Susanna." I smile, gesturing toward the oven.

"Oh . . . yes . . . sorry." She shakes her head and chuckles a bit. I'm feeling a little giddy myself; I wasn't really expecting that greeting. I wasn't sure what to expect. It's crazy—my nerves jumping all over the place and yet, calm at the same time.

"I've got a few calls out to try and get some servers for tonight," Grayson informs us. "I haven't heard anything yet."

"I put a few calls out there, too. I've got three teenagers coming," Susanna says apprehensively.

"Eh . . . that could definitely go two ways. Say, Becca, would you like to earn some extra money tonight?"

"Gracie!" Hazel snaps. Yes, I just got pissed too, but then I remember who I'm dealing with.

I turn to face them. "Why, Grayson, you know I live to serve you—no pay required." I wink.

"Well, aren't you a tough shell to crack tonight?" He smirks.

"Do you always try to aggravate her?" his mom asks with exacerbation.

"Oh, he succeeds most of the time, but it's usually when he's not trying," I enlighten her.

"I'm glad you found a girl who gives it back to you." Susanna pokes at his chest.

"Yes, well, we're working on that, darling, aren't we?" He waggles his brows, soliciting a laugh from me.

"Oh, Gracie!" Hazel smacks his arm. "Do remember your mother is in the room!"

"What-I-say?!" The Brit sounds extra British, causing my body to react.

"You know exactly what you said." She shakes a finger at him, trying not to laugh at his boyish grin. "C'mon, Susanna, let's give these two lovebirds a few minutes before everyone starts arriving."

"Yes, please do, so that we may christen the kitchen at once!" Gray states, earning another smack from her before they head out. He watches as they leave, and once they've made it over the threshold, he turns his focus back my way; his hands grasp either side of my face and his mouth slams up against mine. My lips part for him, willingly. I reach up and weave my fingers into his thick, almost black hair, bringing him closer.

Grayson growls and rips himself from me. "Damn it!" he swears. "I said I wouldn't do this if you came here; I wouldn't give in. I'd make you wait it out so you'd know I was still pissed! But then I see you and my plans to keep you at arm's length do what they do every time—go right out the bloody friggin' window! Damn it, I hate the hold you have on me!" he yells. Yes, I have to say, he's looking pissed enough to match that yell.

"Grayson, you've held out the past few weeks. You know I feel terrible. You know I wish I could take it back. You *know* that I love you." I try to reason with him. "There's only one thing you *don't* know," I let on.

"What's that?" he barks angrily.

"I have," I start waving my hands over each other, "absolutely *no* panties on," I finish. He stares blankly at me, and as he goes to speak, I cut him off. "No—it's open to the breeze! Bare too! I got a Brazilian. I've never had one before. What with the no panties business going on, the slight breeze, and the effects of you turning me on—I'm feeling sexy in the underworld," I state matter-of-factly.

"You're overwhelmed? This is a joke?" he asks me calmly, like he's trying to figure me out. I'm half disappointed that he's not laughing at my announcement.

"I am overwhelmed, but it's not a joke," I say quietly. "Geez!" I gasp as he grabs my hand and yanks me to follow his lead. He brings me (drags, really) into the bathroom by the kitchen. He closes the door and locks it. Turning me aggressively, he unzips my dress. I chew back a ball of nerves.

"Jesus H. Christ!" Grayson gasps when he discovers my truth. "Step out of it," he commands and helps me. The Brit places my gown on the towel rack before feasting his eyes on me. How does he always manage to get me completely naked? My cheeks feel like they are on fire. Grayson's fingers tread lightly down my belly. My breaths come in a short, rapid pace. "Better brace yourself, sweetheart; I'm about to devour you," his voice is full of lust as he slowly gets to his knees. I whimper with need when his fingers reach my clef. "So smooth," he breathes. His face inches closer as his two fingers push through my folds. Retrieving them, he sucks the taste off. "So delicious. Always ready for me, aren't you, sweetheart?" Grayson gives me a crooked smile before pressing on, his tongue darting out to sample more.

"Oh God!" I groan as he lifts my left leg, placing it over his shoulder before face planting. I look around helplessly for something to grasp a hold of. I settle on his head, fisting his hair. Closing my eyes, I focus on the sounds around me: the sloshing of his mouth against my heat, the tempo of our breathing, his groans of contentment, mine of ecstasy. My core tightens and the most intense, beautiful pleasure rushes through me. My hand smacks across my mouth to keep me quiet. Grayson reaches up and yanks my arm, uncovering my mouth just as I peak. "Oh God, baby!" I cry as my hips thrash wildly, grinding into his face. *Oh, fuck!*

Grayson slows down, lapping all of my taste up sweetly, helping me to calm down. He flattens his tongue against me, taking the last of it slowly. He sucks on my clit, then gives me a soft peck before pulling away fully and coming to a standing position again. "*Always* let me hear you," he says sternly before collecting my lips. "You understand me?"

"Yes, Grayson," I submit.

"Becca." He chucks my chin, and my eyes flutter up to his. "We're done." My eyes widen as I feel panic boiling up inside of me. He takes in a deep breath and shakes his head slightly like there's more. "We're done with the chasing. We're done with ignoring feelings. We are done being *apart*. Do I make myself clear? You are *mine*—say it!" he demands.

"Yes. I'm yours," my voices shakes.

"Because I can't do it anymore, Becca—I've reached my limit. I'm done—do you hear me?" It's like he's just not expecting it to be this easy.

"I love you, baby. I'm ready; I promise." I reach up and palm his cheek. "No more," I add.

Forehead to forehead, he holds me as we stare into each other's eyes, breathing in this moment. The moment we finally landed on the same page in our own story. I can't help but get choked up; I'm staring at my forever and I'm overwhelmed by the joy my heart is feeling. *I'm home.* I see it in his eyes. I feel it in the warmth of his arms. I hear it in the sound of his voice.

"What are these for?" He thumbs my tears away.

"Me—saying goodbye to my wall and hello to my future." I chew on my bottom lip.

"This," he pulls it from the clutches of my teeth, "is my job." And with that, my bottom lip is being deliciously nibbled on by much stronger teeth.

"Grayson!" Derek pounds on the door, causing us both to jump.

"What now?!" Grayson barks.

"Guests are arriving," he informs us.

"Ugh . . . for fuck's sake," Gray grumbles. "Let's get you dressed, shall we?" He plants a kiss on my forehead before turning for my dress. He helps me back into it and after zipping me, reaches for the door.

"Grayson!" I say in a panic.

"What?" He turns back.

"You have to wash your face!" I turn the faucet on and point to the soap.

"Right . . . I definitely don't want to share any part of you with anyone." He smiles and then heads to the sink for a good scrub.

Chapter Nine

GRAYSON

I keep my eyes peeled for a glimpse of her. She's been working the room since the party started, as my girlfriend and cohost. She's a natural, making sure everyone has everything they need and that they're enjoying themselves. I can't help but feel proud. I think, or at least hope, that came across in the interview with *People*. They are here, having the exclusive to my after party. Clayton Stern, the reporter for *People*, seemed thrilled to add an impromptu interview with Becca and me, as well as a small photo shoot. She was fantastic, especially when he asked her why she wasn't at the premiere. Leaving out the part where I was a jerk, she told the truth—that she stayed here to cater the party with my staff due to a scheduling faux pas.

Usually, I hate these functions and whatnot. I always feel *off* about them: people laughing at dreadful jokes, niceties that are full of all things phony, et cetera et cetera. Tonight, though, I'm actually enjoying myself. I feel balanced; calm. She calms me, which is odd given our relationship and all of the hoops she's made me jump through. I'm not naïve enough to believe she won't have some more in the future.

"Grayson," Derek says urgently, a little out of breath.

"What's the matter?" I turn to him, and become concerned with the look on his face.

He leans in, "Violet's suffered a terrible stroke. Your mum is on the phone with your cousin now."

"What?!" I ask and immediately rush off to find my mother.

"She's in your study," he calls after me.

My steps quicken, my chest tightens. Aunt Violet is like a second mum to me. In fact, she's my Godmother. I'm just as close to her as Mum, if not more at times. "Mum?" I call out as soon as I enter the room. She seems just to be hanging up the phone.

"Oh, Gracie!" she cries, "We have to go home straight away. She's not doing well; not responding."

"Absolutely, Mum," I agree as I cross the room to her and pull her into my arms.

"Grayson!" Becca says from behind me. "What's the matter?"

I look over my shoulder at her, "My Aunt Violet has had a terrible stroke. We're getting on the first flight available for London, sweetheart, so make sure you have everything packed."

"I'm so sorry." She walks up to us, giving us both a hug. "Which room is yours, baby? I'll start packing your things," she offers.

"That's not necessary; I have clothes there. Can you please inform our guests that we are cutting the evening short?"

"Absolutely." She gives me another squeeze before letting go. "Do you need me to look at flights or is someone on it already?"

"Derek and I will take care of it. I really need you to handle the guests. I don't want a million questions. Is that all right?" I pull my mum in tighter as she continues to cry.

"Yes, of course. I'll go do that now." She presses up on her toes and gives me a quick peck. I watch as she leaves the room.

"She really is a wonderful girl, Gracie." Mum smiles up at me through her tears.

"Isn't she, though?" I agree. "Aunt Violet will love her." That statement only makes her cry harder. "Mum," I grab her upper arms gently. This is Aunt Violet we're talking about—she's stubborn as a mule! She *will* pull through this. I even bet she'll be awake and talking everyone's ear off when we get there," I encourage.

"I hope you're right, sweetie. I just . . . I'm not ready to be in this world without my sister too. I can't take anymore loss right now." Her chin quivers.

"Don't think like that! Besides," I chuckle. "Dad's up there right now, convincing St. Peter that it's not her time yet. If I'm going to be honest—he's begging for them to keep her here longer!" Mum laughs and nods her head in agreement.

My dad and Aunt Violet "tolerated" each other because of my mother. They were like oil and water, those two. They'd had some knock-out scraps over the years. Yet, besides my mother and me, she cried the hardest at his funeral. Just goes to show—you can never really define anyone's true feelings for them because they often will surprise you and maybe even themselves.

"Come now, let us get ready; I have to check flights."

"Okay," she sighs. We head out and both discreetly try to get to our rooms.

"Hey!" Becca grabs my attention and quickens her pace to get to me. I hold my hand out for her to join me.

"That was quick." I kiss her.

"Derek already started informing the guests. Between him, Susanna, and Sam, they cleared them out pretty quick," she says as we enter my room.

"Okay, well, let's get changed and then I have to look at flights." I work at my bow tie.

"I have to wait till I get back to Derek's." She leans her hand on my bed to pull off her heels.

"What are you talking about?" I shoot her a look, confused.

"My stuff is there."

"*What*. In. The. *Hell,* do you mean your stuff is there?!" I roar.

"I'm staying there, so naturally that's where my stuff is." She stops pulling her last heel off.

"Why? Tell me right now why you are staying there!" I get in her face, seething. I don't like this—not one bit. I don't like how close they've become. I hate feeling this way but I can't help it, especially after her recent behavior. Is Derek her fall back guy?

"I wasn't sure I'd still be welcomed here." She stares up at me as she finally pulls her heel off. "I was staying with him. That is until I felt that I was, indeed, still welcome."

"I should hope our time in the bathroom earlier cleared that up for you!" I bite.

"Yes. Nothing says 'welcome committee' like a good round of cunning linguistics." She smirks. I soften my stare. "I had full intentions of bringing my stuff here tonight . . . tomorrow the latest." She reaches up, palming my face. "You're getting so worked up over something so little, acting as if…" She stops, her smile fading. And as if she could hear my earlier thoughts, she gasps lightly in shock, I think. She lets go of my face and turns to walk away from me.

"Becca, wait." I grab her arm and turn her to me. "I'm sorry," I plead.

"I love Derek like you do, Grayson, like a brother . . . a friend. I would never . . . it's just—*no!*" I can see she's fighting back tears. I'm truly disappointed in myself. I'm already ruining things.

"I apologize," I say again, not bothering to mask my vulnerability.

"Let's just get you ready for your trip." She wipes the tears that were threatening.

"Our trip," I correct her sternly. Is she really not going to go with me now because of one irrational thought?

"I can't go to London with you, Grayson; I'm sorry."

"I made a small mistake, understandable given your recent behavior!" Anger takes over me again. "I've told you about my aunt, how important she is to me! You're going to hold this little thing over my head while I'm heartbroken and need you by my side?!

Now, what do you have to say for yourself?"

"I'll tell you what I have to say for myself!" She pokes at my chest, charging forward. "I don't have a passport, you asshole! I can't go, no matter how much it kills me to *not* be there with you!"

"Well, that makes bloody good sense!" I yell in a lower octave.

"Imagine that!" she gives it back.

"Christ, Becca." I rub my face in frustration. I let go, feeling her arms wrapping around my waist. My arms enfold her, and we stand here, embracing for several minutes. "I don't want to be without you," I admit.

"I wish I could come with you."

"You have *no* idea how badly I want you to *come* with me tonight," I groan, just realizing my plans of taking her slowly tonight will not be happening. I shouldn't be thinking about this with Aunt Violet so poorly—but, at the end of the day—I'm a man. Same man whose been dying to have this beautiful woman warm his bed in a biblical sense.

"I'm going to smack you if you are insinuating what I think you are." She tries to be serious, but there's a giggle undercurrent.

"I'll have everything of yours moved here tonight, so I can, at least, know you are in our bed." I kiss the top of her head. She quickly looks up at me and furrows her brows. I lean down and kiss her nose, then her lips. "I hope you find it comfortable. I know you like the mattress to be soft, so that's what I ordered."

"You ordered a new bed . . . according to what I like?" Her eyes light up with a twinkle. "You're really not lacking anything in the confidence department, are you?"

"I'd be lying if I said 'no.' Truth is, I've laid in this bed so many nights, wondering if you'd ever be lying beside me in it. More so these past few weeks," I wholeheartedly admit.

"Do you have a t-shirt I can borrow?" she asks. Not a surprising question; Becca always has a way of asking or mentioning things that have absolutely nothing to do with the topic at hand.

"Yes, of course, darling." I head over to retrieve one from my drawer. I turn back to find her back turned to me.

"Unzip me, please." She glances over her shoulder.

"Who zipped you up today?" I can't help it; the little green monster is growing again. Her shoulders slump at my inquiry. "Never mind, I'm being silly," I add and make quick work of her zipper. "God, you're beautiful." My lips dance across her shoulders. I hear her swallow hard.

"Shirt, please." She holds up her hand.

"Turn around; I want to dress you," I command before licking the shell of her ear. She shivers before obliging. I help her to step out of her dress again and am taken aback by her small fit of laughter. "Care to explain yourself?" I raise a brow, biting back my smile—her laughter is infectious.

"You're running quite the record of getting me naked. I'm a little jealous; I've yet to see you." Suddenly, the shy side of Becca comes out. It's not a side that sees the light of day much, but when it does, it's rather sweet.

I palm her face, "I had full intentions of you not only seeing me tonight but watching you explore my body. I feel awful saying it but, my aunt has picked a fine time to do this."

"How rude of her, really." Becca teases me, making me feel slightly better about my selfish thoughts.

"That aside . . ." I lead, not sure how to ask her. I know that she is a virgin (made so much sense out of a lot when Max told me); I just don't know if she's truly ready to not be. Part of me wants to go in like a Neanderthal, taking what's mine, regardless of whether she's unsure or not. The other part—the fully evolved man (mostly)—wants to make sure that it is something she will never regret, lives up to the expectations that most have for their first time, and finally, make sure I don't do anything that will cause her to walk out of my life for it. Fully evolved man wins. "Are you . . . ready, darling? I mean . . . for what I'd like to happen in this very bed." I feel them—my eyelids—buggers can't keep a normal pace to save my life. Her eyes laugh at me again, noticing my eyelids. She always teases me about it. "Stop," I complain lightly.

"I've been ready for you for quite some time, Grayson. You

don't have to ask me again," she takes on a serious tone. "As a matter of fact, I'd prefer you didn't ask me again." I go to open my mouth, but she places her fingers over my lips. "If, for any reason, I want you to stop, I will tell you—I promise." I kiss her fingers, taking in a deep, appreciative breath. She is more than I ever thought I'd want. I position my shirt and pull it over her. She's swimming in it, and she looks so beautiful.

"Call Derek and ask him to look at flights," she says as she begins to unbutton my tux shirt. I pull my phone out and call immediately. I ask him to look into the flights and mention that Becca will not be coming—this time. My eyes roll to the back of my head as Becca's mouth runs a hot trail across my chest. She pushes my shirt off my shoulders. "You have the most amazing shoulders, baby. They're broad, strong, and defined; I love 'em." She nibbles at them between her words.

"Sounds like I should text you instead of barging into your room," Derek says on the line.

"Yup . . . have to go, mate." I hang up, toss my phone, and attack her mouth with mine. Becca feels for the button on my pants and zipper. I help her, and we push them off, our mouths re-locking after the slight separation. She begins to head towards the bed. I graciously follow her lead. Every inch we get closer seems to match the growth in my shorts. I'm so hard, it's painful. I feel the Neanderthal trying to climb his way to the surface. "Becca," I pull away. "No . . . we can't," I pant.

"I know." Her breath matches mine. "But we can lie in this bed for a few, in each other's arms. I can give you that tonight." She slowly climbs on top of it. I watch as she turns on her back. This no-panty-wearing business is killing me. I flash her a wicked smile and free myself from the confinements of my boxer briefs. Her widened eyes tell me that she is very impressed with the state of my arousal. A flicker of concern passes across her face, as well. She's probably wondering how it will fit. My chest may have just puffed out with pride (blame the Neanderthal). I climb up on the bed and begin a slow crawl up her body, tasting every inch as I go.

"Open," I command, parting her knee. She opens without a thought. "God!" I groan as her excitement glistens before my eyes.

"Baby . . . please," she pleads, her pelvis already gyrating at my barely-there touch.

"I want every part of you, sweetheart. How am I to hold back tonight?" I close my eyes tightly, fighting off the vicious beast that wants to devour her.

"Lie on your back." She tries to push me. I allow her insistence and roll onto my back. She climbs on top of me, her green eyes a million shades darker. I quickly pull her shirt off, drinking in the sight of her. She nibbles on that delicious bottom lip of hers, staring into my eyes as she lowers herself. Releasing her lip, her mouth caresses my skin, working her way down my chest.

"You're so beautiful," she murmurs and traces the lines of my abs with her tongue.

My breath is quickening to a level I almost don't recognize. The anticipation of what she might do is killing me. I run my hand through her hair, encouraging her as she licks up my v-line. My hips surge off the bed. "Becca, darling . . ." I plead.

"Grayson." Her eyes find mine. "I've never done this before, either. If it's not right or you need me to do something differently, please don't hesitate to tell me. I want to please you, baby. It won't hurt my feelings."

"For fuck's sake, sweetheart, I'm ready to come at the *thought* of you doing this." That's all the reassurance I have for her at the mo. She's killing me. She and that sexy, fecking mouth of hers.

I watch as she takes me in her hand—that alone may cause me to be undone. It's like slow motion as I watch her tongue slide through her lips, reaching out to taste me. It swirls around my tip, collecting my pre-cum. Fuck, she just groaned like it was her favorite meal. Becca's sweet, full lips slide down, taking in my length, and I see stars. My free hand joins the one already threaded through her hair, and I hold on, guiding her—encouraging her.

I've never been the type to get high, but I imagine it feels like this: falling into complete bliss. I watch as her hand works around my base, and she ramps up the pace. Every once in a while, she frees me from the clutches of her mouth to "check in" with me, make sure she's doing things proper. I whisper several words of encouragement: *amazing, brilliant, Jesus, and Becca*. I get rewarded with a coy smile and the return of her mouth.

"Becca—Jesus—fuck it all to hell! Darling, what the—" I practically yell, feeling her tongue massage the area between my arse and balls, all the while, still working at my happy fellow. The tightening rips through me, my rapid gasps complimenting it.

"That's it, baby, c'mon," she eggs me on. I lift my head to double check that this is still my Becca; that I'm not in some sort of fantastic dream. The surge rips through me. Becca takes me deep into her mouth again. I erupt, groaning like I'm dying the most pleasant of deaths. She takes every drop I offer her. I'd cheer her on like the champ she is but I'm too caught up in what I'm experiencing at the moment.

I feel my chest heaving, trying to capture some oxygen. Never. I have *never*—feck—that was amazing. "Baby?" She climbs up my body.

I can't even look at her. "Where in the feck did you learn to do that so well?" I ask, my arm across my eyes.

"Really?" she asks, pride and excitement in her voice.

"Becca, where?!" I demand, now looking at her.

"Um . . . *HBO* special? *Real Sex: Forty-Three* or something." She giggles.

"I'll be sure to send *HBO* a thank you note," I say, still in disbelief but then laugh at her infectious giggle. "I can't believe you swallowed," I say after finishing my last bit of laughter. I really can't but probably shouldn't have said it, either.

"Me either." She furrows her brow. "But . . . it was you. I couldn't imagine not tasting you . . . taking it all," she states, seemingly baffled. "I love it. I loved tasting you. It was amazing," she adds.

I palm her face. We stare, locking eyes. There are *no* words. "I love you." Except those particular ones. It's the first time I've ever said them to a woman. It's not nearly as scary as I thought it would be.

Just then, my phone alerts me to a text message, bringing us down from our cloud. "Must be Derek." I reach for it. "Flight leaves in less than two hours. I have to go, sweetheart." I turn to her, feeling just as disappointed as I think she may.

"Go. I'll be here when you get back." She leans up on her elbow and kisses me.

"Don't say that. What if I'm not back for two weeks or so?" I bring us down to reality.

"I will make sure I am here when you arrive back," she states with a certainty in her voice.

"Really?!" I ask, hopeful.

"I promise." She gives me another kiss, quite dramatically, if I may add.

"Alright, time to get me off, then." I sigh.

"Um . . . sorry, but didn't I just do that?" she teases.

"Oh . . . you *most certainly* did." I grasp her chin between my thumb and forefinger. "And I can't wait to return the favor." I rub my nose against hers as my hand falls to her leg, traveling up it.

"Don't!" Her hand grabs my arm to stop me. I begin to tickle her to release it. I love to hear her laugh.

"Grayson!" My mum's voice matches the urgency of her knock. "Almost ready? We have to leave."

"Give me five minutes, Mum; I'm nearly ready," I shout, guilt setting in.

"Call me when you land. When you've seen her . . . every chance you get," Becca fires her requests at me.

"Absolutely, love. I'll need you, you know that." I kiss her once . . . twice . . . *mmm.*

BECCA

Slowly, I stir. Mmm, this is so comfortable. I feel as if I'm on a cloud. This is so much nicer than my bed. I open my eyes in a panic. Oh . . . mmm . . . I stretch. I look over at the clock. It's been seven hours since Grayson left for London. I miss him terribly. *You've only been awake for two minutes!* So?

I decide to start my day rather than argue with my inner thoughts. Noticing my bag near the door, I jump out of bed and head over to it. I roll it over to the bed and unzip it. A shower is definitely in order; my hair is like cement from all the hairspray.

I toss my hair up in a clip before heading down the hall to the kitchen. "There she is!" Susanna offers me a huge smile.

"Good morning!" I say cheerfully.

"Coffee?"

"Yes, please," I practically groan.

"Have a seat, sunshine."

"Any news?" I ask as I sit at the small dinette.

"They've just arrived. Violet is still not responding, but her vitals are stable." She sets a cup of Joe in front of me.

"Thanks." I palm it, noticing she's already fixed it for me. Strange. I bring it up to my lips, take a good swig, and sigh happily. "How did you know how to make my coffee?" I tilt my head at her.

"The same way I learned what to make you for breakfast." She winks before turning. He never fails to surprise me. Susanna starts pouring batter onto a griddle.

"So what is it I want for breakfast this morning?" I ask, leaning up in my chair without standing to eye what she has going on over there.

"Pecan and banana pancakes with extra crispy bacon." She glances over her shoulder at me. I groan. *God, I love him.*

"I'll need—"

"A glass of milk," she finishes for me. *Wow.*

"You're going to join me, right?"

"It's not really proper for me to do so."

"Oh, that's okay; I left my tiara at home, remember?" I giggle.

"I'd love to join you, Becca, but you know, you shouldn't get into that habit. You'll be making friends here. One word that you share your meals with the help and..." she trails off.

"First of all, Grayson has never referred to you as 'the help', only as if you were family. I instantly felt the same way. Secondly, I don't give a rat's ass what anybody else thinks!" I state. Honestly, I'm a little hurt that she would automatically put me in the same category as those other people, "friends" I haven't even met yet.

"I didn't peg you to care, Becca," she starts as if she can read my thoughts. "I just try to remember my place."

"Yeah, well your place is at the damn table with me."

"Are you upset with me?"

"Yes," I huff. "If I was anything like those people, do you think I would've rolled my sleeves up like I did last night?" I ask her truthfully.

"You're right; I apologize." She gives me a shy smile.

"Forget it." I wave my hand. "I know where it came from; I understand." I try to lighten up for both of our sakes.

Within a few minutes, Susanna is sitting across from me, laughing as I do my happy chair dance. When I love something I'm eating, I just can't help it. "So what do you have planned for today?" she inquires.

"Probably do some proof reading for Gray. Does he have an office that he works out of?" I pop a piece of bacon into my mouth.

"He works out of the study. He has an office upstairs, but he hasn't set it up yet." She scrapes up the last bit of her pancakes.

"Why not?"

"He doesn't know how he wants it. I guess he has an idea but isn't sure. He wants to hire someone but hasn't gotten around to it yet."

"Hmm . . . I think I'll take a look."

After breakfast, that's just what I do. I open the dark, wooden door and step in. It's a great sized room with dark built-in shelves, taking up the entire wall, on the right, from floor to ceiling. There are exposed beams going across the ceiling, matching the bookshelves. Other than those features, the room is boring, not a hint of color; lifeless. I walk around the boxes, really taking it in. I can already see the color it should be. I peer into some of the boxes; mostly books and some knick knacks. Suddenly, I'm struck with a brilliant idea. However, I'm not sure how I'm going to pay for this idea. Hmm, I wonder if Susanna could help.

I head back out and rush down the stairs to find her. "Whoa! Where's the fire?" she calls out as I run past her.

"Oh!" I turn. "Susanna, is there a house credit card?"

"What?"

"Do you have a credit card that you use for household things?"

"Why?" She crosses her arms, studying me curiously.

"I want to surprise him. I want to do his office. I just don't have the funds to cover it."

"I can't authorize that—he'd have to."

"It's a surprise, though."

"Becca, he will be alerted to anything out of the ordinary."

"Damn it," I mumble. "Ok, I'll text him." And with that, I turn to head toward his room. I grab my phone.

> **Me:** Morning, baby. I hope your flight was ok. Are you seeing Aunt Violet now? When you get a chance, will you please let Susanna know that I can use the house card? I have a few things I would like to pick up. I love you! Call me when you can!

I hit send and unpack my clothes, hoping for a quick reply. My phone rings just as I finish that thought and I quickly grab it off the bed. "Hey," I answer.

"Hey yourself," he replies. "Now, what is this that you need?"

"It's a surprise," I say gleefully.

"You want me to buy my own surprise?"

I stay silent. He just brought my level of excitement down several notches. "Forget it," I finally say. "How's Aunt Violet?" I try to change the subject.

"Becca?"

"What?"

"How much are we talking?"

"I don't know. I haven't priced it out yet. It's for the house—not me. Look, just forget it; it's ruined now." I sigh in frustration and slam a drawer shut.

"Well, Becca, how do you expect me to respond? You haven't been there twenty-four hours yet, and you're already acting like the lady of the house," he tries to defend himself—poorly, mind you.

"How's Aunt Violet, Grayson?" I ask through my teeth.

"She's responding more and more."

"Good, I'm glad. All right, give me a call later." I grab my empty suitcase and go to toss it . . . in . . . the closet—or, the small boutique attached to his room. *Holy shit.* "Grayson, could your closet be any bigger?!"

"Why are you in my closet?"

I pull the phone away from my ear and give it (him really) a strange look. "I'm putting my suitcase in here. Why are you acting so weird? You're the one who wanted me to stay in your room."

"You're right; I'm sorry. Strange behavior is due to a past relationship. Bear with me, please."

Hearing Hazel call to him in the background, I decide to let it go. There are far more important things to worry about right now. "Okay. Well, go ahead. I'll talk to you later." I close the closet door.

"Ok, love. Have a nice relaxing day." He seems to lighten up.

"Bye." I hang up. That was *absolutely* the weirdest conversation I've ever had with him.

I walk out of his room and run right into Sam. "Oh good!" I laugh awkwardly, as one does when they run right into someone.

"Did you need something, Becca?" He smiles.

"Would you mind taking me to a few stores?" I ask.

"Sure!"

"Great, thanks. I'll just grab my purse."

"Well, you've been busy!" Susanna greets me at the door.

"Yes. Sorry I kept your husband from you most of the day." I kick the door closed with my foot as she grabs some of the bags from me.

"What did you buy?"

"Oh . . . a little bit of this and that. Can you help me bring these upstairs?"

"Uh . . . sure." She seems apprehensive.

"If he doesn't like it, he can make it boring again." I roll my eyes and head on up.

"Speaking of . . . he's less than impressed that you left your phone here," she says, climbing behind me.

"Shoot! Well, he'll get over it." I open the door and find a spot for the stuff we have.

"What color is that?" She eyes the paint cans.

"One I hope he loves." I wink. "Now, shoo!" I fan my hands out at her, sending her off. She puts her hands up and turns to leave. As soon as she closes the door, I get started, moving all of his boxes into the center of the room. I throw a cover over them and get the paint set up.

After a few hours, I am loving what I'm seeing. It's a steel blue (some pun intended), and I can't imagine a better color to suit him. I've just emptied the last box in the room. I framed his Manchester United poster and have the perfect spot to hang it up. That'll wait till tomorrow; I really need to let the paint dry. All-in-all, it looks great on the measly little budget I had. It's not like I would've gone overboard with his card; I just really needed it to purchase a desk. I'll see if Sam can take me around to some antique shops. If I find what I'm looking for, maybe they'll let me hold it with a small deposit till Gray gets back and gives his final approval.

Resigned to that idea, I decide to call it a day in here. Besides, I haven't eaten a thing since breakfast.

Chapter Ten

GRAYSON

"I wasn't going to say it, but I may explode or something if I don't," Derek states as he takes his drink from the stewardess.

"What's that?" Christ, do I really want to humor him? I grab my drink as well and notice a phone number on the beverage napkin. I look up at her, and she gives me a wink.

"Bloody hell! I spend the time putting all my charm on, and all you have to do is breathe! Where is the justice in that?"

"Is that what you wanted to tell me?" I smirk.

"No. I was going to say that if your family waited a minute to cool their jets, we wouldn't have all rushed out there so fast only to come home the next day."

"We have a very small family; we don't want to take chances." I swirl my Jack around and take a swig.

"Really?"

"Ok—we're not in the middle of the Sudan War but still . . . maybe my going was the very thing that pulled her out? Had I stayed home, she would've still been unresponsive! What do you say about that?" I quip.

"I say they better get a bigger door on this plane, or you'll never be able to exit."

"Oh, shut it!" I laugh. "Let me see your napkin." I grab it, pull my pen out of the inside of my jacket, and proceed to write a number down. "Here." I hand it to him. "I happen to find you very charming, mate." I smile.

He chuckles, looking down. "You could've at least made it more authentic with your real number. All you girls are the same, giving the right number to the wrong guys."

"I may need another one of these to tolerate your arse on this flight." I raise my glass, teasing him.

"I'm not the one wanting to fly this plane quicker so that I can get to my girlfriend," he points out.

"Very true."

"Did you talk to her today?"

"Yes—briefly. She's working on some sort of project at the house."

"I know. She called me for my credit card today. Rambled so quickly, I just gave it to her," he says nonchalantly as he reaches past me for his bag of peanuts.

"What's this, now?!" I turn my head sharply to him.

"She asked me for my credit card. What?" He opens the bag and proceeds to retrieve a few.

"She wanted your card to purchase stuff for *my* house?" I'm reaching a level of pissed off that probably shouldn't be reached on a plane.

"No, you daft arse; for my house! She told me the other day she would fix it up. Is that okay with you, your royal highness?"

"Bugger off." I sigh and watch as he takes more peanuts. "Derek! Please just empty the bag into your mouth! Watching you trying to fit those fat arse sausages into that tiny bag is one of the most ridiculous things I've ever witnessed. Stop being a pansy and eat them like a man!"

He stares at me and slowly dives his fat fingers in again. I shake my head and look away. He snickers. I stay silent. He snickers more and despite myself, I feel a crooked smile stretch across my lips. *Wanker.*

I rub my face as Sam inches the car into the garage. I've barely been gone for forty-eight hours. However, with Becca at my house—in my bed—it feels as if I've been gone a week. All I've been thinking about the past few hours is how she will welcome me home tonight. She's not expecting me till the morning, but I was able to get an earlier flight. I did this for two reasons, really. One: I wanted to get back to her ASAP and two: I've barely talked to her since I've been gone, and it's got me completely mad. It does feel as if she's ignoring me on purpose, no matter what Susanna says!

"Glad to be home, sonny?" Sam winks at me in the rearview mirror.

"Yes, I miss Susanna's cooking terribly," I tease. I *do* love her cooking, but we both know the real reason I'm glad to be home. As soon as he turns off the engine, I grab my laptop case and get out of the car. Rushing to the door when I open it, Susanna is there to greet me.

"Where is she?"

"Well, hello to you, too?" She laughs.

"Sorry, Susie." I cringe at my thoughtlessness. I'm not trying to be rude; I'm just anxious.

"Oh, it's ok." She pushes out at the air in front of her. "I just checked on her, actually. She's fallen asleep in bed while proofreading; poor girl." She sighs.

"Why do you say 'poor girl'?" I walk with her into the kitchen.

"She's been working herself to death. That girl doesn't know how to sit and relax."

"What the hell has she been doing? She's been so secretive about this bloody project; it's driving me mad," I admit.

"You'll love it, Gray. She finished yours today, then headed over to Derek's and began working there." She grabs her tea off the counter and takes a sip.

"Can I peek or is it something that's wrapped up?" I may be getting a little giddy like a child on Christmas morn.

"It's not wrapped up." She laughs. "But, I do know she wants you to discover it for yourself." She raises her brows.

"She doesn't want to show me what's she's done?"

"Nope." She shakes her head.

"Actually . . . that sounds very much like my Becca." I smile then clap my hands together and rub. "Now . . . would you be so kind as to point me into the right direction?"

Susanna brings her cuppa back to her lips then shoots out a thumb, jerking it upwards. *Upstairs? Upstairs . . . my office?!* "G'nite, Susie!" I briskly kiss her cheek, then run off to the only stairs in my house. I climb them in two's; I'm ridiculously excited. I stop before the door, hesitating at my realization—no one (outside of my family and Derek) has ever just *done* something for me—just because. Certainly no girlfriend before Becca. I am the luckiest bloke in the world. I shall remember to never forget it.

I take in a final deep breath before opening the door. My lungs deflate quickly, prompted by the sight before me. I walk in, unable to believe it—*she's captured me.* Holy fuck! This is just how I wanted it without being crafty enough to come up with it on my own. I won't even mention the thousands she's saved me not having to hire anyone. *Ok, I mentioned it.* But, good Lord! I look around, taking in every detail from the color of the walls (my favorite) to the tiny details of framed pictures in front of the books on the shelves.

"My poster!" I almost shout. One of my most prized possessions. I got that at the very last game my father and I went to before he died. He somehow managed to get me in to meet the team and have them sign it for me. I'll never forget it. I can't believe she framed and hung it up to show my pride in the team. If she only *knew* the sentimental value behind it. God, I think I've fallen more in love with her at this very moment.

I spin slowly, really taking it all in and stop at my new desk.

What the—? *God,* it's gorgeous. I run my hand across it. It looks antique and majestic. How did she even do this? I was such a stubborn, tightwad about letting her have my card. I couldn't help it, really; thoughts of yester-girlfriends impeding logical thinking. I *know* Becca is nothing like them, yet I can't help the little guard that comes up every once in a while. I need to ask her about this. I study it some more. Wait a minute! This desk looks oddly familiar. Oh my God—is this? Yes, I believe it is! It's a replica of the Resolute desk in the Oval office. My God—she *never* ceases to amaze me. I've seen enough. I need to see her now—*all* of her. At the door, I take one last glance before flicking the light off.

I take the steps slowly, already beginning the process of unbuttoning my dress shirt. I have full intentions of consummating our love tonight. Just the thought has my trousers stretching painfully. I lick my lips, thinking of her amazing taste. My breathing is already changing tempo at the echoes of her whimpers in the past, when I've brought her to the edge, how they will probably be more intense tonight when I finally take what's mine. I grab the knob on my door and pause to pull myself together a bit before I open it. After a moment, I proceed.

I have a clear view of her; the lamp is still on, my manuscript still in her hand, her head turned to the left, and I can hear her soft breathing. I lock the door quietly behind me. I prowl, slowly removing my shirt, pants, and knickers. The bloke below is at full attention—saluting the love of my life. I hear The Cure softly playing on my stereo and it triggers the memory of information I received a while back. On Becca's very short bucket list is the song "Lullaby" by this band. She's wanted to have sex during that song since the first time she heard it at fifteen. Girls are funny like that; everything that has to do with romance, planned out years in advance.

I head over to the stereo and put that song on loop. *Fuck . . . it is hot.* I walk over to the bed and gently pull my MS out of her hands. I climb onto the bed, as she is almost center. She has a simple PJ short set on. Only, her top is a button one, though sleeveless. Slowly, I begin to expose her skin. Completely unbuttoned, I push away the material to reveal her sweet, soft skin to me. Leaning over her, I retrieve a nipple into my mouth, sucking it in a slightly possessive manner before giving the other the same attention. Her chest rises to meet me, soft groans escaping her throat. I cup both breasts, taking turns tasting them. "Grayson," she murmurs in her sleep. I look up at her. She is, indeed, still asleep. To know that I am the one invading her dreams, only adds fuel to my fire. I attack her breasts again but make sure my tongue travels down her belly. I grasp the band of her shorts and tug to pull them off. She lifts her hips. I pull them off completely. The final effort to get her naked wakes her up; her eyes widen in panic.

"Shh…" I try to calm her. She relaxes and allows me to continue with my travels. Her hips jerk up in the air as I lick the apex of her groin.

"Grayson," she groans again and opens wide with my encouragement. I flatten my tongue against her, giving one strong lick up her heat. My eyes roll in the back of my head from her taste. "Baby," she whimpers. Between the song, her whimper, the taste of her, and the anticipation of feeling her stretch around me—stretch for the first time ever—I'm gone.

I climb up her body and attack her lips like I'll never taste her again. "I need you," I groan against them.

"Baby . . . please," she begs. I pull back and stare into her eyes, waiting for her final approval. I reach below and slide myself slowly up and down her slick center. She nods her head as I adjust at her opening. I push in and through, watching her head arch back, listening to the sound that rips from her throat. *Fuck—she's so tight!*

I stay still a moment, waiting for her to acclimate to me, noticing a small tear slip out of the corner of her eye. Finally, she relaxes and stares back into my eyes. I lean down and sweep her lips as sweetly as I can. "I love you, sweetheart," I breathe. She just nods. My guess is, she's too focused on what her body is experiencing right now. I'm focused on that too, wanting to make sure it's perfect for her.

I pull back and, with the patience of God, I fill her again at a slow pace. Her mouth closed, a whimper escapes her nose. I repeat (careful not to hurt her more than I have to) the same sequence several times. Finally, I feel her body fully relax, taking me in. I take on my more aggressive nature, filling her fully at a harsh, yet slow capacity.

"Oh God, baby," she whispers in my ear, and I'm gone—reaching for her to say it again and again. My pace quickens. My mouth attacks her with urgency. Becca wraps her legs around me, her hands on my arse, encouraging me to give her my best. I don't disappoint. "Oh God!" she cries out. I can feel her rise, the way she squeezes me as I pull out, then releasing me as I slam back into her. "Grayson!" she pants as I pick up my pace. I'm lost, in the zone; nothing matters but the end result.

"Fuck!" I yell as I feel the tightening happen, the rush up my shaft. I attack her mouth as I come hard inside of her. She moans as if she approves of being filled with my warmth. Final pump and I drop to her chest, heaving huge breaths.

"Grayson?" she questions.

"You're on the pill. I will *never* wear anything with you, understand me?" I ask, knowing this was her concern.

"Yes, baby," she says so softly, it makes me twitch inside of her. That tone in her voice? Submissive. I fecking love it. I lift my head and stare deeply into her eyes before collecting her lips softly. "You are amazing, darling."

"Was I . . . I mean . . . erm . . . did I do okay?" she stammers.

"Becca . . . you were brilliant, sweetheart." My fingers ghost across her cheek. "Brilliant," I whisper before covering her mouth again.

I take in a sharp breath and open my eyes when I feel the warmth of a mouth, taking my length in. The panic quickly escapes as Becca's eyes smile up at me. "I've died and gone to Heaven," I groan and throw my head back, enjoying her talent. After a few minutes, her hot tongue slides up my v-line, abs; she nibbles gently at my nipple. I slide my hands onto her hips as she straddles me. She sits up, pulling me with her. "Are you sure? Don't you want to rest?" I palm her face and pepper it with kisses. She rises up, takes me in her hand and glides me up and down her center.

"I need you, baby. I need to feel you taking me again," she says seductively in my ear before sucking on my lobe and lowering herself on me. She releases a slight whimper. My right hand falls to her hip again, to help guide her actions. "God, I feel so full."

Bloody hell.

"Becca . . . sweetheart . . . you keep saying things like that and I'll be empty in a mo, leaving us both disappointed in my performance."

She giggles and quickly kisses me. I love that sound—best sound in the world. Soon enough, Becca begins to move upon me. Her pace quickens as she acclimates. I meet her harshly, filling her to capacity. "Oh God, baby!" she cries. I've changed my mind; that's the best sound in the world.

It doesn't take us long to come undone. We fall back to the mattress, breathing as if there weren't another ounce of oxygen in the world. My hands knead her bum aggressively (there's that Neanderthal again) and I add a smack for good measure, causing her to yelp then sigh the most contented sigh I've ever heard. My hands soften, soothing her now. She places intermittent kisses on my chest as her fingers doodle things on it, mostly hearts. I realize something at this very moment: I have everything I will ever need right in my arms. I squeeze her to me and kiss her hair. "I love you. I could stay in this moment forever with you."

"Mmm . . . me too." She smiles up at me. Suddenly, her head tilts to the side, her smile really hitting her eyes.

"What?"

"You haven't told me what you thought of my surprise." She taps my lips with her fingertips.

"You haven't shown me it yet." I try to skate past it.

"I'm sure you managed fine without me."

"Can't get a thing past you, can I?" I bite at her finger.

"Most days—no. Now out with it, Mr. James."

"I was floored . . . am floored. You truly captured me." I try to keep my voice steady.

"I wish I could've done more, but I am happy with how it turned out."

"More? Becca, you have no idea as to what you're talking about." I roll us onto our sides, effectively ending our bodies' union. The expression that blankets her face is sexy as fuck, like the emptiness she now feels is disappointing. I push my naughty thoughts away as quickly as they parade into my mind. I then begin to explain the sentimental value behind the poster. I choke up a bit, which is odd for me; I don't usually allow myself to cry in front of any woman. Her only response to my slip up of emotional sharing is to join me. Of course—she knows *exactly* how I feel. However, I am most certain that if her parents were alive, she'd be fighting her tears just the same. "Now explain to me how you managed to afford that desk. Also, what made you chose it?"

"Isn't it fantastic?!" Her face lights up.

"Yes. You do know what it is, right?"

"Of course I do!" she states as if I've insulted her. "That's why I got it. It resembles the comradery between our countries."

"So, you're saying you won't be fighting me for your independence?" I bait.

"Why—am I losing it?"

"Most of it." I kiss her. "Over time," I add.

"Well, just remember where your bossiness has gotten you with me before." She pats my chest.

"Mm . . . moving along—how did you pay for it?" I grab her hand and kiss the center of her palm.

"Don't worry about it." She lays her head back on her pillow.

"Becca?"

"No—you don't get to ask that! It's a gift, and you're being rude." She's back up on her elbow, challenging me.

"Tell me who you borrowed the money from and I'll take care of it, sweetheart." I try to soften my tone so that she doesn't fly off the handle.

"I'd rather tell you where I hid the body," she postulates and sits up, throwing the covers off. She probably doesn't think I caught her wincing.

"Sore, sweetheart?" I glide my fingers up and down her leg as I sit up with her.

"Of course I am; I've been busting my ass all weekend." She stretches, then her arms drop dramatically as she glances at me. I must not have hidden my disappointment well enough. "Oh, did you think I was grimacing from..." She waggles her eyebrows. I shrug. She leans in close to my face. "I am sore from that too, but it's different. It's more like an 'Mm . . . I can still feel him inside of me' groan." She kisses my cheek.

"Your switch flips at alarming rates, you know this, right?"

"Somebody has to keep you on your toes, Mr. James." She taps my nose before jumping out of bed.

"I hope you don't actually believe you will be showering alone." I climb out after her, reach for her hand and pull her back to me.

"Oh . . . is that part of my independence that I'm losing?" She looks up at me, her green eyes shining.

"One. Small. Part." I kiss her between my words, then spin her to go ahead of me and slap her arse for good measure. Her yelp is quickly followed by a giggle.

Chapter Eleven

BECCA

It's been a while since I heard him typing at his new desk. I look up from the pages in front of me only to catch him watching me intently. I squeeze my thighs together to fight off the instant need building in me. Grayson has this way of looking sexy as fuck in his Clark Kents. And, when he's staring at me like this—glasses in place of a sword—I'm ready to be conquered. We christened his desk two days ago . . . several times (just to be sure it was done correctly). It only seems right to give the new, soft leather couch I'm stretched out on, the same attention.

"When do you think you'll be able to move here?" Grayson finally speaks up. Apparently, his thoughts were not exactly what I thought they were. I'm actually surprised they weren't. Grayson has proved himself to be insatiable. I believe he's created a monster in me, though, because I haven't turned him away once. "Becca, when?" he repeats, circling me back to the question I was trying to ignore instead of analyze in my head.

"I didn't know I was," I say as even tempered and toned as I can. Grayson is very territorial and that can run hot or cold with me, depending on the situation at hand. Because we're both pretty damn stubborn, I've been trying to be more mindful of how to navigate certain conversations so that our hotheads don't explode.

"Sweetheart, we're in love, yes?" he asks patiently (he's been trying too).

"Yes." I bite my bottom lip, curious.

"What did you think was going to be the next step?" He pulls his glasses off and rubs his face. It almost seems as if he's trying really hard to keep his frustration at bay.

"I thought this *was* the next step."

"Yes . . . it was." He agrees with a nod. "But, now we've made that step, as well as another." He smirks. I offer him a coy smile. "So, we're ready to look into the next step," he finishes.

"Why?" I fail to hide my frustration. "Grayson, we don't have to rush everything. Why can't we just enjoy this step for now without thinking of the next one? Our relationship doesn't need a fucking itinerary."

He stares at me long and hard before throwing his glasses back on and bringing his attention back to his screen. "I like schedules," he mumbles.

"I know you do, baby, but sometimes schedules can get in the way of enjoying things that shouldn't be scheduled. Someday, when our youth is but a memory, we'll reflect back to this time. Do you want us to have memories of just being in love and enjoying the little moments that happened, or do you want us to remember us rushing through steps to get to those old people who are reflecting?"

He focuses down on his keyboard, seemingly taking in my words. He lets out a big sigh. "You're right, sweetheart," he concedes. "It's just . . . I'm already mourning the loss I will feel in three nights when you are not here . . . not next to me."

"Stop thinking like that. Let's enjoy the next few days." I get up and head over to him. He spins in his chair toward me and opens his arms for me to walk into his embrace. I sit on his lap. "Would it help if we schedule our next visits?"

"Becca, I know you love Boston. In the long run, though, it makes much more sense for you to move here."

"Stop!" I quietly beg him. "Please, I don't want to think that far right now."

"When is your lease up—can we at least start there?"

"It's now 'at will'." As soon as I say it, I regret it. It's nothing to do with Grayson. It's just that, I'm not ready to consider leaving my life in Boston behind.

"That makes me very happy." He squeezes me to him.

"Gray, besides Stacey, I can't leave Jimmy." My chin quivers at the thought. His smile slowly drops, and he gives me a knowing nod. He's very well aware of how important Jimmy is to me and vice versa. I watch his facial expressions change like someone's turning a dial on him. "You look like you're fighting to say something and hold yourself back at the same time." I run my knuckles down his jawline.

"I am." He winces.

"What is it?"

"Well, it's just—and please don't take this the wrong way— Jimmy seems like a healthy ole chap. I mean, I'd be willing to bet he's got a few years, at least, left in that old ticker of his."

"Grayson," I groan.

"Stop! I like Jimmy; you know I don't want anything to happen to him. Perhaps we could bring him out here to live?" His face lights up at his idea.

"We can't move Jimmy out here, he has family." I roll my eyes.

"Who rarely ever visit him! They'd probably be glad to not have to deal with the guilt trip," he carries on.

"You'd do that? You'd move Jimmy out here for me?" It's a completely absurd idea but to know he thought of it and is willing to implement it, just for my happiness, does things to my heart I didn't think were possible.

"Of course; I'd move Heaven and Earth for you, sweetheart,

haven't you figured that out yet?" His hand reaches up to my face and his thumb traces my lips gently.

"Damn you," I practically whisper against his thumb.

"Damn me?" He jerks his head back slightly.

"Yeah . . . damn you for making me fall in love with you just a little more right now." I lean forward and nudge his lips.

"I'm thinking we should move this conversation to our nice, new couch, sweetheart—sans conversation," he suggests before pulling my bottom lip, sucking it between his.

"I concur, Mr. James." I smile against them.

"God, this is nice." I take in a deep, relaxing breath and close my eyes.

"No fucking shit. When's the last time we did this?" I can hear Stacey continue to slap on sunblock while asking.

"Pre Max?" I question.

"I think you're right."

Stacey and I decided to take a day for just us. What better way to isolate ourselves from our life than to head to Walden Pond? It's a place we've enjoyed since vacationing up here as teenagers. That's the geeky side of us coming out; hanging out at Thoreau's old stomping ground. Let's not forget his buddy, Emerson, down the street. We'll probably stop by his house later. Concord, Massachusetts, in itself, is so rich in our American history, besides well-known authors and transcendentalists. Why, it is the home of where the "shot was heard around the world". Meaning—the start of the American Revolution.

The irony causes me to smile to myself as I am here, starting my own "American Revolution." The Brit has invaded my life even more than ever this past month. I understand he hates being apart, I do too. But, if he's not pressuring me to move, he's showing up un-announced and expecting me to call out of work. This long distance business is causing us all kinds of problems. I almost miss the days when he was just chasing me.

"I hope you're not analyzing shit."

"Wow . . . your ESP is off the charts today," I say half sarcastic.

"There's a reason why we left our cell phones in the car, Bec; no men, no work—just us, celebrity gossip, and anything new on the guys." She tries to keep me on track.

"Ok, ok," I concede. "Speaking of the guys, we need to catch one or two of Joe's concerts." I go right into our favorite topic. Others would call this topic "New Kids on The Block" and categorize it under celebrity gossip. However, they are just "the guys" to us, therefore having their own, more important category of . . . um . . . "The Guys." We're wicked clever like that.

"And Jordan!" she adds.

"Yeah, but he's opening for N'sync, which means we'll get shitty seats and be surrounded by a newer version of our younger selves like we're stuck in some weird fucking time warp," I oppose. "Let's wait till he's doing his own gigs."

"Deal. Better chance of me running into Jonathan anyways." Stacey has always wanted to be the special "hoe" in Jonathan Knight's garden.

"True that." I nod.

"So . . . have you heard from fuck face?"

"Jeremy?" I turn my head to her.

"Yeah."

"No." I turn back to the sun. "I still can't believe he quit like that." To say that Jeremy didn't take the outcome of our "date" too well would be an understatement.

He showed up at our place the next day, saying he was concerned with the way I left, even though Stacey had informed him that I was sick. Of course Stacey actually did this in her own sweet way—something about Jeremy kissing me, repulsing me because I was in love with Grayson, who, being from England, actually spoke the English language correctly. I'm sure this wasn't her exact quote but only what I've been able to summarize from what Jeremy said. That is, after he made sure I was all right. Then, the cursing me out began. I was called every name in the book. It was very uncharacteristic of me, but I stood there and took it all. It was the least I could do after using him for my own jealous purpose. What I did was wrong, no matter who thinks what of him. And, I did tell him that and apologized profusely. *"He's changed you and not for the better. Good luck with dat shit—hope you're happy. I would've given you the world, boo."* And with that, he left. Nice sentiment, but would he have really been able to "give me the world?" No. A cab? Maybe—if the driver could understand him. Anyways, I haven't seen him since. He called work that day and quit on the phone with no notice. Not smart for future references.

"Well, he's never been the brightest bulb in the package. However, his quitting did you a big favor. You know Grayson would've pushed you to leave there if he hadn't." Stacey always knows the best angle to chip away at my guilt.

"No men talk!" I remind her.

"Yeah, right. I say we pull the plug on that thought right now, so we can properly bitch about shit."

"Oh—I so agree!" Thank God! I've got a lot of shit on my chest!

"Well, me first!" She shoots up to a sitting position.

"If you insist." I half-heartedly chuckle at her sudden urgency to unburden herself. Up until this moment, she hasn't let on at all that she and Max are having any issues. A feeling of guilt swoops in like a cloud over my head; maybe she has let on but I've been so wrapped up in my own shit, I didn't even notice. *Bad friend. Bad, bad friend!*

"Max has been pushing the idea around about us taking the next step." She stares out toward the pond.

"Ohh…" I trail off. I'm glad there's no trouble in paradise, but I know all-to-well how the talk of the next step can certainly stir some up.

"Yeah." She fidgets with her fingers.

"Okay, well, not trying to sound like a shrink, but, how do you feel about that?" I ask though I can see she's got some major internal battles going on, what with her body language and all.

"I don't know." She glances over at me. Her eyes are hidden by dark sunglasses, but her face shows her trepidation anyhow. "I mean, I love him." She throws her hands out. "I can't imagine spending the rest of my life with anyone else, but . . . Jesus—I'm only twenty-two. Do I really want this *right now*? I've barely lived."

"Stace, I completely understand your slight panic here. But, let's go over a few things before you hightail it to the nearest border," I start, but wait for the disgruntled couple, I noticed, to pass by. I'm pretty sure they were huffing because they discovered this hidden spot was already taken. Someday, Stacey and I both will have kids that we will bring here. And, we'll sit on the beach parts with all of the other tortured souls. Until then, we always find a secluded area, far from screaming toddlers, fresh kids, and exhausted parents. "Yes, you're twenty-two, but you have a lot of life experiences under your belt already. You've travelled to several countries, you've been clubbing since we were fifteen, you moved to another state, and had your first apartment at nineteen. Most people our age are still living at home. That said, even if you decide to take the next step, your life doesn't have to change much—not right away, at least. It's not like you have to start spitting out babies."

"I always swallow the baby prospects—never spit," she deadpans as I take a break in my speech.

"You're fucking disgusting." I laugh.

"Just sayin'." She shrugs. "Besides, he mostly wants to live together."

"He practically lives with us now." I give her a strange look.

"I know. But…"

"He wants me to be out of the equation," I say it for her.

"You know Max loves you. It has nothing to do with you; he just wants to focus on us. We've spent a lot of time the past several months, helping you along." Instead of looking at me now, she concentrates on her fingers swirling through the sand.

"Wow. Well, thanks for making me feel like a burden." I'm not going to lie; I'm hurt. I never asked them to "push" me along.

"You're not a burden; shut the hell up!" She throws a little sand at my leg for emphasis. "It's not your fault we went on this mission to make you pursue happiness."

"No, that would be Grayson's doing." I huff. Then, like a huge bolt of lightning from the sky, it hits me. "This is *Grayson!* This conversation. Max wanting me out!" *Motherfucker!*

"Wait—what? No, Becca. Grayson didn't say anything to me." She shakes her head adamantly

"No, but you said it yourself, he and Max have become good friends and chat all the time. *This* is Grayson manipulating the situation in his favor through Max!" I point my finger in front of me like I'm jabbing at something. *I'd like to jab at something, all right.*

"That motherfucker…" I can hear the disbelief in her voice as she realized that not only am I right, but she's been duped.

"My sentiments exactly!" I huff.

We spend the better part of the next hour dissecting this latest revelation and what to do about it. I'm not going to lie; I'm pissed. *Control freak.*

At 5 P.M., our stomachs call our beach day to an end, and we head to the Main Street Market & Café in town to stop their growling. We settle at our table, and Stacey hastily types away on her phone. I haven't turned mine on. I'm waiting for Hurricane Becca to settle down a bit. Tropical Stacey, however, is happily morphing herself into a tsunami. I think the wool over her eyes has pissed her off the most.

"Here, read what I'm sending Max." She hands me her phone. I look down.

> **Stacey:** Operation Sugar Shack is successful! Becca will be moving out by the end of the month. You have to give her her deposit back, though. You also have to have half of all the bills for me too. Here's the rundown so you can plan accordingly.
>
> Deposit: 350
>
> Rent: 350

Cable: 50

Phone: 50

Electric: 75

Condo Fee: 50

Water bill: 75

I'll need this all on the first, plus grocery money. I can't wait, baby!

"Stace, we don't pay a condo fee or a water bill." I look up.

"I know that, but he doesn't." She grabs the phone from me and hits send.

"He's going to shit himself." I laugh. She really can be evil. While Max does work part time, all of that is money to spend on Stace. He still lives at home, his parents paying for everything while he maintains a 4.0 at college, getting his masters in advertising. Though Mom and Dad pay his way, it stops at him moving out. That was the deal: they pay for all college expenses and whatnot while he goes to school locally and lives at home. After attempting to do it himself for one year, to experience campus life, he conceded due to the fact that he didn't get to experience much while working all the time. Lucky bastard, if you ask me.

"He sure is," she finally agrees as she continues to text feverishly. "Now, it's somebody else's turn." She hands the phone back to me. I look down and see she's texting Grayson.

> **Stacey:** Hey fucktard, next time you want to manipulate Becca to do what you want, don't go through me and Max! She saw right through your bullshit. I'm pissed that I didn't. Keep pushing her and you'll be pushing her right out the door.

I hand her phone back, and she hits send. I have no problem making him sweat. *Persistent fucker!*

Within ten minutes, our food arrives as well as a ping sound from her phone. "Ha! Figures! It's Grayson. I'm sure Max has read the text and is pretending not to have." She rolls her eyes and reads the message before digging into her burger. "Oh, puh-lease!" She hands the phone back to me and fixes her burger.

Grayson: What in the bloody hell are you talking about?! Why is Becca's phone off? Tell her to call me—NOW!

Just as I'm about to hand it back, it pings again, and I pull it back to read it. Only, it's not from Gray but Max.

Max: Baby!! Are you serious?! That's awesome! I swear I'm having the best week ever! I have great news to share with you when you can call me. I love you! I can't wait to celebrate with you (read: eat the fuck out of that sweet pussy of yours). My heart and cock explode for you. Love, Max-Capacity.

"Jesus Christ, pass the fucking bleach for my eyes." I give her the phone.

"Huh?" She looks down. "Oh." She giggles. "Huh?" she asks again.

"Yes . . . I'm thoroughly confused as well."

She wipes her mouth and calls him. "Hey, curiosity is killing the cat," is how she greets him. "Wait—what?" Her eyes widen. "Are you kidding me? Oh my God, baby, that's awesome! I'm so proud of you!" Her smile is so big, it could swallow her face. It suddenly drops. "Oh . . . well, we'll need to discuss that a little further."

Somehow, I don't think his good news will be so good for me. I decide to feed my face while I wait because that's what emotional eaters, like I, do.

"Uh . . . we may have a problem," Stacey says when she hangs up.

"What's up?"

"Well, first: you were wrong. Grayson had nothing to do with this. Max just informed me that he was chosen for a paid internship.

He was hoping he would get it; that's why he's been bringing all of this up. I didn't know he applied to this one; he wanted to surprise me." She's saying everything so carefully. I know she's thinking the same thing I am—I need to move out. I can't, though.

"I can't move out, Stace! I'm starting school in less than two months."

"I know. I'm going to talk to him later. We'll figure this out. In the meantime, you better turn your phone on and at least let him know you'll call soon." She points to my purse. I should turn my phone on, but I know the wrath of a confused Grayson awaits me. I might as well wait till after dinner.

Chapter Twelve

GRAYSON

"How nice of you to turn your phone on." I fling my glasses on top of my desk and lean back in my chair. I have been texting and calling her for a better part of the day. It's been very irritating, as I needed to go over some things with her. The text from Stacey and then not hearing from Becca for over two hours has left me in a bitter state.

"Hey," she sounds apprehensive.

"Are you breaking up with me?" Why prolong this; let's get straight to it.

"No."

"At some point today, were you considering the idea?"

"No," she states with more oomph.

"Care to explain Stacey's text?"

"I thought you were responsible for something that you had nothing to do with . . . apparently."

"Apparently? Sounds as if you're not convinced."

"No . . . I am. I'm just having a hard time believing that you're not behind it *somehow*. Encouraging Max to convince Stacey it was time they lived together alone seems right up your ally to get me to move out by you sooner," she finally discloses the issues. My heart races and sweat forms in my palms. It's days like this when I feel Becca Campbell is no longer my equal in the intelligence department but completely surpasses me. "Why are you being so quiet?" she asks after a while.

I merely suggested Max to Guy Holden for the open internship spot he had. I may have also suggested that Max would come with an account: Derek's security company. It was just conversation over a golf game. He told me to get Max to apply. I did. Honestly, I didn't believe anything would come of it. I guess it did.

"Grayson!" she snaps.

I take in a deep breath and decide to tell her everything. I've never lied to Becca; I'm not going to start now. To my amazement, she listens without interruptions or hanging up on me. "So . . . in retrospect, I am responsible for him getting a chance to acquire the position, but he must've been well qualified to do so, otherwise, he wouldn't have got it. And, yes, Max and I have had discussions about him moving in with Stacey *when* you move in with me. I did not push him to rush all of this. That was all of his own accord, sweetheart. Becca, believe me, I know how important Jimmy is to you and that you have school starting. Yes, I really want you here, but I wouldn't push it so badly that I'd risk losing you. I love you." I give her a final plea for my innocence.

"I love you too. Gray?"

"Yes?"

"It really means a lot that you chose to be open and honest with me about all of this. You could've just as easily dodged a bullet here."

"That's all I will ever be with you, Becca. I will always tell you the truth. Sometimes, in a very blunt way." She laughs at this and it triggers my lips to jerk into a smile. I love to hear her laugh. When I'm the one who causes it?—jackpot.

"I'm sorry," she says.

"For?"

"Thinking the worst. That wasn't very fair of me."

"No, it wasn't. But I've got a few ideas for how you can make it up to me."

"Oh, do you, now?" she flirts.

I then proceed, over the next half an hour, to engage her with very explicit details. I listen to her come sweetly on the phone and I'm rather jealous of her hand. "Did that feel good, sweetheart?" I try to steady my speech, but I'm beginning my own climb.

"It's not the same, and you would be nowhere near done with me."

"You've. Got. That. Right," I pant. The birth of my orgasm brews in the belly of my balls.

"Are you thinking about me?" she asks in that soft tone that does things to me.

"Only you." It's the absolute truth.

"Are you thinking about the first time you took me? How much I had to stretch to accommodate you? How sore you made me?" *Oh, Christ, does she have my number.* Before I can even answer her, the surge rushes up through my shaft, causing me to groan as I explode. "Jesus, Grayson, I wish I were there to see that."

"Sweetheart, if you were here, this mess would be inside of you and not all over me." I try to regulate my breath.

"Mm…" she moans.

"Have you kept your next weekend off?" I quickly ask.

"Yes, dear," she says with a 1950s flair.

"Good." I wipe myself off with my t-shirt.

"I feel bad that you spend all of this money to see me." This is the first time she's mentioning it to me. Usually, she hints at feeling bad.

"Don't feel bad; you're a deduction."

"So that's why you chased me; I'm just a tax write off to you," she teases.

"Yes, I'm afraid so. I'll even be able to deduct us making love as a form of therapy," I enlighten her.

"Your parsimonious behavior makes me so proud."

"Well, how else could I afford you?"

"Very true. I am an expensive piece of ass," she agrees.

"Oh, but the quality is outstanding; makes it completely worth it," I goad her.

"I'm very happy to hear that, Mr. James, as I do stand by my product, wholeheartedly."

"I know a lot of people who'd like to stand by your product—sample it, even."

"Well, you'll just have to inform them that I only have room for one taste tester."

"Can I apply for that job?"

"You already have it." She giggles.

"Yes, but I'd like a raise."

"I thought I just gave you that."

"Cheeky woman."

"You like my cheeks?"

"Yes—all four of them," I boast.

"All four of them miss you," her voice sullen.

"Becca, why do you do that?" I zip my pants up and grab my water for a sip.

"Do what?"

"Say stuff, like that, in a way that seems like I'm the cause. I'm getting out to you as often as I can. You're the one who is keeping us apart." As soon as I say it, I shut my eyes tightly, waiting for her to bite back.

"How's the new book coming along?"

"Don't change subjects on me," I snap.

"Well, isn't it better to change topics than to constantly beat a dead horse?" she counters.

"Yes, I guess so. Listen, I have work I need to do. I'll talk to you tomorrow. Sleep well, sweetheart." I rush her off the phone.

"Grayson?"

"*Goodnight*, Becca."

"Night," she sighs, sounding defeated.

I don't like to dismiss her like that, but she dismisses me every time I bring up our living situation. I'm rather sick of it.

Two months later

"Hey! Just in time; we have pizza! Want a slice?" Stacey asks as I head into the living room.

"No," I grumble. Stacey looks at me wearily and then glances at the clock. "Is she always this late?"

"This is only her second week, Gray."

"Right. Why does she need to be in a study group already?" I fire back.

"Hey, we know you're pissed, dude, but don't take it out on Stace." Max chimes in, calling me out.

"Sorry, Stace." I head over to her and pull her in for a hug.

"You know, maybe you should just tell her you're coming, instead of surprising her. Then, she'd be home."

"Bollocks." I let go. "I mentioned coming out and she told me to wait."

"She just started school, Gray; cut her some slack."

"I'm worried," I admit.

"It's less than a year. She'll take her boards and then move out by you."

"I don't think we'll make it."

"She's focused on succeeding; she's wanted this for so long. Don't make her question it or push it off because of your own selfish needs, Gray. That's not fair to her." She pokes at my chest.

"My selfish needs? I'm sorry, did you miss the part where I've done nothing but rearrange my schedule around to fly out here to be with her? Or, the many things I've done to make sure she only has to focus on school? *Everything* I've done the past several months has been all about her needs! What part of any of that have I been selfish?" I roar.

"Gray?" I hear Becca's voice coming from behind me. Stacey stares at me wide-eyed.

I take in a deep breath and blow it out aggressively as I turn to face her. "Hi, sweetheart." I clear my throat. "Here, let me help you with that." I rush over to her and grab the bag of groceries out of her arms.

"Thanks." She smiles and leans up for a kiss.

"I thought you were with your study group; why are you in scrubs?" I give her a once over before depositing the bag onto the counter.

"We were supposed to do group but ended up back at the hospital to get all the info we needed for the paper we have to do on our patients this week. It took forever too because charts weren't where they should've been. Then, we had to take turns with the log books." She lets her backpack slide off her arms.

"Did you eat?" I ask.

"Yes."

"Let's go then." I reach out for her hand. "Say goodnight to everyone."

"Goodnight, everyone," her tone condescending. I yank her forward to make her move faster. "Hey!" she snaps at my insistence. I pull her into her room, slam the door, and charge towards her, forcing her up against it. Slamming my hands on either side of her, I lean in near her face. I watch as her pupils dilate. Her breathing comes in small bursts.

"How much did you hear?" I lick my lips, staring at hers.

"Everything you said." She looks down then back up. "Grayson, I appreciate *every*thing you do for me. Even the stuff you don't think I know about. Please don't give up on me." Her eyes fill up. "I know this is tough on us; you more so because of the travelling. But, I promise—no matter what—when I graduate, I will move in with you." Her promise catches me off guard. This is the first time she has committed to a time frame. I absolutely hate that it's nine months from now.

"I really appreciate you giving me a time frame—I do, sweetheart. Can I ask you this, though?" I pause, knowing she'll argue.

"What?"

"Can you try to transfer out to me for the spring semester?"

"I can't."

"You can't or you won't?" My impatience returns.

"I can't. I'm in the LPN program. It doesn't run the same as an RN one. It's a set program for nine months. I'd have to start all over out there." Her eyes hold their gaze on mine.

I huff. "Why can't you move out by me and go through an RN program instead?"

"It's longer. I have none of the pre-reqs done. I'd have to go full time for two years. I wouldn't be able to work," she pleads her case.

"You honestly believe I'd let you work?" I cup her chin. She bites on her bottom lip. I thumb it away from her teeth.

"I may be on the waiting list for a few years, depending on the school."

"Becca, stop looking for excuses." I finally give in to those delicious lips and grab a taste. She releases a slight moan as she opens, allowing me to deepen the kiss. I reluctantly pull away, after a beat. "It's settled then; we'll get you registered at a school near me for spring. You can start on the pre-reqs," I state, then lean in for another kiss.

"I can't do that!" She tries to push me away.

"Why the hell not?!"

She ducks under my left arm and works her way to the middle of the room before turning to face me. "Grayson, I have to look out for my best interest here. If I stay here and finish the program, I can work as an LPN in nine months or so. If I move out by you, start all over and get through a year of school, I'll have nothing. If, for some reason, we break up—I'm screwed! I'll be right back in the same position I'm in now. I'll have the pre-requisites done, but that's it! I need to protect myself," she loses her thunder with that last sentence.

"What am I doing here?" I ask in disbelief.

"Wh-what do you mean?" she stammers.

"I don't know what I'm doing here," I repeat. "It's an uphill battle with you and I'm constantly losing."

"That's not true." She reaches for me, but I push her hands away.

"Yes, *it is*!" My anger approaches center stage. "*I* look at *you* and I see the rest of my life—without question!" I fume. "*You* look at *me* as if I'm a moment in your life that you *know* will eventually pass by. I'm *not* a moment, Becca! I don't want to *just* be a moment in your life—I want to be *all* of the moments in your life; at *least*, a part of all of them!"

"I want that, too!" she cries.

"Do you? Because it certainly doesn't seem that way from this side of the fence!"

"I do, baby . . . I do." She reaches up and palms my face.

"You need to do better, Becca. I need better compromises from you." I close my eyes, letting her touch calm me.

"Like what? I mean, besides what you just mentioned."

I open my eyes and can clearly see the willingness in hers. "First thing's first: come November, you will give notice at *both* jobs."

"Grayson, I—"

"—You will! I am tired of fighting about seeing you when I want to. The holidays are coming; I want you with me. You can still visit with Jimmy and other residents. I will take care of your monthly expenses. All you have to do is concentrate on school and spend all of your breaks with me in California. Take it or leave it, Becca!" With that, her hands drop quickly.

"What's that supposed to mean?" She furrows her brows angrily.

"Just. As. It. Sounds," I state nice and clear for her.

Tears pool into her eyes again. By the way her nostrils are flaring and her teeth are clenching, I can tell they are angry tears. I can't help questioning whether the hand I just played was a smart one. Her chest starts heaving. "I'll take it," she says through her teeth.

"Good decision, sweetheart." I graze her cheek with the back of my hand, and she jerks away as if I've struck her.

"I'm going to take a shower now." She keeps her focus away from me.

"Don't bother dressing yourself when you're done." I catch her rolling her eyes before turning to head into the bathroom.

"Grayson," she says as she reaches the threshold and turns. "This ultimatum bullshit? I'm giving you a free pass this time and this time only because I haven't made our relationship easy on you. But, that is it. If you ever give me one again, trust you will get the answer you are not pushing for. Do you understand me?" her voice is shaky and her nostrils, still flaring.

"Completely."

She nods slightly, seemingly content with my answer, then turns back to go into the bathroom. I decide to give her a few before joining.

BECCA

I let the hot water pelt my face, trying to distract myself enough to calm down. It's not working. I have, however, come to the conclusion that Grayson *cannot* handle this long distance relationship—at all. I mean, I don't like it either, but his need to control things is so much greater than mine. These next nine months are going to be hell.

I take in a sharp breath as a cool breeze hits my back. *Well . . . I knew that was coming.* Grayson slides his hands onto my hips, squeezes them, and then releases my right one. "Gah!" I yelp as his hand comes back down, smacking my hip. His left hand reaches up to my hair, pulling it away from my neck. I feel him wrapping the makeshift ponytail around his hand slowly. He yanks it, jerking my head back, giving him full access to my neck.

Holy shit. This is aggressive Grayson on crack.

"I'm going to *fuck* you senseless, darling," his breath, hot against my ear. "Open!" He slaps my hip again and wedges his knee between mine.

Confirmation received.

He turns me toward the opposite wall. Probably so I won't drown in the stream of water. *He's always looking out for me.* "Hands on the wall, Becca," he commands. I obey. *I'm noticing a pattern here.* He pulls my hips back till it's almost as if I'm bent over something. "Brace yourself." And with that, he slams into me, causing a guttural cry to rip from my throat. It sounds as if he's dragging his breath through his teeth. "Fuck," he lets out with a gust. "I thought you'd be ready for me. I'm sorry, sweetheart. Are you all right?"

"Yes."

"You sure?"

It's amazing how he can go from fierce predator to gentle giant at any indication of my discomfort. Johnny Cash starts singing, "And it burns, burns, burns . . . this ring of fire," which is odd because I'm not really one to listen to Johnny Cash. Also, I'm pretty sure he wasn't referencing a vagina.

"Baby?" he asks softly. My heart may have just jumped into my throat; this is the first time he's ever called me that.

I look back over my shoulder at him with a coy smile. I wiggle my ass a little, "I know I'm new at this, Mr. James, but I hardly believe this is how you fuck someone senseless."

"Eager, are we, Miss Campbell?" He smirks, then leans over, tightening his grasp on my hair, and nips at my lobe. "Let us warm up first, shall we?" He slowly pulls back then yanks my hair again as he slams back into me. My jaw drops as he takes to short thrusts with deep penetrating grinds, like he's trying to get further inside of me. "There's nothing better in the world than the sounds you make when I'm deep inside of you." He bites across my shoulder and up my neck. I'd respond to this flattery, except, I'm too busy involuntarily shaking my legs as I come hard around him. "That's it, sweetheart, say your prayers."

I then pray to God, Jesus, and all the disciples. As soon as I come down, I quickly learn what being fucked senseless means. The slapping sound from said style of fucking is so loud, it may as well be the sound of my head slamming into the tile. Speaking of, I am doing everything I can to prevent a head-slamming incident, using my forearms as bumpers. Grayson pulls my hips higher, bringing me to my toes, as a barbaric yell escapes his throat. *I'm thinking Tarzan when he got balls deep into Jane.* My eyes shut tightly as I play her role to perfection.

One final pump and he stills for probably five seconds though it seems like minutes. Then, he collapses gently onto my back. Both of us gasping for air, we slide down into the tub, my back against his chest. A six-foot-four guy, sitting in a standard sized tub would be the equivalent of sticking an Orca whale in an above-ground pool, I think. Throw me in the mix, and I can assume we won't be resting here for long.

"I'm going to call that piece 'The Call of The Wild,'" I say as serious as a heart attack.

"What?" Grayson laughs.

"I totally imagined us as Tarzan and Jane, going at it in the jungle."

"You are off your trolley!" He laughs harder.

I look down. "Actually, I believe I'm still on it, like there might be a chance at another spin around the block." I grind into him.

"Well, since you're the only passenger, I don't like to rush you off. I'm very grateful for your patronage." His fingers glide up and down my sides, causing me to squirm and giggle. He squeezes me to him. "I love you." He kisses my temple. "I'm sorry for coming off like a big bully out there. I just want you with me . . . always." He lightens up on the squeeze.

"I love you, too." I snuggle back into him.

After a beat, "We're not very good water conservationists," he pipes up.

"Nope. The idea is lost on us," I agree. "Let's get up; I didn't wash yet."

"Christ, what the hell were you doing in here?" He gives me the leverage I need to get up.

"Reciting Socrates, what else?" I quip and help him up.

He rolls his eyes. "Turn; I'll wash your hair," he commands. I oblige . . . as usual.

Chapter Thirteen

"How's your leg, Jimmy?" I ask as I walk into his room.

"It's sore, honey." This is a guy who rarely complains about pain, that is, unless someone is being a pain in his ass. For him to even say that his leg is sore is probably the equivalent to someone else screaming bloody murder.

"I'm sorry, Jim-Jim." I grab his hand. He's lying on his bed with his leg propped up while watching TV. "Janet said I could change your dressing as long as you don't mind." I hold up the wound care caddy and shake it for emphasis.

"I'm just a guinea pig to you now, huh?" he teases. "Go ahead." He holds his hand up to his mouth like he's going to tell me a secret. "I bet you'll do a better job," he says in a hushed voice.

"Shh!" I wave him off and then chuckle. There is not a single resident here that likes to have Janet do their dressing.

I set the caddy down near his leg. He pulls the leg of his sweat pants up, revealing the bandaged shin. I cut away the gauze wrap then pour saline over the section of bandage touching his sore so that it pulls away from the wound without hurting him. "How does it look?"

"There's still some infection here; see the pus?" I show him.

"All that from banging my leg on that damn wheelchair," he tsks and shakes his head.

"That, and your poor circulation problems."

"Oh well, fix me up, nursie!" He smiles.

"Yes, sir!" I salute him and get to work, cleaning his wound.

"Grayson still here?"

"Yeah, I think he's going to stay till I have my three-day weekend for Columbus Day. Then, we'll fly to his home."

"I won't say that I approve of him staying with you like this, not being married and all, but I know he treats you well, so I'll let it go." He winks.

"He's really a great guy, Jimmy. I'm very lucky to have him."

Grayson has been with me for the past month, ever since he surprised me that weekend and gave me the ultimatum. I never ask him how long he is staying for, just if he'll be there when I get home. I think he appreciates that. I absolutely love having him with me all of the time. It's *really* nice coming home to him, and it's done wonders for our relationship to have this long period of time to bond. He helps me study every night and makes sure I'm drinking and eating when I'm bogged down with papers and projects. When I need a break from school work, I get a few chapters of proof reading done.

On Friday nights, we're extra strict about me getting everything done for school so that we may enjoy our weekends. With it being Fall, festivals are a dime a dozen in New England, so we've been hitting some of those or going up to North Conway, New Hampshire for a night. *We haven't argued!* That's one for the record books! He's really sweet—in his way, of course. And, he's doing more spontaneous things, mostly to get a laugh out of me.

"What are you thinking about? You have a huge smile on your face," Jimmy inquires.

"Oh." I laugh. "I was just thinking about yesterday when Grayson and I went food shopping. And, you know how stores play songs over the intercom?" I ask. He nods. "Well, I'm a big fan of New Kids On The Block, and "The Right Stuff", one of their big hits, came on. Grayson immediately grabbed my hands and made me dance around the aisle with him as he serenaded me. He even let go of me to do the side-kick dance move they do. He looked ri-goddamn-diculous, and I was laughing so hard, I was crying." I laugh as I tell him.

"I bet that made his day, making you laugh like that," Jimmy muses.

"I think you're right, Jimmy." I sigh and think twice about telling him what Grayson did in produce. Though, I can't stop thinking about it.

"Sweetheart," he grabs my attention. "I'm absolutely in love with these melons." He holds Honeydew melons up in front of my breasts. "They're perfectly sized, firm enough, yet, soft to the touch. I can't wait to get them in my mouth. What a succulent feast I'll have. I could probably nibble on them all night. Look how nicely they fit in my hands." As he says this, I can hear the elderly lady, nearby us, giggle.

"These are very *nice melons, baby. But, my mind is on this beautiful specimen." I hold up a Butternut squash.*

"That is a huge Butternut." He widens his eyes.

"I like them huge."

"Will it fit in a dish, though?"

"Oh, I like to put this right in my oven—without a dish." I seductively run my hand up and down what would be the shaft.

"But what if it explodes? Your oven will be filled with juices from the Butternut."

"That's when I'll know it's done and ready to go in my mouth. I'll clean my oven after." I pull my bottom lip in.

Suddenly, the elderly woman clears her throat, gaining our audience. "It's nice to see two young kids enjoy their fruits and veggies so much." She winks. "Do yourselves a favor; always take the time to be carefree with each other like this. Life has a funny way of making us forget to remember. Always stay young and in love.

I lost my Pauly a few months ago." Her eyes fill up and her voice cracks. "Sixty-two wonderful years all because we stayed silly and in love. You reminded me of him and I. Thank you. I needed that." She brings a hankie up to her eyes and blots. "Remember what I said. Pauly and I were lucky enough to be given that advice and smart enough to follow it. God bless, you two, and I wish you at least sixty-two years, as well." She sniffles. I put the squash down and rush over to her, pulling her into a big hug.

"Thank you for sharing that with us. I'm glad we triggered a good memory for you." I kiss her cheek.

Grayson hugged her too. We chatted for a few more minutes; saw pictures of her Pauly, their wedding (gorgeous), kids, grandkids, pets, and the fake family picture she left in from when she bought her wallet. She said they seemed like pleasant people; she felt bad throwing them away. Then, she laughed at herself, and we joined in. That will *so* be me in sixty years.

After leaving her, I have to admit—it stirred up my own feelings of loss again, which made me very weepy. That is until Grayson serenaded me with a song by my five other favorite guys.

"Boy, do you have it bad," Jimmy states as I bring myself back to the here and now.

"Yes, I do," I agree, then laugh.

"I better get an invitation to your wedding." He shakes a finger at me.

"Oh, don't get ahead of yourself."

"When I see the way Grayson looks at you, it reminds me of how I felt about my Loretta. I'm sure I looked at her like that." He chokes up. "He'll ask you—and soon. Mark my words," he adds.

"Loretta was a lucky woman, Jimmy." I smile empathetically. I know how much he loved and adored her.

"I was the lucky one." He pokes at his chest adamantly.

"You both were lucky." I pick up the caddy and walk to the head of the bed. I plant a kiss on his oversized forehead (he's only about ¼ bald). "I'll see you tomorrow. Thanks for being my guinea pig." I smile.

"You are going to make a great nurse!"

"Thanks, Jimmy. Try to stay out of trouble, okay?"

"I won't make any promises," he tries to joke, but I can see he can't fully pull himself out of his grief yet. I can understand that.

Jimmy's wound care was the last thing left on my list of things to do before clocking out. I bring the caddy down to the treatment room to put it away, clock out in the nurse's lounge, and bid everyone adieu on my way out.

It's so nice to leave at 5 P.M. Oakwood has been very good about my new part-time schedule. I only work eight to sixteen hours a week. Today was my two-hour shift. Luckily, my Nursing Fundamentals rotation is here. So, after doing eight hours as a nursing student, I clock in and stay for two additional hours, helping with rounds and whatnot. They've been short-staffed between Jeremy leaving and my drastic cut in hours; they'll take whatever help they can get.

As far as Barnes and Noble? I left them two weeks ago. I had to. I hate to admit it, but Grayson was right. It was all too much. Thank God (well, Grayson really) that I was able to save enough to afford these cuts. Not to mention the car he bought me and the bills he paid off that he doesn't think I know about. It'll be a long time before I ever admit that I know. As grateful as I am, it pisses me off just the same. However, I am getting very used to his domineering ways, even finding myself being turned on by it. *Who am I anymore?*

I look up from watching the pavement as I walk to my car. Oh. *I'm the girl completely head over heels for that guy.* Grayson jerks his head up as if he can sense my presence. I suddenly feel like a giddy schoolgirl seeing him there. And, I do nothing to hide these feelings as I jog to him excitedly with probably the biggest grin I've ever produced.

He stretches his arms out for me, and I jump into them, wrapping my legs around his waist. I pepper his face with kisses. "What are you doing here, baby?"

"I thought we'd have dinner out tonight." He looks into my

eyes. His facial expression is full of warmth, happiness, and contentment. "This is quite the reception, darling. I trust you had a good day?" He pecks at my lips several times, preventing me from answering.

"I love you. I'm so happy you're here." I hug him.

"Let me fix that by mentioning that you left your coat in the car. Becca, you can't risk getting sick. I already have to nag you about eating," he scolds me in true Grayson form, though gently.

I rest my forehead against his. "I love you," I reiterate and collect his lips with mine. My tongue slides across the slit of his mouth, urging it to part. As he does, I waste no time deepening the kiss. We both groan with satisfaction.

"Christ, get in the bloody car before we're both arrested for indecent exposure," he says after tearing away from our kiss. He gives my bum a slap for good measure before letting me down. He opens the door for me. Still smiling like an idiot, I get in.

"Where's your car?" I ask as he adjusts and gets in the driver's seat.

"Home. Max dropped me off." He turns the key, places the car in gear, and we head off. "Do you have much work to do tonight?"

"Just the usual for Monday; it won't take me long. I should study a little, though."

"I'm more than happy to help you study for Anatomy and Physiology." He slaps my thigh and leaves his hand there to travel up.

"How kind of you, Mr. James." I laugh, grabbing said hand.

"Anything for you, my love." He glances over at me, flashing his pearly whites.

We arrive at the Sylvan Street Grille, a local favorite in Danvers. Hand in hand, we head in, and since it's a Monday, we're seated straight away.

"How's Jimmy?" He peeks over the menu.

"Good. Still having an issue with his leg." I grab some popcorn from the bowl the waitress supplies us with. "I feel bad about how I left him."

"Oh?"

"Yeah, he was thinking about his wife. He was pretty sad." I frown.

"Don't feel bad. Perhaps he would rather grieve alone." He reaches across the table for my hand. "You have a beautiful soul, sweetheart, and it especially shines through when you mention the people you take care of. You can tell they are not just a job to you."

"They're family," I agree.

Just then, the waitress arrives, and I bite my lip in anticipation of hearing what he will order for me tonight. He always *knows*. It's bizarre. Yet, I find it very *hot*.

He eyes me at first as if that final read will confirm what he is thinking. He places our order and hands off the menu. "Filet Mignon and garlic mashed is a win-win with you."

I gasp. "Mr. James, do you mean to tell me that you played it safe with my dinner selection?" I act shocked. Actually, I am.

"With the range of emotions you just flashed before me in only a half an hour—yes, I played it safe. Besides, you have work to do tonight. If I ordered you a pasta dish for comfort, you'd be comatose by the time we'd get home. So, I ordered your 'happy' and 'comfort' food."

"It pleases you to do this, doesn't it?"

"Immensely."

"It's because you're bossy." I point out.

"And you do love me for it." He waggles his brows at me and releases my hand for some popcorn. I give no reply. His head can be big enough without me encouraging it by announcing that he's right.

"Did you order our plane tickets?"

"I ordered mine for this Wednesday and yours for that Friday afternoon."

"What? What are you talking about?" I'm about an octave below yelling.

"I'm going home in two days." He throws more popcorn in his mouth.

"Why?" No, he can't leave.

"I've overstayed my welcome. Besides, I have things I need to do at home."

"Did someone tell you that?" My blood is beginning to boil.

"No."

"I thought…" I can't finish my sentence. The waitress deposits our soups in front of us.

"Eat up," he instructs.

"Fuck you," I snap under my breath and push the cup forward.

"Certainly. But, I am famished; let us wait till after dinner." He pushes it back in front of me. "Eat!"

I grab my spoon and angrily break through the Swiss cheese on my French onion soup. I'm only eating this because I skipped lunch and am starving. It has nothing to do, whatsoever, with him commanding me and me finding him sexy as fuck when he does so.

"Becca, I have prior obligations, meetings and appointments, otherwise, I wouldn't be leaving," he pleads with me.

"Cancel them or rearrange them."

"I can't."

"You mean you won't," I snap.

"There's too many of them."

"Grayson, please. I need you; don't go," I beg, tears leaving their respective pools. "I'd be lost without you," I add. It's all true. We've formed a routine this past month. Well, Grayson formed it, I followed. But, that's just it—that's the point—I need him to keep me on track. The fact that I'm in love with him only adds to my feeling of loss.

I watch as he texts someone, paying me no attention. Several pings happen with a quick response from him. Then, finally, he puts it away. "It's being worked out," he states before focusing on his soup.

"You're staying?" I am hopeful. *You're pathetic.* You again?

"You are my first priority, Becca."

"Thank you," I'm barely audible. He gives me a slight nod and points his spoon at my soup. I smile and happily oblige.

LAX

Gray and I step off the plane and head down the bridge, hand in hand, to the gate. There, we notice Derek. He's holding up a sign that reads: *Abandoned by best friends; looking for replacements.*

"Bugger off, you wanker," Grayson boasts, yanking the sign out of Derek's hands. Derek's famous hyena laugh ensues, which gets us both laughing. He then pulls me in for one of his bone-crushing hugs. I've missed him terribly. I won't deny that seeing he included me as his best friend makes me appreciate him all the more. "Hey! That's enough now! Get your own girl!" Grayson breaks us apart. He's trying to be playful about it, but the jealousy is all over his face. I really don't understand why he acts as if every man is pining for my affection.

"Let's go before he has us running off to elope in his mind." I roll my eyes and grab a hand from both of them.

"You know, I can hear you talking to him about me." He tugs my arm.

"You can?" I ask incredulously.

"Amazing, I know," he matches my shock. I beam up at him as I head off to obtain our luggage. I swing their hands wildly like an excited child. I sort of feel that way. I love these two guys and my happiness is at a heightened level it hasn't been at in a long time.

"Who wound you up today?" Derek chuckles.

"I'm just really happy," I vocalize.

"About what?" Grayson inquires as he points to our baggage carousel.

"I'm in love," I simply state as we approach and wait for the belt to start. I look to my left and up at Grayson as I feel his thumb softly caress the top of my hand.

He leans down, almost brushing my lips. "I had *no* idea you felt this way about Derek," he utters.

"Yes . . . intensely. Shh . . . don't tell him." I close the gap between us and smile against his lips.

"It's his quick wit and charm; he's beguiled me as well." He sucks in my bottom lip, trapping it between his teeth.

"I'm not deaf either!" Derek announces. "Always the third wheel," he grumbles.

"Hold on, mate; I'll kiss you in a minute." Grayson consoles. I give into the laughter that's making my shoulder's shake.

"Derek." I turn my attention to him. "You are a very important third wheel. Imagine we are a tricycle; where would Grayson and I be if you weren't the big, strong wheel in the front, leading the way for us to travel in perfect harmony together?"

"And now she's explaining things to me as if I'm Forrest Gump." He shakes his head and starts grabbing our luggage that's circled around to us. I continue my laughter. God, I love these guys.

My internal clock says it's after 8 P.M., and I'm beyond starving. With the time change and length of flight, and knowing Susanna was planning a huge feast as we were arriving at dinner, Cali time, we skipped the plane food. My stomach growls in protest of this decision. "We're almost home, sweetheart." Grayson brings our entwined hands up and kisses the back of mine.

"What's for dinner?"

"I'm not sure. I told her to decide."

"That's very unusual for you." I look at him strangely.

"I'm not always a control freak; I like to be surprised, too." He raises both brows.

"Are you hinting at something, baby?" I pull my bottom lip in, nibbling at it.

"I don't know what you are talking about." His smile is suggestive. I make a mental note to come up with ways to surprise him this weekend.

"How you doing up there, Forrest?" I give Derek some attention.

"Very busy being the big wheel, guiding you two home." He winks in the rearview mirror. I smile and rest my eyes as I lean against Gray.

Within a few minutes, Derek rolls the SUV through the open gates to Gray's house and pulls into the garage. "Home sweet home," he announces.

Before we even get the doors open, Susanna and Hazel are making a beeline for us. "Gracie!" Hazel yells with an exaggerated excitement as we climb out. She rushes to him for a big hug.

"Christ, Mum, I was in Boston for a month, not off to war." He laughs at her as he squeezes her tightly.

And then it happens out of nowhere; I flashback to the last time I hugged my mom. I can barely remember what it felt like. It was a year ago. They had come up for the Topsfield Fair. That was the last time I saw them alive. My heart crushes into a million pieces in my chest. "Becca?" Grayson's voice pulls me out of my thoughts.

I quickly wipe my tears away. "Can you guys excuse me for a moment?" Without an answer, I turn on my heel and head into the house, directly to Grayson's room. I shut the door behind me and have myself a good cry.

They are going to miss everything. I'm never going to be able to call and tell them all the new wonderful things happening in my life. My dad will never walk me down the aisle. My mom will never get to see her first grandchild be born. She'll never get to see me being a mom. I'll never hear him call me his "little girl" again. *Who's gonna pick me up when I fall? Who's going to tell me everything is going to be all right?*

Suddenly, I'm swept off my feet. I panic, then realizing it's Grayson, I throw my arms around his neck and bury my face in the crook of it as he sits on the bed with me in his arms. My sobs come in strong waves. He rocks me, holding me close to him. "Everything is going to be all right, sweetheart," he whispers against my hair.

Oh.

I bring my head up to look at him. His eyes are reddened, and I remember that he can easily feel my pain with me because he suffers from the same loss.

"Why? Why did it have to be my parents? Your dad?" I ask,

knowing he won't have the answer, only the same question. He frowns and shakes his head. He frees his hand from my legs and reaches up to wipe my tears away. Satisfied, he palms my cheek and leans in to collect my lips. "I love you," I breathe against them.

"I am *so* in love with you, sweetheart." He closes his eyes and rests his forehead against mine. We stay here—in this moment—for several minutes. Interruption is provided by my growling stomach. We both laugh, as it is quite loud.

"Let me freshen up, and I'll apologize to everyone, okay?" I kiss him again.

"There's no need. Go ahead, though; I'm starved." He helps me up and pats my bottom.

"So bossy."

"One of the many things you love about me," he calls out as I enter the bathroom. I agree, but I'll keep that to myself.

Chapter Fourteen

GRAYSON

"Susanna, please tell me you've made something different for Becca," I plead, trying to keep my cool as I take in the spread across the dining room table. It's *all* seafood. Susanna looks at me like a deer in headlights. "I've told you before—she doesn't eat seafood!"

"Gracie!" Mum yelps, shocked at my tone, I'm sure.

"I—I got her mixed up with the last one," she stammers.

"What?" I yell. "How dare you even put her in the same category as anyone I've ever had here before?" Oh my God, how could she say something like that? Is she trying to sabotage my chances this weekend?

"Grayson, it's okay." Becca tugs at my arm.

"It is not!" I snap.

"It is," she reiterates, looking a bit amused. "Is that cod?" she questions Susanna.

"Yes."

"I like to have fish 'n' chips every once in a while. It's perfect, Susanna, thank you. Shall we eat?" Becca shrugs slightly with her question then claims a seat. I sit next to her, feeling a bit like a big ogre. *Overreact much, Gray?*

Susanna leaves the room. Mum and Derek take a seat. I grab Becca's plate to fill hers first. After a few minutes, everyone's plates are filled. I take my first bite and notice Becca waiting. "Eat." I point to her plate.

"Oh, I don't want to start till after Susanna and Sam sit down." She eyes their empty plates.

"It's a dinner party; they eat in the kitchen." I don't even know why I just said that.

Becca looks at Mum, then Derek. "It looks like a family dinner to me."

"Is that a question?" I choose to not look at her.

"Sometimes you really remind me of a petulant child, Gray." She throws her napkin onto the table and gets up.

"Where are you going?"

"To get the rest of this family!" she snaps and proceeds to head to the kitchen.

"She'll do," Mum says nonchalantly.

"Glad you feel that way, Mum." I finally find my smile. She looks at me curiously. I look over at Derek as he would understand my cryptic message. However, there is food in front of the beast; he may as well not even be here.

Not five minutes go by and Becca re-enters the room with a disgruntled Susanna and Sam behind her. She raises a triumphant eyebrow at me as she holds her stare. I give in and crack a huge smile. "I'm sorry for behaving like a—petulant, was it—darling?"

"Yes—petulant," she agrees.

"Yes. I'm sorry for behaving like a petulant child, Susie."

"There will be no Éclair cake for you, Grayson," she states as she shakes and places her napkin into her lap aggressively.

"Really?" I pout.

"Really."

"Damn." I sulk.

"I can have Éclair cake, though, right?" Derek asks quickly.

"The beast has come up for air!" I announce.

"The *beast* will be enjoying *your* favorite cake," Susie quips.

"Damn," I sigh. She's really mad at me. Derek gives me a shit-eating grin. I can almost hear him singing "na nan a nan na." *Wanker.*

I decide to turn my focus towards dinner, having already got in enough trouble.

"Susie, can I talk to you for a minute?" I almost beg as she does the dishes.

"Grayson, I'm so mad at you; I could really use some time to calm down." She continues washing without looking at me.

"I've never behaved that way towards you before." I ignore her request.

"*Never!*" she agrees, her voice displeased.

"I'm nervous."

"About?"

"I want everything to be perfect for her this weekend. I already had a strike against me when we got here." I rest my hip against the counter next to her.

"How so?"

"Seeing Mum and me, it triggered her sense of loss. The last time she saw her parents alive was around this time last year. Most of the time she's okay, but you know how it is. One moment you're fine, then *boom*—you think of them."

"Yes, I do." She glances my way, a slight frown in place.

"So, right off the bat, the weekend dropped south. I didn't want anything else to go wrong. Then I saw the seafood, and I lost it a bit." I shrug.

"Let's get something straight; you *never* told me she dislikes seafood. You made a mistake, and you tried to make me take the fall for it. *That's* what I didn't appreciate. And, of course, the way you talked to me." I can hear the hurt in her voice.

"I am truly sorry. I thought I had, but it still doesn't excuse the way I behaved. Please forgive me. I promise that will never happen again." I lightly rub her back and give her my pouty face when she looks at me after turning the faucet off.

She turns to me, grabbing the dishtowel to dry her hands. "Why are you nervous?" She ignores my charms.

I crank my neck around to make sure the coast is clear. "I'm going to ask Becca for her hand in marriage," I almost whisper. Susie's face lights up and it makes me so happy.

"What's with all the whispering, you two?" Mum asks from behind us.

"Did you tell her?" Susie mouths. I shake my head. "Tell her!" She pokes at my chest.

"Tell me what?" Mum looks between us.

I look around again, then bend down, so I'm in earshot. "I'm going to ask Becca to be my wife." I stand back up, smiling. Only, it drops, as I am not getting the same delighted face I got from Susanna.

"No," she states.

"I wasn't asking you."

"I haven't had a chance to really get to know her yet," she elaborates.

"Well, you have this weekend to rectify that. I'm not changing my mind." I stand my ground.

"Gracie, you don't want to rush into things like this."

"Pah! Pot—kettle, Mum!" I scoff. This coming from a woman, who was engaged to my dad after a week or so. I'm actually surprised at her reaction; Mum and Dad had a happy marriage that lasted over forty years. "By yours and Dad's standards, I'm way behind schedule."

Mum releases the cute little laugh she does when she's trying not to laugh or doesn't mean to. "Oh, what can I say? You're right. Besides, I may not know her well yet, but what I do know, I adore." Her hands reach up, palming my face. Tears fill her eyes. "I've never seen you so happy and carefree. She's good for you, Gracie."

"So, you give me—us—your blessing?" I place my hands on top of hers.

"Absolutely." She smiles. "When are you going to ask her?"

"Not sure. Derek's picking the ring up for me tomorrow. I'm sure it'll burn a hole in my pocket; so sooner rather than later."

Just then, Becca enters the kitchen. "Groveling properly, I hope?" she asks.

"But of course, darling." I smile broadly at her. "Susie even said I could have my cake back," I lie.

"Nice try!" Susie smacks me with the towel.

"Ow . . . that wasn't nice," I say to Susie as I open my arms for Becca.

"Will you be terribly upset with me if I went to bed early?" Becca asks.

"Tired?" I kiss her head.

"Yes. It's been a long day." She looks up at me. "I'm sorry. I know it's our first night here."

"It's okay, Becca," Mum says. "You've had a full day already without throwing the time difference into the mix."

"Thanks, Hazel." She releases me and gives Mum a hug. I watch; my heart swelling at the sight. I love these two women more than anything in the world. I'm glad to see their affection grow for one another. She releases my mother then gives Susanna a hug. "Night, Susanna."

"Night, Becca." She smiles.

"Gray," she turns back to me, "why don't you and Derek go out for a few drinks or something. He's missing his buddy."

"You truly are a rare breed, sweetheart." I kiss her nose. "Come, I'll walk you to our bedroom." I grab her hand and lead the way. "Derek, get a fire going outside, will you, mate? Becca's heading to bed, and she's been good enough to let me out to play." I slap his back when we come upon him.

"Right-O. Night, Becca." He kisses her cheek.

"Night." She smiles. He goes off to see about that fire.

"Don't you want to go out?"

"What for? I have an outdoor fireplace and bar. There's no need for us to leave." I open the bedroom door.

"Oh . . . okay. That's good; I don't have to worry."

"Nope." I smile. "Arms up," I instruct as I grab the hem of her shirt. I pull it up and over her head. Immediately, I second-guess my plans to hang out with Derek.

"Oh no . . . I know that look." She steps back, pointing an accusatory finger at me. "Go! I can get myself ready for bed."

"But—"

"—No! Shoo!" She sweeps her hand at me, and I can't contain my laugh; she's so damn cute.

"Just a kiss, then?" I plead.

"Just a kiss." She holds her finger up in warning.

"Promise." I place my hand over my heart.

"Okay." She smiles and steps forward.

I grasp the sides of her face and descend slowly, savoring the anticipation. "You're so beautiful," I say in awe. Her tongue peeks out and slides across her bottom lip. I take this as my cue and cover her mouth with my own. I run my tongue across the slit of her mouth causing her to open so I can deepen the kiss. She moans as our tongues do a slow seductive dance with each other, and it's all I can do to hold the Neanderthal back. Becca tries to pull away but I'm relentless and she caves, threading her fingers through my hair and pulling.

Knowing how exhausted she is and how close I am to not giving a fuck about it, I pull away. "Aggressive woman, you; try to control yourself for once, will you?"

"I don't know what came over me," she plays along. *God I love her.*

"Get some rest, sweetheart." I give her a quick peck and slap her arse (as I often do). It's a lovely arse, what can I say?

"Night, baby," she says before entering the bathroom. Becca's been calling me "baby" for months now, but it still makes my heart skip a beat. It's sacred to her and knowing I am the only person she's used that endearment for, makes me appreciate that four letter word a whole helluva lot more now. I give the inner Neanderthal one last shove down and leave to hang out with Derek.

"I was beginning to wonder if you'd make it out here," Derek states as he pokes the fire.

"Sorry, mate," I offer and drop in a seat. "This mine?" I grab the bottle of beer off the table.

He nods and walks over, taking the other seat. "Nervous?"

"Yes and no." I bring the bottle up and let the cool liquid hit my throat. I'm not much of a beer drinker, but I do enjoy having a few with Derek every so often.

"When are you going to ask?"

"Not sure; at some point this weekend." I stare at the fire.

"Are you going back with her Monday night?"

"No. I can't. I've pushed things off already that I shouldn't have. The meeting with John." I give him, for instance.

"The producer?"

"Yes."

"Ohh…" he trails off.

"Yeah . . . not good. I'm lucky he's entertaining another meeting with me."

"Does she know?"

"No."

"Are you going to tell her?"

"That I'm staying here or that I almost lost the executive producer?"

"Both."

"I have to tell her I'm staying here, that I have to catch up on meetings. That is all she needs to know." I put my beer down. "Enough about us, what is going on with you?"

"I've hired a few men and one woman. I'm sending them off to Crucible for training next week."

"Fantastic! Any new prospects for clients?" I cross my feet at the ankles on the ottoman. There's a brisk chill in the air. Very autumnal, which I'm glad for as it is Becca's favorite season. I want her to have all of her favorite things here.

"And then I lit my arse on fire, ran down the street, screaming '*shark!*'"

"What?" I whip my head in his direction.

"Oh, hello! Welcome back, mate!" Derek is at his sarcastic best. *Fuck, I'm an arsehole.*

"Sorry." I wince.

"I love Becca, I really do. But, I miss my best friend." He gets up. "I'll call you tomorrow after I pick up the ring."

"Derek, I—"

"—Save it. It's fine. I'll catch you tomorrow." And with that, he leaves.

"Great," I breathe. I decide to stay out here for a while to finish my beer . . . or two. Besides, the crackling of the fire is very relaxing.

"Gracie?" Mum calls to me quietly.

"Hey, Mum. Come to join me, have you?" I smile up at her.

"Do you mind?" She zips up her sweatshirt before placing a kiss on my head, like I'm five.

"Not at all; have a seat." I point to Derek's empty chair.

"Why did Derek go home? That's unusual," she comments as she sits.

"Let's just say I wasn't very good company."

"Ah. This will pass, especially when he finds someone." She pushes the air out in front of her.

"I hope it happens soon. He desperately needs to get—"

"—Ahem."

"Right—sorry." I chuckle.

"Is Becca okay?"

"Yes. She just misses her parents so much. I understand the pain, but I still have you, so it's not quite the same."

"Does she have anyone else in her family?" She sips her tea.

"Yes. She's very close with her Aunt Tess and Uncle Bill, but they're in New Jersey. I've yet to meet them. I have chatted on the phone with them; they're lovely and great fun. I rang her Uncle Bill the other day. With Becca's dad gone, it only seemed right to ask him for permission to marry his niece."

"How'd that go?"

"Very well, actually. As I've said, we've got to know each other over the phone. I also went into her work and asked Jimmy for permission. He was the toughest on me." I can't help but laugh. I love that ole chap.

"Who's Jimmy?"

"A resident of hers; they are very close. He promised her father that he'd keep an eye on her while her parents weren't around. He's taken his roll a lot more seriously since their death. He's a wonderful man. Becca really knows how to attract and keep wonderful people around her." I nurse my beer.

"Case in point," my mother says as she holds her hand out in my direction.

"You're bias." I laugh.

"I'm right."

"You usually are."

"Are you going back with her on Monday?"

"Can't wait to get rid of me?"

"Don't be daft." She smacks my leg.

"I can't." I proceed to explain why.

"When you are all caught up out here, you need to go back to her. I think that was the smartest thing you've done."

"Really, Mum? That was the smartest thing I've ever done?" I tease.

"With this relationship, yes. Oh, Gracie, the way you were carrying on about her not moving out here right away, it made no sense. You've been the one able to telecommunicate all along. Why you gave her so much grief, I'll never understand." She sets her tea down.

"Look who's getting ready for the millennium! Telecommunicate, Mother?"

"I don't live under a rock, you wally."

"I suppose you're right."

"I thought we'd settled that already," she deadpans.

"Too right. So, Mother dear, what's on your agenda for tomorrow?" I finish off my beer.

"I thought I'd grab Becca for a few hours, have some girl time."

"Sensational idea!" I bring my feet off the ottoman and sit up straight. "It'll be great for you two to really start bonding, and I think it will be good for her to have that sense of a motherly figure around."

"I think she and I are off to a great start." She beams. "I have to admit, I am very excited at the prospect of finally having a daughter, even if only through marriage."

"Good. Maybe you'll stop calling me 'Gracie' then." One could only hope.

"Never! You'll always be my Gracie; I don't care how old you get!"

Now this is a battle I am not only used to losing but expect to do so. Truth be told, it would sadden me if she stopped calling me that. "I love you, Mum." I reach for her hand.

"I love you too . . . Gracie."

"Ready to call it a night?"

"You?"

"Yes." I stand up. "Shall I escort you, me lady?" I hold my arm out for her.

"Why, thank you kindly, sir." She bats her eyes then laughs as she takes my arm. We walk over to the dying fire and I grab the bucket of water, tossing it on there to help it along. I escort Mum in and to her room, then go on to mine. The thought of Becca, sprawled out in bed, already has my arousal on high alert.

Upon entering, I immediately head to our en suite. I undress and jump into the shower. I smell as if I had been camping, or at least I think I do. I have missed this glorious shower, though. I know Becca has too, as well as the tub. After I'm all washed up, I proceed with the rest of my bathroom ritual. I catch a note poking out beneath the hand towel I used to shave. I grab it.

10/ 09 /99

Yours for the taking . . .
Yours always,

Becca
XXXXX

"Huh?" It's dated for tonight. My mind, of course, is going in one direction, but that can't be right; she was bone-tired. In any case, I speed through my production here, curious as hell.

Flicking the light switch off, I enter the bedroom and walk to my side of the bed. I turn the lamp on the lowest wattage, which illuminates the room in a soft glow. I notice Becca, sleeping soundly, her back facing me. I pull back the covers and immediately bring fist to mouth. I bite. Becca is completely naked, and her arse glows beautifully in this lighting. Even if my assumption that she wanted me to wake her was wrong, there's no way I could stop myself.

I pull the covers off completely and slowly climb in. My teeth are itching to bite at the delectable treat in front of me. I let my hand ghost down her left side, stopping at her bum. I squeeze it gently and bite her right underneath the cheek where her thigh greets. My mouth travels up higher, nibbling her some more along the way. I taste her skin with my tongue, and I'm just now noticing the rapid tempo of her breathing.

"On your belly," I command, and I know she'll obey. She always obeys me in the bedroom, and I find that bloody fucking hot. True to form, she lies flat on her stomach. I situate on my knees and make room for myself between her legs. I grasp each cheek and knead them methodically. "Becca." I stare at her arse, wanting it. "You have no idea how badly I want to claim this arse of yours," I groan. She gasps. "Not tonight, sweetheart, but soon."

Her body remains tense and rather than having a discussion, I decide to calm her nerves with a massage. My hands slide slowly up her back; my lips, following their trail. I let my tongue out to taste her sweet skin. She softly moans when I reach her shoulders and add a little pressure, working at them. "Does that feel good?"

"Mmm…"

"Don't fall back to sleep," I warn. I work my way back down to her arse. I'm greeted by it being pushed eagerly into my hands. I squeeze, then smack her right cheek, and am rewarded with another moan from her. She's *not* making restraining myself easy on me. "So lovely," I utter, caressing her pink cheek. I continue with her massage, paying her shapely legs attention. *I love her body.* Every. Single. Curve.

I watch her squirm as I bite at the insole of her foot. Her bum lifting into the air, antagonizing me. I place her foot back down, and my hands gravitate to her arse again. Her body shakes with giggles. I give a good smack to her left cheek to keep things equal and to put a stop to her giggling. It works. And now, she pants. My hands glide over her bum again, and slowly, she pushes up to meet my caress. My right hand rests at the small of her back. With great restraint, my thumb descends down the center while I knead her cheek with my left hand. When she pushes up, I slide my thumb down quickly to cover her opening. "Gray!" she panics, and her hips fall, but I keep placement.

"Shh…" I apply more pressure without pushing my thumb inside of her. I just want her to feel the sensation. After a beat, I keep the pressure but add some circular motion. "Relax, sweetheart. This is as far as I will go tonight," I coax her a little. I can feel the tension in her body dissipate. "That's it, baby," I encourage.

"Grayson," she almost begs.

"Slide your hands underneath you, darling," I instruct. "Make yourself come."

"No." She shakes her head. I know it's because she feels self-conscious.

"Yes. Now!" I command.

Her hands work their way underneath her. I stop the circling of my thumb, waiting to follow the rhythm she takes on pleasuring herself. "Now, Becca!" I smack her arse with my free hand. She begins to move, her hips rocking as she grinds into her hands. "Good girl." I kiss down her spine and work my thumb in unison.

"Can I have your fingers inside of me?" She pants.

"So greedy, darling." I smile then happily fill her request—pun intended. "Christ, you're so bloody fucking wet."

"Oh God!" she cries out, clenching around my fingers.

"Oh God, what?" I demand.

"Oh God, baby." She bucks then holds still as if she's frozen till the wave passes. She exhales and drops.

"Again." I bite at her skin, tasting the sweet saltiness of her sweat. Before she starts, I pull my fingers out, bringing her lubrication up to her bum. "Let's go, Becca. Pleasure yourself one more time, then I will have a go at it." I return my digits to her welcoming warmth. She puts her hips back in motion. My thumb follows her lead, which may be the cause of her whimper.

"There are no rules in our bed, sweetheart. It's all about our love and showing that love through pleasure. There is no guilt in giving and receiving pleasure from one another. Leave all of those thoughts outside our door where they belong." I know this is why she gets timid sometimes. "Do you understand me?" I nip at her lobe.

"Yes, baby."

"Do you have any idea how fucking sexy you are? How much you turn me on, submitting to me?"

"Please," she begs, and I know she's climbing. She pushes back against me and I take the opportunity to push my thumb in. "God!" she screams. I finger fuck her hard, and she is wild, all circuits being worked.

"That's it, darling; come for me," I coach. And she does—*hard*. "This is going to be quick," I announce, retrieving my fingers from her and yanking her hips up high. I slam into her and shift right into relentless-pounding gear. I feel her clench around me again, and I join in her rise.

She says her prayers, so sweetly, as I fill her up, gasping with each thrust. I push inside of her one last time before collapsing on top of her. Buckling under my weight, she sprawls flat onto the mattress. I kiss at her back as I pull out and roll onto my back. "Come," I call to her. She turns and snuggles up to my chest, sighing with contentment when I wrap my arms around her. "You okay?" My lips graze the top of her head.

"Mmm hmm," she hums. My fingers ghost up and down her back. Within a few moments, her breathing evens out and I know she's drifted off.

"Graaay-seee. Graaaay-seee, wake up," Becca coos. *Gracie?* Wait—what? I let my eyelids flutter open. "Good morning, sleepyhead." She leans over me and gives me a chaste kiss.

"How did this happen?" Becca never wakes up before me. I look over at the clock. Crikey—it's 10 A.M.!

"I guess someone wore you out."

"You should've woken me."

"Why? You needed the sleep." She brushes my hair away from my forehead.

"Did you call me 'Gracie'?" I look at her curiously.

"I did."

"Ugh . . . you've already been around my mother too much, then," I groan.

"I think it suits you." She taps my nose.

"I think *you* suit me." I lean up and brush her lips.

"Likewise. Anywho, I came in to let you know that your mom and I are heading out to shop."

"Oh good." I sit up and grab my wallet. I open it and retrieve my black Amex. "Here, whatever you want, sweetheart, for the house or yourself. Just put it on here." I hand it to her.

"Stop." She pushes my hand away and stands up.

"The card, Becca," my voice stern.

"Fine; just in case I see something for your house." She takes it.

I roll my eyes and grasp her face, bringing her close to me for a kiss. "I'll see you later this afternoon. I love you." I give her another soft peck.

"I love you, too."

Chapter Fifteen

BECCA

"I like what you did with Grayson's office." Hazel picks up an old ceramic bowl, inspecting it.

"Oh, I'm glad. I thought it came together well. Look at these sconces. I think they'd be gorgeous refurbished in white." I hold them up for her.

"I think you're right, Becca. Let's get them for the study. Now that Gracie has his office, we can claim the study for ourselves." I guess she's planning on me being a permanent fixture in Grayson's life. This makes me happy beyond words. So far, Hazel is a dream for a mother-in-law. No, that's not exactly the right title. Mother-in-courtship? Yeah, that sounds regal, like Grayson.

I tilt my head. "Do you think he'd let us do that?"

"Me? Maybe not. You? Without the slightest hesitation." She smiles at this.

"Oh—come on!" I try to call her on her bluff.

"You, my dear, have been given full carte blanche. I kid you not." She puts the sconces in her basket. "Grayson hasn't gotten around to much decorating. He only bought the house a year ago, maybe a little over." She looks as if she's trying to work out the dates. "In any case, what you see is what the previous owner did. He has ideas about what he wants but hesitates. You captured his thoughts for the office. I'm sure he will be delighted, if not relieved, for you to slowly do one room at a time." She starts heading over to the buffets. I follow her, thinking about everything she just said.

"That must be why he gave me his card, to get stuff for the house," I surmise.

"And whatever you want. He texted me," she answers before I even ask.

"Is Grayson a lot like his dad?"

"In some ways, but I'm afraid he gets most of his personality from me, so you're really stuck with the two of us," she says almost as if she's treading carefully.

"I can't think of two better people to be stuck with." I put my arm around her shoulder and squeeze her toward me.

"I'm so happy to hear that, Becca." She pats my hand and smiles at me.

I let go and we continue to peruse the antique shop, talking color schemes and concepts for our new and improved study. It's strange in a good way, the ease of our new relationship. The more time we spend together, the more I feel as if we've known each other forever. At the same time, I do have my guard up. Not because she makes me feel as if I should, but more of a reality check for me. She's *not* my mother; she's his. He will always come first. Seems like a silly and weird thing to be thinking about, but I'm very aware of my feelings. I'm craving that mother/daughter relationship. Hazel seems more than happy to fill that void for me. While that is wonderful, if I don't make it a habit now to remember her loyalty, it will hurt that much more, later, when and if she ever had to reveal it. Lines can get blurred. I need to keep my heart at some distance.

"What do you think he will say about all of this?" I ask as we watch a few men load up the small truck Hazel had Sam rent. To say we got caught up in a moment of inspiration would be a flat out lie. It started out as a moment; it morphed into a shopping frenzy.

"I don't know, to be honest." She giggles.

"Is there an empty room we can store it in while we sort and place?" I'm trying to focus on the here and now, but my mind keeps wandering off to various scenarios that may happen when we get home. All of them include him screaming his head off—sounding extra British—demanding receipts.

"You mean *hide* it all in?" She covers her mouth and really gives into her laughter. "Oh my, Becca, it seems like we are a very bad influence on each other," she admonishes.

"He's going to lose his shit, Hazel." I panic. "Oh no!" I groan as I watch more stuff being brought out. "We really bought all of this?"

"Stop! We are grown women. We will not allow him to chastise us. It's all stuff for the house. He would've spent a lot more hiring a designer. It'll be fine!" she comforts me, I think. She could be trying to comfort herself. I just cross my arms, rubbing them up and down, nodding. Hazel retrieves her cell phone from her purse and begins dialing. "Derek, are you at the house? Oh good! Stay put; Becca and I need your help. Okay, see you soon." She hangs up.

"You will have to ride in the truck with me to get the car," Sam says as he walks over to us.

"Shall we get in now?" Hazel brings the strap of her purse up higher on her shoulder.

"Yes, ma'am. We're just about done here." He nods.

"Becca." She holds her hand out for me to lead the way.

The butterflies in my stomach have morphed into the alien from *Spaceballs* as we approach the house. I pass the truck and park the Mercedes in the garage. Hazel touches my arm and I know she's saying something to me, only, I can't hear her because the *Spaceballs* alien, that wants to burst out of my stomach, is already singing "Hello my baby, hello my honey, hello my ragtime gal…"

real loud in my head. *Oh fuck! I think I'm having a panic attack.*

"I can't breathe!" I yell, unfastening the seatbelt and reaching to get the door handle. I lunge out of the car and exit the garage quickly; gasping for air once I make it outside.

"Becca, sweetie, are you okay?" a very out of breath Hazel asks once she makes it to me.

"He's going to flip out. We have to return this stuff. What were we thinking?" I blather on as I find a small garden bench. Maybe it's a stone seat? This would look much more in place if it had a gnome sitting on it. It would also accommodate a gnome's ass better than mine, but I sit anyhow and force my head between my legs, trying to pull myself together. I feel Hazel's hand rub my back. It's not really the best thing to do when someone is in any stage of a panic attack. A neon sign should light up that says "Don't touch me." I'm about to tell her this, only "Did we buy a gnome?" comes out instead.

"I think we missed that section," she says with much thought.

Clearly, I've either worked myself out of a panic attack that was starting or . . . I'm just plain fucking crazy. I'd have to go with the latter at the moment.

"What are you two hens going on about over here?" Grayson's booming voice makes me jump up. He eyes me curiously. "What's the matter?" He walks up to me. He must've come from the side of the house and not seen the production carrying on in the front. The slam of the truck's ramp, hitting the driveway, makes Grayson's head jerk in that direction. "What the...?" he trails off. He glances back at me quickly before going off to investigate.

The alien comes back as soon as I see a look of disbelief come across his face. Grayson brings his hands up to fist his hair and puffs his cheeks out with a big exhale. "Oh, for the love of Pete!" Hazel snaps under her breath. "I love my son, but he's such a tightwad." She makes her way to him. I release a nervous giggle. There's something about the way she calls her son a tightwad that is priceless. I follow her lead.

"What's the meaning of all this?" I can see he's trying to remain calm.

"Your girlfriend and I saved you thousands of dollars. You won't need to hire an interior designer." I am in love with Hazel's approach. I feel certain that I will be learning a lot from this woman.

"I thought I'd try to get a room done or at least started with each visit until I move in," I add.

"All of this is for the house?" his voice is quite unreadable.

"Yes." I nibble on my bottom lip.

"What did you get for yourself?" He lets his hands drop and pockets them.

"Well, your mom and I have decided to make the study our own, so we bought these fancy sconces and chandelier that I will refurbish."

"There was a desk she was eyeing, but I couldn't get her to buy it." Hazel pipes up.

"Why?" He keeps his eyes on me. I shrug. "That's not an answer."

"I wasn't sure I wanted it."

"She went back to look at it ten times—I counted." Hazel is relentless. I widen my eyes at her like you would when secretly telling a friend to shut up. Clearly, we're not at that level yet.

"Mum, can you call the store and order it?" Grayson takes a step closer to me.

"I already did. It'll be here tomorrow," she quips, widens her eyes back at me, and then turns to go inside. Ok—guess we *are* on that level.

I bring my attention back to Grayson and gasp when I realize he's practically on top of me. His hands grasp my face. He descends slowly upon me. My heart races like it's trying to beat out of my chest as his lips find mine, painting them softly, coaxing them to part. His tongue slides over mine at a pace that is hypnotic. I easily lose myself in this kiss with him. It's the best place to get lost. My hands slide up his chest, and I fist at his shirt as the kiss becomes more urgent.

"For fuck's sake, can you two control yourselves long enough to help out here? I mean, this is *your* shit, is it not?" Derek calls out to us, effectively interrupting our moment.

"God, he's been a bitter arsehole these past two days," Grayson grumbles near my ear.

"Well . . . he's right." I try to straighten out the wrinkles I caused in his shirt. "Go. I'll go inside and make sure everything is sorted according to what room they will end up in." I give him a final kiss, slap his ass, and laugh.

"Hey now—that's *my* calling card."

"Go!" I demand.

"Very bossy! Also *my* calling card."

I smile and turn to go in, but quickly look over my shoulder. "Gray?"

"Yes, love?" He turns back to me.

"Thanks for not getting mad at me for all of this." I point to the truck.

"Day's not over, sweetheart; I've yet to see the receipts," he reminds me, raising one eyebrow up pretty damn high. I'm impressed.

"You gonna spank me, Gracie?"

"Well, since you're asking for it and all." He smirks.

"I'm not."

"You're goading me, therefore, you are. Would you like me to do it now, in front of everyone?"

"Oh . . . I think I hear your mother calling me." I raise my hand up to my ear. "Be careful; don't pull your back out. Though . . . it is a good night for a ride," I say and quickly run into the house as he was getting ready to charge toward me.

I look ahead and see Sam turn down the corridor on the right; that's where all the guest bedrooms are as well as Hazel's, Susanna and Sam's. Funny, the ranch seems big from the outside, but you don't really realize just how big it is. Straight at the end of that corridor, past all of the bedrooms, is Grayson's gym. I should probably block out some time to spend in said gym. I'll start Monday. *Right after you leave?* Is there a better time? *Lazy-ass.* Fuck off.

Hazel waves to me from outside the last room. "We're organizing in here."

"Good thing there's an empty room," I say with exasperation as the line of men, following me with furniture, pass by to deposit it in there.

"I know. Go in and direct them please. You know better where everything will go."

"Sure." I smile and follow the guys.

Within a half an hour, all furniture and knick-knacks have been moved in. Grayson even managed to keep his hands to himself, though his eyes did ungodly things to me. "You know, sweetheart," he pulls his shirt up to wipe his sweat, "when I had thoughts of getting hot and sweaty today, I knew you would be the cause of it, but in not one of my fantasies did I ever picture this being the reason why." He leans down and gives me a chaste kiss. "You did a lovely job, though. I like everything I can understand."

"Why, Mr. James, that sounded very much like a backhanded compliment." I laugh.

"Well, depending on what some of these things end up being, I'm afraid it will have to stay as one." He looks around.

"Not nice." I smack his stomach.

He grasps my chin between his thumb and forefinger, raising it so I look him in the eyes. "I can do nice, sweetheart. Why don't we start with a nice shower?" He nudges my nose with his.

"Then what?" I run my fingers above the waist of his jeans. He growls, grabs my hand and drags me out of the temporary storage room, down the corridor, and then left to our room.

"Did you enjoy that?" Grayson looks over at me as he guides me down the steps to the Simi Valley Cultural Arts Center.

"That was so much fun!" I throw my free hand out. Grayson brought me here for the production of *Ghost Tour at Strathearn Park*. It's a play, new this year, where we were led on a walking tour. At each of the thirteen stops, we were greeted by historical apparitions. We not only learned a lot of local history from these ghosts but gained many laughs as well. Only Grayson would find something unique like this to combine my love for history and theatre. I think I'll keep him. *Like you have much of a choice.* Will you just butt out?!

"I'm so happy you liked it. I wasn't sure, with it being new and all." He pulls me to him as we get to the sidewalk and throws his arm around my shoulder.

"What's next?" I look up at him as we walk.

"Next?" he lightly groans. "You're not tuckered out yet?"

"No." I pout.

"I'm just kidding, darling. How 'bout we find a little dive with live music?"

"Hmm . . . a coffee bar?"

"Coffee? Becca, it's almost 10 P.M."

"Take me to a diner for cake and coffee." I give him a toothy grin.

"A diner? Ugh—you are impossible!" He opens the passenger door for me as we just arrived at the car. I get in and watch as he walks around the front. "Not sure we'll find any diners at this hour besides IHOP or Denny's," he states as he climbs in on his side.

"Really?"

"Really."

"What the hell? It's tough being a Jersey girl in a non-Jersey world! Why haven't 24Hr diners caught on everywhere else? There are people starving at 2 A.M., damn it," I protest.

"Yes, you're right. It's a travesty, and we should approach our congressmen and senators immediately."

"For real," I huff.

"The campaign slogan should be: *Forget starving children— feed the drunks!*"

"You'd win with a slogan like that." I push the vent to direct the heat at me.

"Surely," he agrees and turns the heat up.

"Casa de James for coffee and éclair cake, then?"

"Now *that* is a solid plan." And with that, we're on our way home.

"Here you go, love." He hands me my coffee he insisted on making. I decided to come out here on the patio and get a fire started.

"Mmm . . . thank you." I palm the mug and bring it to my lips. "This is hot chocolate." I give him a look.

"I thought it'd be best since you changed your mind about the cake." He sits next to me and wraps me in his embrace. "You've got the fire going—I'm impressed."

"Besides being a girl scout, I've gone camping with my family most of my life."

"I believe that fire would've been roaring even if you didn't have that history. That's just the kind of woman you are, baby." He kisses my hair and uses my sacred word.

"Perhaps," I sigh and snuggle into him, hypnotized by the crackling of the fire.

"Becca, I need to talk to you about something."

"Oh?" I glance up at him.

"I can't go back with you on Monday," his voice apprehensive.

I clear my throat so that my voice doesn't crack. "Why?"

"I have meetings that I can't reschedule again. I want to be there for you; believe me. But, there are things I can't do on the East Coast. Grayson James is not just a man but a business. As an author, I have many obligations: promotion, meetings with the publisher and movie producers, so on and so forth. I can't do all of those things in Boston." The more he speaks, the faster his blinking gets.

"I understand." I put him out of his misery quickly. "Do you know when you'll be able to get out by me?" I can't believe how well I'm handling this. Maybe it's because I have two more days with him. I'm sure by Monday I'll be having the reaction he was expecting tonight.

"As soon as I wrap everything up here. I'm shooting for the beginning of November at the latest." He pushes my hair behind my right ear. "Then, we can fly back here for Thanksgiving," he adds.

"Um . . . about that." I sit up and out of his arms.

"What?"

"Can we have it by me?"

"No."

"Wait; please listen." I put my hand up.

"No, Becca. I won't budge on this. It's not like you have family, whereas I do! Now, I've bent over backwards for you at every chance, but not this time! The answer is *no*!"

"You fucking asshole! I can't believe you just said that to me!" Oh . . . I'm wild. I'm like a bull—seeing red—scraping my hoof on the ground, getting ready to charge. I stand up. "My parents went to my aunt and uncle's for Thanksgiving, first off! Second, I have been hosting this holiday for the past few years for my other family, which are my friends and Jimmy! That is why I wanted to stay! If I don't, then Jimmy is stuck at the nursing home. His family never brings him home for any holiday." I start to cry.

"First, I am very sorry for what I said, or really . . . how I said it. It was not meant as a dig. Secondly, Jimmy is not your responsibility." He is being so calm right now; I want to rip his hair out. How can he behave so calmly when I'm two seconds away from turning into Linda Blair?

"It's settled then; we will celebrate Thanksgiving without each other." I hit him back with the calm though I'm sure mine has a hint of crazy attached to it.

"No," he stands up as well, "that is *not* what we're going to do!" He's all teeth and anger in my face.

"Then you'll stay with me for it?" I'm hopeful even though he seems almost to be foaming at the mouth.

"No! *You* are coming *here*!" he seethes. "What are you going to do next year and the year after that, when you are living here—fly back to host?"

"I don't live here now. Grayson, you and I both know that

things could change in the blink of an eye. What if Jimmy's not with us next year? I know I'll have to make certain adjustments once I live here. I don't have to this year." I need to rein us in. "Can't we just fly everyone out to Boston?"

"You've got to be joking me! You are actually standing her, suggesting that *I* fly everyone out to you, after you've just had your way with *my* credit card today?! What's this 'we' business? The shoes are worn in now, aye? You're getting quite comfortable with spending my money?" He pokes at his chest. "It's not *our* money; it's *my* money!"

"I meant it as a couple," my voice shakes.

"Oh . . . you'll pay half, then?" he mocks me.

"I…"

"Yeah . . . that's what I thought. You can't even pay for your own ticket, or your bills, or your car." He's so condescending. "I'll go broke, courting you any longer."

I gasp.

What the fuck is happening here? We were so happy not twenty minutes ago. "I'll return the stuff I bought today," I can barely hear myself.

"I'm sure those were, most likely, final sales," he's curt. "Are you coming here for Thanksgiving, Becca?"

"No."

"Wrong choice," he snarls. "Night." He turns on his heels and goes into the house, leaving me to deal with the fire.

IT'S AFTER TWO in the morning and Gray is still not in bed. Of course, I haven't been able to sleep a wink. Instead, I've been wracking my brain the past few hours, trying to figure out what happened. Grayson and I haven't argued like this in a long time— months. And even then, it didn't seem this bad. Something's really off with him. *Enough!* I'm gonna go find him!

Just as I get up, he enters the room. "I was just coming to find you." I walk over to him. He ignores me and gets PJ bottoms out of his drawer. "Grayson." I touch his arm, but he shrugs me off and goes into the bathroom. I climb back into bed and keep a watchful eye out for him. After a beat, he's back out and turning my lamp off without a word. He climbs in on his side of the bed. "I love you," I say softly.

No answer.

After all of the nasty things he said to me tonight, I should welcome that. I feel a small pang in my heart that is just strong enough to cause a crack in it.

"Becca, if you're gonna carry on over there with that sniffling, then, please, go sleep in one of the guest rooms."

Who *is* this guy that is talking to me like this? His behavior only makes me cry a little harder.

"Off you go! Go on—get out!" he barks from behind me. "Now!" he yells, causing me to jump. "Out!"

"Grayson?" I can't believe my ears.

"Now, Becca, or I swear, I will pick you up and put you outside the door myself!"

I thought my heart was breaking a moment ago. I was wrong. This is what it feels like. I don't even bother grabbing my robe. I just leave. I go to the only guest room I saw that was done and vacant. I plop onto the bed and have myself a good cry.

Chapter Sixteen

GRAYSON

I give in to the need for a big stretch then roll over to pull her into my arms. I sit up quickly at the realization. God Save the Queen—I've royally screwed up! I was an arsehole to epic proportions last night. What the feck was wrong with me?! I have to fix this straight away!

I don't normally make a habit out of running through my house half naked. Susanna spectating and laughing simultaneously is probably at the top of my reasons why. I can't be bothered enough to slow down. I check the first room—empty. Second—empty. I jog out to the kitchen, hoping she's there. Just Susanna. "Have you seen Becca?" I ask quickly, fighting off the terrible feeling I have at the pit of my stomach.

"No." She gives me a quizzical look. *The office!* I leave Susanna without an explanation of my search. I climb the stairs by two and barge through the door when I make it to the top. Not here. *Not here!* Even more panicked, I run back down the stairs and into my room. I close my eyes and take in a deep breath before opening the closet door. When I do, my world stops; her suitcase is gone. *Sam!* I rush off to find him. I don't have to go too far as he's in the kitchen with Susie.

"Sam, did you drop Becca off somewhere this morning?" I am desperate, and I'm sure it's all over my face by the look of theirs.

"No, Sonny." He holds his hands out and shrugs in that "what gives?" way that most Italian men do.

"She's gone," my voice cracks. "I don't know where she is."

"She's on a plane, heading home," Mum pipes up from behind me.

"What?" I turn to her in disbelief.

"I drove her a few hours ago," she admits. I immediately run to the box on the wall that houses the keys to the cars. "Where are you going? Her plane left two hours ago."

"Why? Why did you take her? She wasn't due to leave till to-morrow; you know that!" I yell.

"You watch your tone with me, Gracie!" She stalks towards me, pointing her finger. "You want to know why?"

"Yes," I say through my teeth.

"Because the way you talked to that poor, sweet girl last night made me sick to my stomach!" she chokes on her words.

"I was awful, but I was—"

"—Awful? You were supposed to be asking her to marry you, professing your undying love for her, not *debasing* her! All because she said no about Thanksgiving? Shame on you!"

"Yeah, I got mad, Mum! I have the bloody right to! It's always about her and what will make *her* happy!"

"You foolish, foolish boy." She shakes her head.

"Boy?"

"Yes—boy! You are behaving like a child! Everything is about her, huh?" She gives me a condescending look.

"Yes."

"Funny, all I heard from her yesterday was whether you would be pleased with this or that. First time she came out here, dressed for the ball, she happily stepped up to get you out of a pickle, even though you embarrassed her. Lord only knows how she's treated you in Boston."

"I'm your son. You're supposed to guide me through things—protect me—not help shatter my heart!" *Fuck these damn tears.* My mother has this impeccable talent for always making me feel like I'm twelve.

"I am guiding you, Gracie. You're never too old to learn a lesson, and I'm wise enough to know I need to teach you one." She sits down at the dinette.

"Did you make her leave?" This is unbelievable.

"No. She wanted to go. I thought it best you had time apart."

"Sam, I'll be ready in ten minutes for the airport." I look over at him.

"I told her we'll all be there for Thanksgiving. Until then, you will stay put," Mum informs me.

"No!"

"You have meetings this week," she reminds me. *Shit.*

"I'd better not lose her, Mum." I point an accusatory finger at her.

"If you lose her, it will be due to your own stupidity." She sips at the tea Susie just brought her, cool as a cucumber . . . dismissing me. I grit my teeth, fist my hands, and offer her a growl before leaving the room. See?—Twelve.

I'm running out of ideas. Outside of my dreams (when I do manage finally sleeping), I haven't heard the sound of her beautiful voice for three weeks. I miss her so much. I ache for her like nothing I've ever experienced before. Everyday flowers arrive for her whether at home, school, or work. Each card relays a memory, passage from a book, lyrics from a song—anything I can think of to encourage her to give me another chance. I'm not even sure what our status is anymore.

I have, however, figured out why I went ballistic on her. I was more nervous than I let on, even to myself. I think, for some reason, I took her rejection over Thanksgiving as a possible rejection towards me asking her to be my wife. So I behaved irrationally, trying to protect myself. *Stupid fool!* Now, I'm on the verge of losing her . . . if I haven't already.

Since she left that morning, I seem to be on the verge of losing a lot of other things, and people. Derek's irritation with me climaxed after my behavior towards Becca. He'll only talk to me if I stay clear of all discussions about her. It's difficult, as she is my favorite subject. I know he talks to her all of the time (I may have checked his phone when he wasn't looking). Mum talks to her all of the time. And Stacey has told me, in her words, "You can officially fuck off, Grayson!"

Being in purgatory has not helped me career wise. The meeting that I rescheduled was disastrous. It's just as well. I can't focus on a movie right now. I know it will happen once the right team is in place. I'm not in a rush.

I've missed the deadline for my new book. Becca was supposed to finish the last few chapters. I've grown quite dependent on her proofing eyes. Of course, I did try this angle to get her to talk to me. All else aside, I have paid her for this very job she has not finished. I mentioned that too because what else could I lose?

"Gracie?" Mum calls out to me lightly. I look up and see her head peeking in my office.

"Yes, Mum?"

"It's time for dinner, sweetie."

"No thanks."

"You haven't eaten all day."

"So what?" I murmur.

"Cheer up, Gracie. You'll see her soon." She comes further into the office.

"No I won't. Let's face facts, Mum; she doesn't love me anymore." I say this more to give her a guilt trip and not because I actually believe it. I have been questioning it a lot lately, but I don't want to believe it's a possibility.

"Oh, you know that's not true. Why do you allow these thoughts to creep in?"

I scoff. "You really have to ask? Oh, that's right—you haven't a clue because you and her are chums, aren't you? Do me a favor, Mum, and leave me be."

"Tell her how you feel," she suggests.

"Yes, thank you, Mum, that's a brilliant suggestion. I'll get right on it." I roll my eyes.

"You're getting into a bad habit of disrespecting me lately. If your father were here," she chokes up. *Christ.*

"I'm sorry." I get up and stride across the room to her. I wrap my arms around her. "I'm just upset. I love her. This is killing me, Mum. I don't know what else to do. I have been trying since she left. I've got groveling down to an art." I rest my head on top of her white hair.

"Write her a letter. Tell her how you really feel. Not these little snippets of things you've been sending. You have to write to her like you're a man in love, going off to fight in a war you know you may not come back from," she explains.

"You've been reading your old regency romance favorites, haven't you?" I chuckle.

"Shut up." She does her famous giggle. "I mean it, Gracie; write the letter." She looks up at me.

"Okay." I kiss her cheek.

"Now, let's go and get some food into you." She breaks away.

"All right—you win." I follow her lead.

Mum was right. *How unusual?* I needed to sit down and really write her what was in my heart. I poured myself over it for hours. I wrote about things that I never gave much thought into. By the time I finished writing the letter, I realized how truly in love with her I am. I mean, I knew I was in love with her. But to see the true depths of it is outstanding. *She. Is. Everything.*

I reach into my pocket and pull out my buzzing phone. Ha!

Mum. It certainly took her a bit to call me. "Hello, Mum," I answer.

"While you're out, could you stop by Pamela's? She has a package for me from Genevieve."

"Normally I wouldn't mind, but I'm nowhere near Pamela's."

"Where are you?"

"Delivering Becca's letter." I can't help my smirk.

"Oh, you're at the post, then?"

"No. I'm hand delivering it." I glance up as I hear the doors of Becca's school open and students coming out.

"What?!"

"Yes, Mum, I'm here. The idea of me not being here was killing me. There's too much of my heart and soul on these pages. I couldn't risk it being lost. And, I couldn't bear the idea of her ignoring me. I have to go. She's headed this way now." I don't wait for her reply; I hang up.

Just as I do, Becca notices me and stops in her tracks. My heart plummets. I've got rather used to her face lighting up as she'd run to me when I'd surprise her. I'm not quite sure how this is going to play out.

BECCA

I can't believe he's here. It is taking every fiber of my being to not run to him and jump into his arms. I've missed him terribly. It's been torture not talking to him. But, Hazel was very adamant that he needed this time to really re-ground himself. She said I gave him too much power, flattened myself out good so he could walk all over me. I didn't feel like I was a doormat, but if this is what *others* saw, maybe it was true. Stacey and Derek jumped on board, as well. Talk about a fucking intervention. In the midst of my heartbreak, I have stopped and wondered how he's been managing without his sidekicks.

Ok, I've been standing here like an asshole long enough. *You think?* Ugh! I readjust my backpack and start my way toward him.

He's leaning up against my car, legs crossed at his ankles. Usually clean shaven, he now has a beard. It's maintained and . . . it's sexy as fuck. His blackish-brown hair is combed perfectly with a part on the side. With jeans that fit loosely in his legs and a cocoa-colored corduroy sports jacket to complete his ensemble, he is what dreams are made of . . . or *GQ* magazine. If my panties could give off a weather alert right now, they would be donned in a raincoat and galoshes.

"What are you doing here?" I tighten the hold on the strap to my backpack for support. He uncrosses his ankles and stands up fully, towering over me. He reaches for the strap to my backpack and slides it off my shoulder once I let it go. Taking my hand, he leads me to the passenger side, opens the back door, throws my bag in, then closes that one and opens mine. "Where's your car?" I ask as I get in.

"I took a cab here. Buckle up." He closes my door and takes his time walking around to the driver's side.

"Where are we going?" I ask as he climbs in. "Do you need my keys?" I pull them out of my purse.

"Spare set." He dangles them in front of me. *Right.* I resolve to just stare straight ahead. Grayson starts my car up and makes his way through the school parking lot. I wave at some of my friends. "How are your studies going?"

Small talk? Is he kidding me?

"Well."

"Did you finish up that paper?"

"On dementia? Yes."

"What did you get for it?"

"A."

"Good girl."

"How did your meetings go?"

"Not well."

"I'm sorry."

"Are you?" He glances over at me.

"Yes. Clearly, it was my fault they didn't go well," I snip.

He stays silent.

Boom—my answer.

I avert my eyes to the side window, fighting tears back. "What are you doing here and where are you taking me?" I ask when I feel I can safely do so without choking on my words.

"I need to read something to you. I thought I could do that while we enjoy the foliage at Endicott Park. Then, if all goes well, I'm going to take you home and make love to you until you're begging for mercy."

"What makes you think I'll even want that?" I snap, turning my neck toward him.

A slow smile creeps up at the corner of his mouth. "Because, darling, your legs have been clenched shut since the moment I stepped into this car."

Damn it! I unclench them as he pulls into a space at Endicott Park. He turns the car off and stares at me. "What?" I finally ask, feeling self-conscious.

"I've missed you more than you can imagine. I guess I'm relishing this moment, having you here next to me," his voice sincere.

"C'mon." I nod towards the outside and grab my handle to get out. As soon as I do, I cross my arms and start walking. There are leaves everywhere; it's gorgeous.

"Warm enough?" he asks, catching up to me. I nod. "Why don't we sit on that bench over there?" He points out.

"Okay," I agree and head in that direction. Grayson's hand lightly touches my back and slides to the small of it. Even through clothes, my skin reacts, sparking into a raging fire, traveling throughout my body. I swing around and quickly sit down, crossing my right leg over my left. Grayson sits next to me and begins an interesting pattern of breathing like he's in a bucket of ice and running his hand through his hair. It almost seems comical. "Calm down. Take a deep breath." I reach out to touch him, but think better of it.

"I rather you would."

"What?"

"Touch me," he murmurs. "Your touch has a calming effect on me."

"What do you have to say to me, Grayson?" I entwine my fingers, keeping them busy and away from him.

"I have it written here." He unbuttons the top few buttons of his jacket and retrieves an envelope. "I didn't want it to get lost in the post." His eyelids blink like mad. So much so that he actually brings his hand up and applies pressure with his fingers. "Bloody hell," he whispers. I giggle. I didn't mean to. He looks back up at me sharply.

"Sorry."

"Well, you're in the lead for apologies. I may just take an extra moment to bask in this." He gives me a shy smile.

"Ba—Grayson, c'mon." I shuffle a finger at the letter.

"Now that's promising."

"Just habit." I look away.

"Right, then. I'll start."

"I can read." I look back at him.

"Congratulations! The world is your oyster now!" he quips.

"Shut up," I grumble, but despite myself, a small smile creeps across my lips. He pulls the letter out of the envelope and unfolds it. He looks down at it and clears his throat before beginning.

"Dearest, sweetheart,

I was told I should write to you as if I were a soldier going off to fight a war I know I may not come back from. I teased this person about their description. But, as I sit here now, trying to muster up the right words to describe my feelings for you, knowing this may be my last shot; the irony is not lost on me.

"I have been smitten with you since that bone-chilling, cold day last March. You lit a fire in me that I wasn't aware was dormant. As you know, my obsession with you was instantaneous. What you don't know is that it all started with your bum."

He looks up at me with a mischievous grin. I shoot him a strange look, trying not to smile. He holds the letter up.

"There I was, minding my own business, and out of my periph-

eral vision, I saw it wiggle to gain my attention. I vaguely remember it chanting my name, as well. I thought to myself, 'Good God, that's a fantastic bum.' Then you turned around and I mentally fell to my knees. Not an ounce of make-up on, you had tendrils of hair falling everywhere, and you looked pissed off about dealing with gardening books."

He eyes me when I let out a chuckle. I was pissed. I hate that section.

"You were bloody gorgeous. I had to talk to you. So, I came up with my poppycock story, thinking you'd know who I am. I was met with that smart mouth of yours. It had been a long time since anyone went head to head with me besides my family. I was completely mesmerized by this—still am.

"Trying to court you was as much of a nightmare as it was an amazing journey. There were moments that you would let your guard down and relax with me. I fell more and more in love each time it happened.

"I'll skip over the event that finally brought us together. But, it definitely had its importance in our timeline.

"Since then, things have been truly amazing. That is, until I was completely possessed by some demonic monster. Becca, I have replayed that night over and over again in my head. I'm sick from my behavior. Everything I said was so off base—so wrong. It's no wonder you left me. I can't take any of it back. All I can do is give you the explanation that made most sense to me."

He stops again and glances at me. I do nothing to hide my tears. I, too, have replayed that night over and over again. The worst was when he kicked me out of the bedroom. I take in a hiccupping breath and avert my eyes. "I'm so sorry, sweetheart. I…" He tries to reach for me, but I jerk back. "Right," he breathes and goes back to the letter.

"That night, I wanted to ask you something. I was extremely nervous, more so than I realized. The argument over Thanksgiving wasn't because of the holiday, per say. You saying no to the holiday with me felt more like you saying no to me in general, as your

family."

"You're speaking in riddles, Grayson!" I scold.

"Please." He holds his hand up. I cross my arms and huff.

"It's completely ridiculous; I see this now. Does one ever be-have irrationally on purpose? I didn't, at that time, know where it was coming from. I can't tell you enough times how sorry I am. I can't forgive myself, I don't know how you will, but I pray you do.

"Becca, you have become my best friend, my better half, the rhyme to my reason. I have never *felt this way about anyone before in my life. I honestly didn't know you could feel for someone at this level and magnitude of love. You are the center of my world; what was missing from my life. Every time I look at you, I see my future. When you smile or laugh, and I know I'm the cause of it—jackpot.*

"I love this newer version of me when I'm with you: slightly deflated head, makes silly jokes as such from previous comment, feels suspicious when people agree with me too quickly. You remind me to stop and smell the roses, hold tightly to the ones I love, and never give less than my best. I could easily write a book about how wonderful you are and how much better I am for having you in my life.

"You see, the thing is, I can't picture my life without you. There's no one else I'd want to wake up next to every morning. I have never looked into another woman's eyes and seen my children. It happens every time I look into yours. I can't imagine growing old with any-one else. I love you, Becca. More than I can bear."

He folds it and puts it away. "I think I'll take it from here." He takes in a deep breath. "That night, like I said, I wanted to ask you something. My question was sitting in my pocket, burning a hole in it." He gets off the bench and onto one knee. "I made a huge mis-take that night. My intentions have always been to keep you, not push you away. You are the love of my life, Becca. I don't deserve this at the moment, but if you agree to be my wife, I promise to earn the privilege of being your husband every day for the rest of my life. Please forgive me. Please say you'll be my wife." He opens the box to me.

I had hoped. I had dreamt of this moment for months. It's always only been *him.* But, to go from that night to this? A month ago, I wouldn't have hesitated. "Can I . . . I need a few moments," I stammer as I quickly stand. He looks up at me and gives me a nod, disappointment all over his face. I walk around and head toward the pond, kicking up leaves in my path.

Think, Becca, think! *What do you need to think about?* A lot—being a doormat! *Chicken shit.* You're not helping me! *Do you love him?* Yes. *Do you want him to ever not be a part of your life?* No. *Life is short, remember?* Yes. *Don't waste it on bullshit.* But—he hurt me. *File it and pull that shit out to show him at the most irrational times.* Why? *Because it drives men crazy.* Who are you? *Your inner bitch.* I kinda like you. *Good—you're kinda stuck with me.* I guess so. *There's more of us.* What?! *Shh... go pull him out of purgatory.* Right!

I turn around and watch him sitting on the bench. He seems so lost. I stride toward him. He suddenly jumps up and approaches me at a quick pace. "Becca, I'm sorry. I shouldn't have just done that to you. I—"

"—Ask me again." I put my hand up to stop him.

"What?" he sounds as if the wind has been knocked out of him.

"Ask me again," I repeat and offer him a soft smile.

"Becca, will you—"

"—Wait. On your knee, please." I stop him.

He bites back a smile. "You just love to see me grovel."

"Yep, pretty much."

"As you wish, my darling." He gets down on one knee and re-opens the box. "Becca Kirsten Campbell, will you do me the honor of becoming my wife? Marry me, sweetheart—please?"

"Yes, Grayson, I will marry you." I smile through my newly formed tears.

He takes the ring out of the box, slides it on my finger, then stands up, lifting me off the ground. He kisses me over and over again. "Woohoo!" he screams. "She said yes! She said yes, everyone!" He spins us around.

"Gray . . . we're the only ones here." I laugh.

"There are ducks right over there." He points. "They seem very excited about my announcement."

"Funny, you're the only quack I see around here," I deadpan.

"God, I've missed this smart mouth of yours," he says then attacks me again with another long, drawn-out kiss. Mmm…

Chapter Seventeen

BECCA

Grayson and I barge through my front door, our mouths still connected, and our hands already working at each other's coats.

"Can you two hold that thought? I like having popcorn with my porn," Stacey calls out to us.

"Shut up, Stace," we both say as we head to my room.

"No, no! What's he doing here?" She gets authoritative as if she's just remembered. I hold up my left hand and wiggle my fingers.

"*Oh my God!*" she screams with excitement.

"I know!" I break away from him because, after all is said and done with the proposal—it's girlfriend time. It's an unspoken rule amongst women everywhere: when you lose your virginity, become engaged or pregnant—run, don't walk, to your BFF to give a full report.

"All right, listen, you two, I haven't seen or touched her in three weeks. We are going into our room now to rectify that. Afterwards, you two can spend hours ogling, rehashing how I asked, chanting, or whatever the hell it is you hens do when a girl gets engaged. Right now—she's mine." And with that, he picks me up and throws me over his shoulder.

"I agree! Go on and confuckuate your engagement. I have to call Max and tell him he's in deep shit." She follows us to get every word out.

"Bye." Grayson turns once we're in the room and closes the door.

"Confuckuate?" I laugh as he puts me down.

"I may have to steal that word." He grins. Grasping my face, his mouth is on mine again. I manage the last few buttons on his coat and slide it off his shoulders. He works mine off, as well. We pull away from kissing as the need to get our clothes off becomes urgent.

I grab at the hem of my shirt, pull it over my head, and toss it to the side. Grayson is pulling at the straps of my bra before I can even get it unsnapped. "Excited to see the girls, huh?" I tease.

"I'm excited to see *everything*." He grins, sliding my bra off. I nibble on my lower lip as he takes in the sight of me. I slowly unbutton my jeans and turn around as I shimmy them down at a seductive pace, giving him a show. "Christ," he whistles through his teeth. I step out of my jeans and am greeted by his hands on my hips. His hot breath hits my neck with great promise and a shiver runs down my spine. My right arm reaches up behind and around his neck, encouraging him to devour the nook in mine.

"You're still dressed," I murmur.

"I got distracted." He nips the sensitive area below my ear, his hands traveling up to be filled with my breasts. My lips find his. They part, allowing the intrusion of his tongue. The caress of his tongue is slow, seductive, and urgent all at once. I moan into his mouth as he tweaks my nipples in a painfully good manner. Breaking away, I spin back to him. I take to stripping him. "Eager as always, Miss Campbell," he muses. I give him a smirk and the rise of one eyebrow as I whip his belt free from him.

I fold it in half and smack his ass with it. "Why, yes I am, Mr. James." He gives me a look of shock. I toss the belt and make quick work of depantsing him. I bring them down to the floor. Grayson steps out and I let my hands travel up the outside of his thighs as I trail hot kisses up them. I grab his "man of steel" and flatten my tongue against the base, sliding up it with one good lick. As soon as I reach the tip, I swirl my tongue around it then take him deep into my mouth. I can't begin to describe the satisfaction it brings me to hear the pleasure in his groan. I pull back, adding pressure with my tongue as I suck then plunge him back in as far as I can take it.

"Becca, darling, please . . . God, you're amazing. But, I need to be inside of you . . . you know . . . the usual way. Becca, please stop!" he says urgently and stops me from continuing. Damn, I had a good rhythm going, too. *You're becoming a real champ at this; I'm impressed.* Thank you, Inner Bitch. *I'm Inner Whore, but you're welcome just the same.* Oh, for fuck's sake! *Exactly. Carry on, now.*

Grayson pulls me up to him. His mouth attacks mine again as he walks me back till the bed hits the back of my legs. He pushes me on the bed a bit more aggressive than usual, but there is a fire in his eyes that I've seen many times. Keeping my eyes locked on his, I crawl back. My heart feels as if it will beat out of my chest. The anticipation is killing me. Every inch of my body is aching for his touch, the way he possesses me.

Grayson—in general—has an over-the-top personality, and he never shies away from showcasing it. However, his powers have no hold over me, and I can often be found challenging him. That is, except for in the bedroom. For some reason, I am perfectly happy to relinquish my control to him there. I'm not sure if it's my inexperience or that submitting fully to him somehow heightens the pleasure I receive. I don't know. Maybe someday I will. What I do know, is that right now, I'm about to be devoured and sent to a level of ecstasy I never knew existed before I met Grayson.

I feel the dip in the mattress as he climbs between my legs. He breaks our stare, glancing down at my lady business. "So wet," he whispers and glides his index finger down my center. My obsequious hips leap up. "Feel good?" He licks his lips.

"Yes."

He then slides two fingers inside of me, meticulously massaging my upper front wall. I grasp at the sheets for strength. My hips rock to the pace of his touch. "I love to watch you, the pleasure you're experiencing at my hand." Grayson's voice is soothing and sexy. "Do you have any idea how bloody fucking sexy you are? Look at the way you move to my touch, sweetheart. Knowing I'm the only man who's touched you like this—who will ever touch you like this, there're no words to describe the feeling. *You* are mine. *This* is mine. *Your pleasure* is mine." He applies his free thumb to my clit, sending me through the roof. My orgasm surges through me out of nowhere. I was so busy listening to him, I didn't notice myself climbing. My hips thrust into the air rapidly, fucking his fingers and yelling out my prayers. "So bloody gorgeous." He climbs above me, pulling his fingers out of me when I finish my last quake. He grabs my right leg, wraps it around his waist and plunges deep inside of me. My neck jerks back involuntarily. My mouth gaping open as one last spark is lit from my previous orgasm. *Holy fuck!*

He grinds deeply into me several times before grabbing my left leg and wrapping it around his waist as he gets more on his knees, lifting my ass off the bed. He grabs a hold of my hips for leverage, beginning a slow succession of thrusts until he switches to harsh pounding. I throw my hands over my mouth to quiet myself. "Hands off!" he yells.

"Oh please. Oh please," I cry (the good kind) as he pounds harder.

Grayson grits his teeth but a feral groan rips through them anyway. His face scrunches up. "*Fuccccckkkk!*" he yells as he explodes inside of me. I'm not far behind him, clenching to rush myself there. One final deep thrust into me and he holds it there. I can feel him pulsating inside of me. His thumb works at my clit. "C'mon, Becca!" he commands. And like magic, the tightening occurs, rushing through my core. I cry out, rocking on his dick. I still, riding the last wave with him deep inside of me till, finally, I collapse. Grayson follows, crashing on top of me. We lie here, trying to steady our breath.

"So . . . when do you want to get married?"

I grab his hair and tug to make him look at me. "*You* are relentless." I kiss his forehead.

"You know me; I have to have all my ducks in a row." He crawls up a bit, so he's looking into my eyes.

"The pond's not gonna go missing, Gray. We've been engaged for barely two hours." I play with his hair. "You've got great hair," I mention. I do love it. It's thick and rich in color.

"I love when you group sentences together that have nothing to do with one another." His fingers trace the curve of my clavicle bone.

"If I don't say it, I forget to. That's my clavicle bone, by the way." I glance at his finger.

"Are you trying to seduce me with your medical wit?" His eyes smile at me.

"I have a very sexy brain; consider yourself warned."

"Sexy—scattered. Toe-may-to—toe-motto. Let's just call the whole thing off," he quips.

"You're so mean to me; I don't know why I stick around." I pout.

"It's the Clark Kents. Anytime you muster the courage to say *enough is enough*, I slip those bad boys on and you can't even remember your name. They are your Kryptonite." He nudges his nose against mine.

"Indeed, they are." I lean up for a kiss. "I have a little secret, though."

"What's that?"

"The Clark Kents have no power unless they are on a very specific person."

"I better tell Derek to cancel his order then," he says wide-eyed with a panicked frown. I roar with laughter. "Every time this happens I'm in shock and awe."

"Every time what happens?" I furrow my brows.

"Every time I make you laugh like this—it's remarkable. I don't think I've ever made any woman laugh sincerely like this."

"You're a very funny man." I run my hand through his hair again and settle on playing with his earlobe.

"That's very odd to hear that. No one's ever defined me as funny." He grabs my hand and turns his face into it, kissing the center of my palm.

"I think everyone has different traits that only step into the spotlight when they are around certain people who may provoke it. Just think about several of your closest friends and how you are with each of them when you are alone. I know for me, I'm a little different with each one. Maybe it's different interests or different comfort levels; I'm not sure which."

"That makes a lot of sense, actually. Sort of goes with the old saying 'you'll know when you know'. You're the only woman I have ever wanted to marry. Maybe it's because you bring out the traits in me I didn't know existed." His fingers play at my lips. His eyelids start going into Morse code.

"Why are you getting nervous?"

"I'm not. I was nervous. I thought I lost you once and for all. We've been together roughly seven months now, and I've had that concern twice. I can't say that I'm not worried it will happen again." He slides off of me a bit. My diaphragm is grateful.

"Grayson, we can't let the 'what ifs' of life paralyze us." I turn on my side and lean up on my elbow. "The first time was due to miscommunication and information. This last time, I didn't break up with you. I just needed time. You really hurt me. I felt abandoned, and it stirred up all of the feelings I've had over losing my parents. Your loved ones *aren't* supposed to abandon you. Through no fault of their own, my parents did. Your father did. It seems silly to think of it like that, but it's part of the grieving process. It wasn't so much the terrible things you said to me on the patio, it was the way you kicked me out of your room . . . your bed. Dismissing me like that made me feel like I was a toy you were done playing with. I felt cheap, used; I felt like a fool. Worse than any of that, I felt like, for some reason, I wasn't worthy of love. How could I be when everyone, who's supposed to love me unconditionally, abandons me?" my voice cracks with a slight sob. Grayson stares at me, seemingly speechless, but I can see the hurt all over his face from the pain he caused me; his eyes are reddened and his jawline is twitching lightly.

His left hand palms my cheek, thumbing away my tears. "I fought so long and hard for you to trust me enough to love you. To hear how one stupid, irrational moment—on my part—swooped in and destroyed all the hard work and dedication I poured into making you mine . . . to make you comfortable enough to be mine, it kills me. I went to your Uncle. I went to Jimmy. And to make sure I covered all bases, I talked to your father just in case he could hear me. I asked these three men to *trust* me with your heart. I *promised* them that I would *never* hurt you. I *told* them that I was a good man, that I would *always* put your happiness before mine. I said you would always have top priority in my life. I'm a fraud," he sounds so broken up.

"Grayson." I shake my head.

"Listen, please!" he gets stern. "I didn't make all of those promises knowing I was a fraud. I made them all because I found them very easy to make as, up until that night, I already lived up to them. But, I was cocky. I forgot that of all the things you bring out in me, insecurity is one of them."

"What?!"

"It's true, Becca. I worry a great deal about whether I'm good enough for you, whether I deserve someone like you. You are *very* different from anyone I have ever been with. You see *me*, not the persona. And, it's scary. I'm so used to the superficial. With you, things are so deep. Becca Campbell, you dirty little thing, get your mind out of the gutter!" He suddenly laughs, catching my thoughts through my facial expression, I'm sure.

"What can I say? You say things are deep with me; that's where my mind is going to wander. I can't help it."

"I'm being serious," he almost pleads.

"I know. I'm sorry." I kiss him.

"What I was saying was you've peeled layers off of me I wasn't aware existed. Through you, I am learning who I am . . . who I want to be, besides what I've put out there for the world. And well, I explained to you what happened that night, how far and where I took that rejection. That was the insecurity I feel at times and I buckled under the pressure from it. I looked out for myself first. In the meantime, I hurt you and proved myself to be a fraud to those three important men in your life. But I'm aware now. I'm still learning, Becca. However, I can say, with utmost certainty, that I have never been a man who makes the same mistake twice. At least, I try not to. I will do better at proving myself to them, to you . . . to me. From this day forward, I will make sure your happiness always does come first or I will die trying to make it so." The passion in his declaration knocks the wind out of me. And I truly believe every word. There's just one problem; he's missed the reason why we've had any of these issues: communication.

"Grayson, all of that to the side, we're not discussing our biggest issue," I tread lightly.

"Please tell me something wonderful is going to come out of that smart mouth of yours and not something else for me to think on."

"I'm afraid not." I give him a half smile. "When the whole pregnancy fiasco happened, it was due to you not telling me in the first place. In return, I wouldn't listen to you. This last time, you felt insecure and instead of telling me how it made you feel, you set out to hurt me, protecting yourself. Bottom line, baby? We need to do better at communication. The lack of talking things out has been the nasty seed all along."

"So, basically, it is all my fault—both times." He almost seems a little perturbed.

"No. Well, yes—to a point. I'm not an angel, though. It's just . . . if you would've told me why you were getting angry, we could've possibly worked through it. Part of the problem is that you are a take charge kind of guy. You're used to handling everything. You *like* to handle everything. You can't handle *us* because we're an 'us'. That means two people, one relationship; we are both responsible for nurturing and protecting it." I release my elbow from its duty and slump my head onto the pillow.

"Communication; okay." He nods. "I'm going give it a go right now," he announces. "While I feel really good about us clearing the air, I can't help but feel like there is yet *more* for me to let go of or give. I've given a lot more to this relationship than I ever imagined I would to any. When is what I give going to be enough?"

"I'm sorry you feel that way." I look down. "You have given a lot . . . let go of a lot." I look back up. "I've only had a few hang ups. I've let most of them go or am in the process of doing so to be with you. Your biggest hang up is control. That control rolls into most areas of your life, of our life together. And that is why it seems like you have to do so much more than me. You say jump; you expect me to ask how high. Life is not like that, Grayson. I'm not a business deal; I'm a person. A person with a life and goals before you ever came along. I can't just merge everything with yours or relinquish it at the snap of your fingers. It's very unrealistic of you to think so. I'm sorry that it seems you are doing more than me. Just try to remember that I'm on the other end of it, dealing with your irascible behavior." I tap his nose.

"Irascible behavior?!" he shouts.

"Case in point." I raise a brow.

"Damn it," he says under his breath. I laugh lightly and lean in for a kiss. "Okay, we'll *both* work harder at this. I do have one final question before we get back to the business of merging."

"What?" I eye him suspiciously but more because I'm wondering if he's talking about the same "merging" I'm think of.

"You talked a lot about feeling abandoned."

"Yes."

"Did you . . . did you say yes to me because you really want to marry me or because you don't want to feel abandoned?" His eyelids are going a mile a minute again.

"Both," I answer quickly.

"Care to explain in more detail?"

"I am very much in love with you. I can't picture my life without you. I almost said no—that's how badly you hurt me. But then, if I did that, I'd be the one abandoning us. In essence, I'd be abandoning myself, as well. Life is too short, Grayson—we both know that. I don't want to be without the people I love. I don't want to mourn for the rest of my life. And I would . . . I would mourn the loss of you greatly. Why do that to either of us then? What point would I have made? Yes, I want to marry you, Grayson. There are many things in my life that I am unsure about, marrying you is *not* one of them. You are the great love of my life. We're not fairytale perfect, but we're perfect for us. I love you," I say through my newly formed tears. I do, I really love this man more than I could've ever imagined. He has been my light through the darkest year of my life, and he shines so brightly.

"I love you, too. Thank you." He rolls me onto my back and holds my face in his hands.

"For what?"

"For your honesty, for loving me, for just being the amazingly frustrating woman you are, for everything right down to the merger that is about to take place." He went from sweet and sincere, to silly and mischievous in two seconds flat. But that's just part of his charm; I'll take it . . . and the merger that's growing with great enthusiasm. The prospects of it are limitless...

To Be Continued....

Acknowledgements

There are so many people to thank, but at the top of my list are my diehards for this series. These women have been supporting me in every way possible through the journey of storytelling. They have been patiently waiting (read: nudging me every so often) for the beginning of this particular story. They fell in love with Becca, Grayson, and Ray just as much, if not more than, me. As a writer, knowing about and feeling this love from them, it's indescribable how much this means to me. In no particular order: Wendy Colby, Heather Routh, Tammy Becraft, Leanne Wright, Amy Barbagallo, Debbie Baardsen, Jennifer Siegel, Nicola Spears, Shell Williams, Ange hall, Shelli Reid, Christi Lofton, Karen Shenton, Annette Holland, Olivia Hayes, Anna Roselli, Lheanne Spicer, Jennifer Inglehart, Arianne Addicks, Joely Bogan, T Bird and Rebecca Gegenheimer. I hope I didn't forget anyone!! Thank you girls for all of your support!!!

There are two ladies that I couldn't do a thing without. They've been my biggest supporters from the beginning and, more importantly, they've become my dearest friends. Wendy Shatwell and Claire Almendinger, I'd give you one of my kidneys! I wish there wasn't that big damn pond separating us. *Throws another nickel in the "private jet" fund.* I love you both like you're my sister(s) from another mister.

To all of my friends (not of the book world), thank you for always cheering me on, reading my books, and saying how proud you are of me. It means so much! Roll Call: Jennifer Bedet, Kaitie Gifford, Karen Lincoln, Amanda Lavita, and Darlene Donovan.

All of my close Author friends (you know who you are), to go through this journey with you is nothing short of an amazing experience. I love you crazy bitches hard!

Robin Harper, you blew another beautiful cover out of the water! I can't thank you enough for all you've done for me. You've gone above and beyond! I cherish you, lady!

Stacey Blake, I can't wait to see the magical things you will do with this book. As I'm writing this, I must admit: I'm wearing pants. Oh the shame… lol. *Holds wine glass up to you* Cheers, lady!

Christy French, thank you for taking me on! You're an awesome assistant, virtually and cyberly (shh…I'm a writer, I'm allowed to make up words! Lol).

Claire Almendinger, ooh a double mention! We must add a stripe to your pink cape! It was a complete blast working with you as my editor on this! You did a great job, though we struggled at times with the language barrier. Hahaha! #BritishEnglishVSAmericanEnglish #TheStruggleIsReal Love you, chickie!

A big thank you to my family who cheer me on and help me when I'm off to a signing! To all of the readers I've met this past year at the signings, so happy you boarded this crazy train! It's been beyond amazing to meet all of you!

Lastly, to the most amazing kids a woman could have, never give up on your dreams no matter how many curveballs life throws at you. I love you guys more than my heart can stand.

About the Author

I am a domestic engineer (born and raised in New Jersey) whose sole responsibility is guiding three young, impressionable kids into becoming phenomenal adults. This challenging yet rewarding work requires a lot of love (coffee), patience (wine), and determination (periodic exorcisms). I work all of this magic from the beautiful state of New Hampshire.

Before becoming a domestic goddess (not really), I spent over a decade working in the medical field, where I wore more hats than the queen.

I have loved the written word and the great escape it provides since I was a little girl. When I wasn't reading about people and the places they lived, I created my own characters and adventures.

Having found myself again, through my writing, with The Lost & Found Series, The One, and The GEG Series, has been nothing short of a dream come true. Also, it makes people feel better when I laugh randomly or talk to myself, knowing it's my characters and not "the voices" . . . that would be creepy.

www.authorjacquelynayres.com
Spotify playlist: http://spoti.fi/1WIvHeA

https://www.facebook.com/JacquelynAyresAuthor
https://twitter.com/JacquelynAyres
https://www.goodreads.com/author/dashboard?page=1
https://plus.google.com/u/0/+JacquelynAyres/posts

www.ingramcontent.com/pod-product-compliance
Lightning Source LLC
Chambersburg PA
CBHW02094518O626
46814CB00003B/935